ANYONE
BUT
NICK

OTHER TITLES BY PENELOPE BLOOM

The Anyone But . . . Series

Anyone But Rich

Anyone But Cade

Anyone But Nick

The Objects of Attraction Series

His Banana

Her Cherry

His Treat

His Package

Her Secret

Stand-Alone Novels

Savage

The Bodyguard

Miss Matchmaker

Single Dad Next Door

Single Dad's Virgin

Single Dad's Hostage

BDSM Themed

Knocked Up by the Dom

Knocked Up by the Master

ANYONE BUT NICK

PENELOPE BLOOM

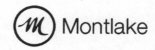

 Montlake

Published by Montlake, Seattle
www.apub.com

Amazon, the Amazon logo, and Montlake are trademarks of Amazon.com, Inc., or its affiliates.

ISBN-13: 9781542018890
ISBN-10: 1542018897

Cover design by Caroline Teagle Johnson

Printed in the United States of America

ANYONE
BUT
NICK

Chapter 1

MIRANDA

If I closed my eyes and listened to the clatter of falling bowling pins, the dated soundtrack of easy nineties hits, and the hum of arcade machines, I could imagine I'd slipped back seven years. *Almost.* If I'd really stepped into the past, I'd feel the slight pressure of a pair of boring granny panties digging into my cheeks. I would also be wearing the infamous cardigan-and-camisole combination I'd thought was the height of fashion.

Nowadays, I was far more sophisticated. I'd traded the granny panties for ass floss and the cardigans for silky blouses and power jackets. I'd learned to stop apologizing for being intelligent and hardworking. My philosophy was that I needed to feel like I could step into any office in America, bust down the door, and start kicking corporate booty. Figuratively, at least. I'd tried self-defense classes once, and the only technique I was halfway proficient at was blowing the rape whistle.

I looked down at the soggy paper tray of nachos in my left hand and the hamburger and fries in my right. I even had a water bottle awkwardly wedged between my elbow and my side. Tonight, I wasn't a door kicker. I was the third wheel—or, more technically, the fifth wheel—on a double date.

The more I thought about it, the more the sounds around me stopped feeling nostalgic. All they did was remind me of how different

I was now—how much things had changed, and maybe not all for the better.

I could hear the deep laughter of Cade King and the rumble of his twin brother's voice, even over all the chaos. That was enough to snap me into full awareness as surely as an ice-cold toilet seat at three in the morning.

Just down the short stairway leading to the bowling alley, my two best friends, Kira and Iris, were smiling and laughing at something Cade had said. It was getting harder and harder to be a good person—the kind of friend who would see their happiness and smile right along with them. Instead, watching them have fun felt almost accusatory. *They* had figured it out. *They* had found that special someone. So what did that say about me if my life seemed to be cracking apart at the foundations?

Be glad for them, Miranda. I repeated the thought a few dozen times in the hope that it'd overpower my gloominess. After all, why shouldn't they be happy? Iris still worked as a cop, even though she'd recently paired off with Cade. Kira still loved her job as a teacher, and she was in a seemingly perfect relationship with Richard King. They'd found their happily ever afters—their kisses on the beach with one foot kicked up behind them. So what if I was currently buried up to the neck on that same beach while little crabs made nests in my hair and seagulls stole my food? At least I could be glad my friends weren't screwed too.

A young kid who looked around middle school age bumped into me. I spun, did a teetering balancing act, and watched helplessly as Cade and Iris's nachos fell to the carpet.

"Sorry, dude," the kid said in a tone that was so far from apologetic it was actually insulting. He looked up at me with a strange mixture of confidence and blind panic, then *dabbed*. I expected him to run off, but he just stood there, looking at me.

I glanced down at the nachos and felt a swirl of unexpectedly strong emotions swelling up. The kid was watching me curiously, almost like he knew something was about to happen.

Normally, I would've composed myself, pushed down any emotions I felt, and handled this like a proper woman.

Normally.

I lunged forward and started stomping the nachos. For a few seconds, all I saw was pure-white rage. I stomped so hard it sent shock waves up my leg and made my knees hurt. When I was done, there was just a cheesy, crumby paste on the ground.

I stared down at the mess in numb fascination. "Taco salad," I whispered.

The kid was still staring at me, but his jaw had dropped. "You're a psycho."

"Listen, you little turd. I just got out of a long-term relationship a week ago. And yesterday? I lost my job. Do you have any idea what it feels like when everybody thinks you're so perfect? Can you imagine what it's like when you realize one day that you're trapped in someone else's illusion? That your whole identity is dictated by the expectations of a stupid small town and your friends, but you're in too deep to do anything about it?"

The boy thought about that, then his eyebrows scrunched up. "I play this online game, and I told a girl I met that I was in high school and the captain of the football team. She wants to meet in person now."

I sighed. "Those were rhetorical questions. The point was you bumped into me and made me drop my nachos. You saw what I did to those nachos when they pissed me off, didn't you? What do you think I'll do to you?"

For a second, I thought he was about to cry, but then I saw him start to lift his arms.

"And don't you dare dab at me again," I warned.

The kid turned and ran. I couldn't tell if he was laughing or crying, but I felt like I'd lost my mind either way.

"Wow," Cade said.

Apparently, he had been watching everything from the stairs at my side. He clapped his hands slowly. "Amazing. That was really just amazing. Oh, and is it okay if I grab one of these, or should I worry about what you'll do to me?"

"If you repeat any of that to anyone, I'll—"

"Stomp me?" he asked. He bent down, fished out a miraculously intact nacho, and popped it into his mouth. "Don't worry. I enjoy dramatic irony. If I told everybody Little Miss Perfect was actually falling apart on the inside, watching you struggle to keep up appearances wouldn't be nearly as fun. Secret's safe with me. But, really, you could've at least given him some advice about his online girlfriend. That was just rude."

Cade casually headed back down to our bowling lane to take his turn, as if he hadn't just witnessed me having a mental breakdown. Clearly, something inside me had become unhinged, and I was only barely holding it all together. I had never been the type of person to let my stress show—or be a jerk to little kids, for that matter. If there were an Olympic event for internalizing problems and putting on a calm face for the world, I would've been the most decorated gold medalist in history by now. I let out a slow, controlled breath. I could absolutely do this. I'd even gone as far as writing it down this morning as a daily goal: *Survive bowling night with the happy couples. Show no weakness. Do not get grilled on the breakup, and do not talk about getting laid off.*

Easy. Everything in the world was easy if you pretended it was. Cade was a slight hitch in the plan, but I believed him. He'd keep quiet, and nobody had to know I didn't have everything under control. I repeated that to myself as I resumed my slow walk back to our lane.

Calm face, Miranda. Calm face. It was just like losing both of my thumbs and one eye but then having to watch all my friends give thumbs-up and carefree, happy little winks to everyone they saw. Sure, I'd be happy for them, but I wouldn't be able to stop thinking about how it was not winking if you had only one eye. All I'd ever have was blinking, and wasn't there something tragic about that?

Iris noticed me coming and pretended to jog toward me in slow motion. She also started *saying* something unintelligible in slow motion, complete with exaggerated tongue movements like she was a dog with her head out the window of a moving car.

I waited impatiently for the full minute it took her to travel a couple of feet. To her credit, she stuck with the slow-motion theme all the way through the part where she noticed I didn't have any nachos.

"Hey," she said. "Where are the nachos?"

"Maybe I ate them," I said dryly.

Iris laughed. "Damn. What crawled up your ass and converted it into a rental property?"

I must've looked particularly pathetic, because Iris's eyebrows scrunched together, and she put her hands on my shoulders. "Hey," she said more softly. "Are you okay?"

As much as I wanted to smile and nod, I knew Iris would see straight through the lie. "A kid ran into me and made me drop them. Then I stomped them into the ground and made him run off laughing or crying—I'm still not sure which. Okay? And I was really mean to him. I normally like kids. So stop interrogating me about it. That's everything."

Iris looked like she was trying to keep a straight face, but she wound up laughing. "I'm sorry. It's just that I'm picturing you stomping the nachos. What was going through your head, exactly?"

I put my hands on my hips. I wanted to be mad at her for laughing, but I couldn't stop myself from smiling too.

"But really. Why did you stomp them?" she asked.

"Because I was pissed? Can we talk about something else?"

"Iris," Cade called. "Your turn." I didn't fail to notice the wink he gave me. *Helpful bastard.*

"Are you winning yet?" I asked Iris.

Iris turned and squinted at the scoreboard, where the names of our little group were on display. If there was any doubt of my fifth-wheel status, all I needed to do was check out the scoreboard. Cade and Iris had entered themselves as a team named "Snakes on a Lane." They had even come up with a cringeworthy handshake where it looked like they were trying to pretend their arms were snakes in some sort of fight, complete with hissing sound effects. At least it would've been cringeworthy if Cade wasn't so obnoxiously confident. He probably could've pretended to be a chicken in the middle of a crowded room, and women still would've swooned.

In typical Richard King fashion, he and Kira had gone with a more down-to-earth team name: "Rich and Kira."

Then there was me. I'd tried to enter my name without a team designation, but Cade had gone to the liberty of editing it while I was making a food run. I was apparently now a member of the "Rolling Solo" team. *Great.*

"Yessss," Iris said in a poor impression of a snake. "Sssseems we're going to win."

"You are such a dork," I said. I was too annoyed to want to laugh, but I couldn't help at least smiling a little. No matter how lost I felt at the moment, the one thing that had always been an anchor in my life was my friendship with Kira and Iris.

"Then you're going to lose to a dork," Iris said. "What does that make you?"

"Bad at bowling?" I guessed.

Iris took a fry from Rich and Kira's tray, burned her mouth, and strung together a creative line of swear words. "Thanks for warning me they were hotter than Satan's asshole."

"Maybe you should stop trying to steal other people's food. It's karma," I said. "I'd also be curious to know how you have experience with the temperature of Satan's rectum."

6

"Rectum," she said, laughing. "You're such a proper dork." Iris reached for another fry. I swatted at her wrist, and she pulled her hand back, then shot me a dirty look. "You can't control me."

I rolled my eyes. I found a spot on the cracked-leather bench behind our alley and sat down. I set Rich and Kira's food to the side and watched as Iris joined into an argument Cade and Kira were in. They were debating if it was against the rules for Cade to lie on his belly and push the ball instead of doing it like a normal human being. He was getting way too far into character as a snake.

"You good?" Rich asked.

"I'm fine," I said. I still wasn't used to talking to any of the King brothers. Seven years ago, I'd sworn an oath with Kira and Iris. We said we'd never date them again, no matter what. Even if they came back on their knees and begged us to forgive them for what they put us through—even if they wound up famous and dripping with cash. Apparently, my friends had decided solemn oaths sworn on hilltops in the dead of night were negotiable. I guessed I'd missed that particular memo. Now the oath that held the three of us together felt more like an anchor tied around my neck.

"I've just been thinking about everything lately," I said.

It was almost silly for me to even care anymore. It would be different if Nick King had shown any interest in me since coming back to West Valley, but he seemed content to take over his brother Cade's role of the town playboy. It still turned my stomach to think about. The Nick I'd known seven years ago was thoughtful and intelligent. He didn't jump from woman to woman for a quick thrill. I knew people changed, but looking at who he was becoming felt more like admitting the boy I'd known back then was dead. The only glimmer of solace I could take was the rumor about how he was becoming notorious for never sleeping with any of the women he was dating. I wasn't sure if I believed it, but it was confusing to find I wanted to.

Rich was the put-together, mostly normal twin brother of Cade. Like all the King brothers, he was offensively hot. They were like the three brothers of the apocalypse, at least if apocalypses could be caused by raging female hormones. Rich would bring destruction to all the women with traditional taste. He was smart, funny, and kind. He'd charm your mom and dad, be great with the kids, and probably help fix your dad's 401(k) while he was at it. Cade would charm your mom in particular, piss off your dad, and wind up talking one of the kids into doing something reckless that resulted in broken bones.

The Nick I'd known in high school was harder to figure out. He had seemed nice enough, but there was also a dark cloud around him if you looked closely. You'd never quite known what his goals were, but he was so viciously intelligent that we'd all known he was destined for something incredible.

"Thinking about everything, huh?" He stroked his chin thoughtfully. "People don't usually think about everything unless it feels like *everything* is going to shit, I've found."

I laughed softly. "Fair point. And maybe that's not so far from the truth."

He raised an eyebrow. I couldn't blame him for looking surprised. The few sentences I'd muttered to him had probably been the most open I'd ever been with him. I wasn't even sure why I suddenly wanted to confide in him. Normally, I would've at least talked to Kira or Iris about this. For some reason, I felt the floodgates threatening to open for Rich instead. Maybe it was knowing that Cade, of all people, was the only person who really knew what was going on with me. Well, Cade and the traumatized middle school kid.

I sighed. "It's just that I was kind of used to the idea of having *steady boyfriend* checked off my list. You know? My whole life has always been about checking off boxes. Get good grades. Get into my first choice for college. Get a degree. Get a job. Get promoted. Work harder until you get promoted again."

Rich nodded. "At some point, you realize it's not how many boxes you check, but which ones you check, and how well you check them."

Now it was my eyebrows that crept up. "Spoken like somebody with experience."

Rich flashed a smile that didn't completely make me decide to start liking him, but it came close. "Why do you think I suddenly dropped everything to come to West Valley and win Kira back?" he asked.

"Kira said you never admitted she was the reason you came back. I thought the official story was something about business opportunities on the East Coast."

Rich looked a little coy. "Maybe letting you in on that little secret will get you to stop glaring at me all the time."

I bit back a smile. "Maybe. But if you told me what got Nick to agree to come back, I'd consider it a done deal. No more glaring."

"Nick, huh? As the last surviving member of the Overlook Point Oath Squad, I wouldn't peg you as the one to be curious about Nick— you know, considering he's supposed to be the only man in the world you'd never date."

"Maybe curiosity and a desire to date aren't necessarily synonymous?"

He held up his palms. "Point taken. But I guess I'll have to deal with more glares, because Nick's reasons aren't mine to share. If you want to know badly enough, maybe you two will have to stop playing chicken and finally talk."

My water bottle crinkled between my fingers when I thought of Nick. When I really thought about it, Nick made me feel pathetic more than anything else. It had been seven years since I had had a crush on him. Seven years since he had asked Kira out instead of me and made it painfully clear that he wasn't interested in me that way. It might not have all seemed so humiliating if I hadn't written him that stupid poem the day before he had asked Kira out. I still cringed when I thought about it. Either way, it wasn't the sort of thing that should've warranted an eternal grudge. And if I was honest with myself, anger wasn't what kept me from wanting to fix things with him. It was the fear that he'd break my heart again.

When Rich had come back to West Valley, he'd practically gone straight from the plane to Kira's school and tried to apologize for what had happened seven years ago. Cade hadn't been in as much of a hurry, but he'd still found his way back to Iris. Nick, on the other hand, had avoided me like the plague.

That didn't normally bother me, but I guessed I was feeling a little sorry for myself, considering the events of the last twenty-four hours. I'd broken up with the boyfriend everybody thought was perfect for me and lost the job everyone thought I was amazing at.

I might not have been certain of a whole lot at the moment, but I knew one thing: all I wanted was for things to go back to normal, even if I was starting to have more and more trouble figuring out what normal was.

"Hmm," Rich said. He was watching me with an annoyingly perceptive expression, like he knew exactly how *not fine* I was. He pointed to my hands. "It looks like you're thinking about taking that poor water bottle into the bathroom and interrogating it."

I relaxed my grip on the bottle. "I've been better," I said. "But, no offense, it's not something I really want to talk about."

"Just remember that it's not good to bottle it up forever. You've got me, Kira, Iris, and even Cade—if you feel like venting to a brick wall that spits out bad puns and laughs at its own jokes, that is."

I smirked. As if on cue, Cade grew considerably louder. Both Rich and I stopped talking to look toward him.

Cade's palms were pressed together, and he was doing some kind of swimming motion, maybe still imitating a snake. Kira was pressing her hand to her forehead, and Iris was watching with a confused expression.

"Do you mind apologizing to everyone for me?" I asked Rich. "I've got a big day tomorrow. I think it'd be best if I head home and get some sleep."

He watched me with a funny expression. "You sure everything is okay? Aside from the obvious issues, I mean."

"Fine," I said, and then I laughed after a short pause. "And that's not code. Really, I'm fine."

But I couldn't help thinking how far from fine I was as I headed out of the bowling alley. I didn't let myself dwell on any of that. All I had to do was what I'd always done. Look forward. Focus on working my ass off and chasing my goal, even when the thought made me want to curl up and aggressively breathe into a paper bag.

I can do this.

The only slight hitch in my plan was my friends would *all* laugh their asses off when they found out where I was planning to interview tomorrow.

Chapter 2
NICK

Everybody lived for something. Some spent their whole lives searching for that something; others found it but never quite reached it. I'd found mine a long time ago, and I woke up every day hoping for another taste. I lived for a challenge. It was my drug. When I was younger, it had been enough to find something hard and overcome it.

I'd always been clever, and that let me overpower almost every obstacle I'd come across. Then I realized it wasn't enough to just overcome the obstacles. There were countless ways to get through a locked door, but only one perfect way: the key. My addiction evolved until it wasn't enough to succeed. I had to succeed in a clean, precise way. *A perfect way.*

Take my man-child of a brother, Cade. Keeping him alive was a challenge that probably should've required a full-time staff of handlers and experts. It probably should've also required specialized tools like cattle prods and traps to keep him under control during his more adventurous moments. But it was technically a task that could be accomplished in any number of ways.

I believed there was a perfect solution to every challenge. Finding it was what gave me a rush. I loved the process of searching for the secret, whether it was subtly convincing my brother it was actually a bad idea to ride a shark—yes, even if he was wearing full-body chain mail—or finding the one faulty cog in the complicated machinery of a failing company.

I craved the perfect solution. Precision. There was a kind of poetry in the efficiency of doing something just right—without an ounce more or less effort than was required.

My brothers and I owned a company called Sion, and our work was all about that kind of precision. We found businesses that were on their way to financial collapse and turned them into virtual money-printing machines. When we showed up with checkbooks and wrote down enough zeroes, they were always willing to sell off their burden to us. After that, my job was to trim the fat. When necessary, I'd step in as a temporary CEO until I could find the key to getting the company back on track. Nothing ever quite matched the feeling of finding the one loose thread—that sometimes-minute adjustment to let every other piece fall back into place.

Today, Bark Bites was going to become Sion's newest acquisition. It was a restaurant franchise where the menu also included a selection of items for your dog. The dogs were given a little doghouse beneath the table and a tether to be leashed. Based on the information I'd seen, Bark Bites was about six months away from declaring bankruptcy, whether the management knew it or not. They weren't a publicly shared company, so the hostile takeover route was off the table. Instead, I was going to go the simple route. I had a meeting scheduled in half an hour, and I was going to show up with a fat check in my hand.

My brother Cade sat beside me in the lobby. It was rare for him to join me on business outings. For that matter, it was rare for Cade to do much work in general. My brother had an unfortunate tendency to attract disaster and avoid responsibility. Unfortunately, the work he *did* do was borderline genius, and we always knew we could bring him in when negotiations reached a standstill with important clients. Cade could convince just about anyone to do just about anything. If he wasn't so annoyingly useful, we could've just told him to stay home and skipped the hassle. But becoming a father seemed to have pushed him to be a little more proactive in being a regular part of the business. He'd never admit as much, but I wondered if he was trying to be a better example for Bear.

I always felt slightly obligated to spend time around Cade, if for no other reason than to keep him from accidentally offing himself. I imagined it wasn't much different from being in charge of a two-year-old, at least if that two-year-old was hypercapable and clever in the dumbest ways imaginable. I'd saved him from countless near-death experiences. There was the time he'd called to complain that the constant beeping of his carbon monoxide detectors was giving him a headache and making him nauseated. There was also the time he plugged in a drenched extension cord outside to prove it was safe—it wasn't—and if I hadn't kicked him away from the cord, I'm not sure he would've been able to let go.

Cade leaned his head back against the wall while he played a game on his phone that looked like it was designed for children.

"Can you at least turn the volume down?" I asked.

Cade shot me a withering look. He and my brother Rich were twins. Cade's life of mischievous living and trouble had somehow managed to make the two of them pretty easy to tell apart. Cade was the one who looked like he'd throw a party at a moment's notice, and Rich was the one who looked like he'd shut it down and tell everybody to get back to work. They were as close to polar opposites as you could get, but I supposed that wasn't a shocker from identical twins. Everyone wanted an identity, but twins had to work harder to carve out their own since they were always being compared.

Cade tapped the buttons on the side of his phone, and I was fairly sure the game got louder. "How's that?" he asked.

"Remind me again why you decided to tag along for this?"

"Because of your little speech?" He tried to change his voice to imitate mine. "Rich and I are so busy pairing off and getting in relationships that we're going to neglect the business." He paused, mimicking pushing a pair of glasses up his nose. "*Blah, blah.* You're worried that it's going to all fall on your shoulders. *Blah, blah.* You have a fetish for women dressed as pirates, and you fantasize about what they'd do with their peg legs. What was it you said, again? 'I want 'em hilt deep in me dark star'? Or was it 'elbow deep and h*arrrr*d.' Emphasis on the *'arrr.'*"

I sighed but couldn't help grinning a little. "Why is that so weirdly specific? Also, that's disgusting. Dark star? Do you seriously talk about assholes enough that you need to get that creative in nicknaming them?"

"Every good fetish is full of details. Like I knew this woman once who wanted me to role-play a crow." Cade leaned in and lowered his voice. "But she had clipped my wings, and she was keeping me prisoner. Like a sex slave. But a crow, so I had to kind of—" He started trying to do something to me with his arms outstretched like two big, stiff wings.

I stared at him, and the look on my face made him trail off. "I was going to say you should be less specific, because it makes me wonder if you could make something so obscure up. But now I see you're just pulling from past experiences."

He shrugged. "You've never been with somebody who was into the pirate stuff?" He made an imaginary hook with his index finger and tried to pull my shirt open while making vague, raspy pirate noises. "Where do you keep the booty?" he demanded.

I chuckled and slapped his hand away. "Jesus Christ. No wonder we stopped trying to talk you into working more. It's like bring-your-kid-to-work day."

"You wish I was your kid."

"What is that even supposed to mean?"

"Don't worry your pretty little head about it. Just know that if your genius plan to give Dan a huge check fails, I'll be right here with my unstoppable negotiation skills."

"The big-check plan never fails," I said. "Give me two minutes in there, and Bark Bites will be ours."

"*Bark Bites will be ours*," Cade mocked. "You sound like a supervillain."

I shook my head and tried to get my head back on the work. This wasn't the typical company we tried to flip at Sion. Usually, we aimed for the big, national kind of companies. It had always amazed me how even the biggest failing companies had one problem at the root of all their issues. If you identified all the symptoms and worked your way backward, you'd eventually find that single, glaring problem. *The key.* Sometimes, it was an employee, a company policy, a branding error, or even a clerical mistake. Whatever it was, I loved the challenge of finding it and fixing it.

The door to the lobby opened, and I stared for a few moments before I realized who I was looking at.

Miranda Collins. The afternoon sun blazed in behind her so at first all I could make out was the vague, glowing outline of her. I had to stop myself from thinking she looked angelic in that moment. It was just a trick of the light. She walked a straight line past the bench where Cade and I sat. Her head was held high, and her eyes never so much as flickered from staring straight ahead.

Seeing her always made me feel strange. I knew she still wanted nothing to do with me, but she took it a step further. Miranda was aggressively indifferent toward me, and not just the kind of indifferent that meant she'd intentionally avoid saying *bless you* if I sneezed in front of her. No. It had gone far, far beyond that. There was a kind of hatred in her eyes that, like good wine, had fermented and grown stronger over time. On the rare occasions I'd caught her looking at me since my brothers and I had come back to West Valley, I could've sworn my soul had tried to shrivel up and hide from the intensity of those eyes.

But, I had to admit the fact that she loathed me so much was also a little bit sexy. I also couldn't help thinking that she was the Mount Everest of challenges. I mean, what possible key could there be to a problem that complex? What could I find in that tangle of old, sour bitterness she called a brain that would get me in? Sometimes, I thought

16

the only way to fix what had gone wrong between Miranda and me was time travel. Hell, maybe that was why I'd always had such a nerdy fascination with the topic.

Without going back in time, how could I possibly fix what was broken between us?

It was an old question I'd asked myself a dozen times before, but it didn't stop me from looking at it again. I studied her as she passed, as if some subtle hint in her body language might hold the key. She wore her long blonde hair in a braided ponytail down her back. Her outfit was crisp and pressed, like she'd somehow managed to commute here without sitting down and putting the slightest wrinkle in her skirt. I distantly decided I wouldn't have put it past her to own a portable steam press to touch up her clothes throughout the day.

She was beautiful, confident, and successful. None of it surprised me. Seven years ago, I'd had a massive crush on her when we'd gone to high school together. I'd often thought about how things played out back then. It seemed like one or two different decisions could've set us all on a different course. Instead, I'd wound up dating Kira after she'd written me that poem out of nowhere. Cade had brought those idiotic pot brownies for Iris, and Rich had ratted Kira out to his coaches. In three fell swoops, we'd managed to set off the romantic equivalent of a nuclear bomb between ourselves and the girls. It had all culminated in the infamous vow Kira, Iris, and Miranda swore on Overlook Point. No matter what, they'd never date me or my brothers. Except Miranda seemed to be the only one who still cared about the oath.

I waited for her head to turn or even her eyes to shift toward me, but she didn't so much as glance our way as she passed.

Cold, as usual.

Cade leaned over and whispered, "Go to her."

As much as I hated doing anything my brother suggested, I knew the curiosity was going to eat at me if I didn't try to talk to her. I wasn't chasing after her for the reasons my brother probably thought, though.

Yes, she was the challenge of all challenges, but I also wasn't planning on tackling her—or the challenge she presented—yet. Part of what made me good at what I did was my patience. I knew if I just waited long enough, an opportunity would present itself.

To do my job well, I needed as much information about Bark Bites as I could get. The moment Miranda walked through the door, she'd become a piece of information. That was all. *For now.*

The lobby led into a long hallway lined with doors, most of which seemed to be offices. I was about to call out to Miranda when I saw her pause outside the door at the end of the hallway. Her back was still to me. She took a few deep breaths and half turned like she was about to head back the way she'd come, but then she reached for the door. She pulled her hand back suddenly and muttered something under her breath.

Why was she hesitating? My brain quickly churned through the most likely outcomes. A job interview she was nervous for? Delivering bad news to someone in that room? A boyfriend who works here?

I was surprised when the last possibility made me feel tight in the chest. I knew she'd been dating Robbie Goldman for a few months now, and I hadn't felt anything when I'd heard they had recently split. So why would her finding a rebound guy bother me in the slightest? Besides, I'd been dating my way through every eligible woman in West Valley to get my matchmaking parents off my back, even if I was currently single. I was the last person who had any right to be jealous if she had already found someone new. Except maybe it wouldn't feel as loveless and cold as all my failed dates had felt. Hell, I hadn't even slept with any of the women—a fact that was getting me an unfortunate reputation around town, but I hardly cared about that.

Without warning, Miranda turned and yanked on a door handle to her left. It didn't budge, so she tried another door. When it opened, she stepped inside and closed it behind her.

I had been curious before, but now I was intrigued. The Miranda I knew was the kind of well-oiled machine I had always admired. She knew her purpose, and she pursued it relentlessly. Whatever I'd just seen in the hallway didn't add up. No matter the reason, she had hesitated. It was a chink in her icy armor of indifference.

I walked slowly down the hallway until I was standing outside the door she'd gone inside. I pressed my ear to the wood and listened.

There was a strange rustling sound inside. I frowned as I tried to imagine what it could be. An aluminum can crunching? Papers brushing together? But there was a chewing noise too.

I slowly pushed the door open and looked inside.

Miranda was sitting on the ground with a bag of pretzel sticks in one hand and a chocolate candy bar in the other. She took a violent bite of the candy, then tipped the bag of pretzels back and practically inhaled a few. Once she was done chewing the pretzels, she put the bag to her mouth and started hyperventilating into it. She had to stop and cough after a few seconds, probably from inhaling pretzel salt at a high velocity.

I was about to slowly back out of the room when her face turned red. She had been coughing, but now she was just leaning forward and clutching soundlessly at her throat.

I hurried to her side, slid my arms around her from the back, and pressed my fist into her just below her breasts. She coughed again, and something half-chewed launched out of her mouth and stuck to the back of a chair.

For a few seconds, neither of us did anything except wait for the glob of half-chewed food to slide down from the chair and fall to the floor. Once it fell, I realized I was still crouched behind her with my arms around her. I could even feel the weight and warmth of her breasts just above my hands.

I was the first to recover from the shock, so I stood back up, brushed off my knees, and offered her a hand up. She took it uncertainly and then stood, brushing pretzel crumbs from her skirt.

"Hey," I said. "You're not the first person to show up for a big interview and choke."

Miranda looked like she wanted to do anything in the world but laugh. Her lips quivered, and she finally smiled and shook her head. "Thank you. For saving me."

"I'm just sorry I was too late to save those poor pretzels and the chocolate bar. I could've sworn you were only in here for a minute before I came in. Are you training for an eating competition?"

This time, she didn't appear to have any trouble not smiling. "I missed breakfast."

"I'm not surprised. I'd miss my food, too, if I could inhale it that quickly."

"If you're done making fun of me, I have an interview in a few minutes, and I need to get ready."

"See you in a few, then."

"What?" she asked.

I bit back the smile that wanted to come. "Nothing. Good luck."

Once we'd left the conference room, Miranda fast-walked toward the bathroom.

I took a few seconds to process what had happened. I'd just seen Miranda Collins double-fisting junk food. This was the same Miranda who only ever ate salads and drank water. The same one who exercised religiously and was the poster girl for perfection. A pang of concern ran through me when I realized she might have taken the breakup harder than anyone thought. I almost called after her to apologize but decided against it.

The most confusing part had been the way I could practically feel the air crackling between us when we talked. I just wanted to find out if that had been the electrical charge of an imminent explosion, or the potential for a chemical reaction. I guessed maybe there wasn't much of a difference between the two.

Either way, I had a feeling that opportunity I'd been waiting for was getting ready to present itself. It seemed like it might be time to tackle the Mount Everest of challenges, after all. The question was whether either of us would survive the process.

Chapter 3
MIRANDA

Damn it.

My throat still stung from whatever I'd inhaled during my little freak-out. No, it wasn't a freak-out. It was a calculated, rational decision to lower my heart rate and calm my breathing before a big interview. Hadn't I read something about salt and sugar being beneficial to proper brain function?

Probably not.

I needed to face the facts. I was far from being in control, no matter how hard I wanted to pretend otherwise. I still couldn't believe that Nick King, of all people, had to be the one to walk in and catch me choking on pretzels and chocolate. Why couldn't it have been a janitor?

The postsnack guilt was already creeping in on my walk to the restrooms, but I often thought of my little junk food frenzies as a sanity-retention mechanism. In less fancy terms, I'd go crazy if I couldn't at least let loose in private every once in a while.

Everybody expected me to be so damn perfect all the time. I could barely remember how it had all started anymore. All I knew was that somewhere along the way, it had stopped feeling like me. It was more like getting caught up in a current and realizing I'd been carried so far from where I'd started that the only thing to do was continue floating along. And now I could hardly order a hamburger without imagining the sarcastic jokes they'd make. They'd assume I was having a mental breakdown if I skipped a workout or had a stain on my clothes. I'd been so damn predictable and seemingly perfect for so long that the town of West Valley would've ground to a halt if I slipped up.

Get ahold of yourself, Miranda. I took a few more deep breaths—minus the pretzel bag, this time—and tried to shake the nerves out. I knew I was putting too much thought into it. I always did. It wasn't that everybody else had me in a cage. I'd put myself there, but it had been so long ago that I had no hope of finding the key anymore.

By the time I made it out of the lobby and passed the elevators, I was composed and focused again. If there was one thing I was good at, it was compartmentalization. Like a kid shoving her toys into the closet until the doors barely shut, I scooped up all my insecurities and stuffed them in a dark corner of my brain. I even used the mental equivalent of the old jump-rope-around-the-doorknobs trick, just to be safe.

I was me again. Calm, focused, and ready to kick ass. Except I nearly collided with Cade King as I turned the corner toward the restrooms.

"Whoa," Cade said. "I guess I lose the bet."

"What are you talking about? No—" I closed my eyes and tried to gather myself. "Better question. What are you doing here?"

Cade squinted. "Like in an existential sense? I guess I'm just trying to leave the world a little less uptight than I found it. You know, fighting the good fight—pulling sticks out of asses. Speaking of which, do you want any help with that?" He actually had the nerve to lean to the side, as if he were trying to look for a stick jutting out of my ass. "It's in there pretty deep. Might even be a two-man job, but if you push and I pull, I think we could—"

I jabbed my finger in his chest. "I'm about to have a very important interview, and I don't need you messing with me right now."

"Interesting," he said. He leaned forward and sniffed slightly. "You smell aroused. Why is that? Why do you reek of . . . *passion*?" He made a show of thinking deeply, scratching his chin and furrowing his eyebrows. "I know it's not because of me. *And* I saw Nick sneak into that room with you a few minutes ago, presumably alone. *Miranda!*" he said suddenly in exaggerated shock. "Your buttons aren't even done up properly, you *harlot.*"

I glanced down and remembered I wasn't wearing anything with buttons. "Could you please move? I really have to pee."

"Somebody with a guilt-free conscience wouldn't have had to check their buttons, you know. Just a thought." He wandered past me, whistling obnoxiously.

I used the bathroom and then saw Cade was sitting in the lobby once I came back out. He was watching something loud on his phone with a disinterested look on his face. He glanced up at the sound of my footsteps, shot me a thumbs-up and a wink, then went back to focusing on his phone.

Unbelievable.

I stopped outside Dan's door again. I wished I could say I was more calm and collected, but now my thoughts were buzzing with questions. I'd been so confused by Nick barging into the conference room that I hadn't thought to wonder what he was doing at Bark Bites. Seeing Cade made me even more curious. Were the King brothers planning to acquire Bark Bites, even though it was a fraction of the size of the companies they typically looked for?

I raised my hand to knock, but the door opened before I could. Dan Snyder, the president of Bark Bites, shot me a sheepish look and then walked straight past me. I watched after him, openmouthed and searching for the right words.

"Come in," a man's voice called from inside Dan's office.

I slowly stepped inside. My blood turned cold when I saw who was sitting in Dan's chair.

Nick King.

Suddenly, Cade wandering around in the lobby made complete sense.

"No. This is not happening," I said.

"Dan says you were looking at the VP job, right?" Nick asked. "Sit. Please."

I blinked a few times, half expecting Nick to vanish. It was just a stress-induced mirage, as if all that stuff I'd shoved in my mental closet had caused the doors to burst open, filling my brain with fantasies. But Nick sitting in that chair wasn't a fantasy. It was a nightmare—a deceptively beautiful nightmare, but a nightmare nonetheless.

As if on cue, he made an expectant gesture toward the chair across from his desk. "We can do the interview with you standing, but your knees don't look too trustworthy right now. Then again, I am certified in CPR in addition to my familiarity with the Heimlich maneuver, so . . ."

I cleared my throat and walked across the room in a daze. I sat down in the chair and had to drag my eyes up to meet his. "Mouth to mouth won't be necessary. I'm fine." My desire to get as far away from Nick as possible was at war with how badly I wanted this job.

He looked painfully good as he sat there and studied me. His shirt was a dark charcoal gray with a silver tie speckled with teal slashes of color that brought out his eyes. *God.* Had he always seemed so intimidating? I had to physically force down the urge to fidget in my chair.

Nick carried a presence that I knew I could've still felt with my eyes closed. He just *looked* like he was destined for great things, as if a man so painstakingly perfect couldn't possibly exist just to have an ordinary life. I hated how small he made me feel. I especially hated how that smallness didn't also go hand in hand with a sense of wonder.

"I just have one question before we start," I said. *Why didn't you love me back all those years ago? Why Kira?* I mentally willed myself to cool it. Being a hysterical idiot, even if it was only in my own head, wasn't going to do any good.

"As long as it's appropriate," he said.

"What? Why would I ask you something inappropriate?"

He shrugged. "I just wanted you to know it wouldn't be professional for you to ask me if I was currently single, for example. Then again, we don't technically work together, yet, so I suppose the line is still delightfully blurry. Scratch that. Ask me anything."

My mouth was hanging open. "I was——" I clamped my mouth shut. I couldn't even remember what I'd been planning to ask anymore. Was he actually flirting with me like nothing had ever happened? I bit back the temptation to ask him that. It was a verbal minefield I wouldn't survive stepping into, and I knew it.

"Yes?" he asked, leaning in.

"I'm not going to ask if you and your brothers bought Bark Bites, because seeing you sitting there makes that pretty clear. But . . . how did you know I was planning to interview here?"

Nick tilted his head to the side as a slow smile spread across his handsome face. He chuckled softly. "Oh, I see. You think this is no coincidence? Wow. I'd say I was flattered, but it sounds more like you're flattering yourself. You think I'd buy an entire company just so I could fulfill some creepy power fantasy and become your boss?"

I blushed. "When you say it out loud, it sounds ridiculous. I'm sorry, no, that's not what I really——"

Nick drummed his fingers on the table. "The real question is whether I'd use that power to punish you for vowing to avoid me, or to try to seduce you into breaking your vow."

I felt thirsty suddenly, and the heat in my cheeks was spreading to my chest. I was appalled at how obviously flirtatious he was being—and also secretly thrilled by it. I wasn't sure if he was really flirting, though. In some ways, it felt more like he was planning to lure me into a kind of emotional trap.

"Wouldn't the third option be that you're not planning on abusing the power you'd have over me?"

"That would be a third option, yes," he said flatly. "It would also be the least exciting option."

"So when does the interview start, exactly?"

"As soon as you're done investigating my personal life. Also, to answer the question you were too afraid to ask: no, I'm not currently seeing anyone."

I chose to ignore that. "One more question. Why Bark Bites? I've seen the list of companies Sion has acquired. This is way lower profile than anything you guys have ever set your sights on before."

"My brothers and I have our reasons, but those don't concern you."

As perfect as everyone tried to make me out to be, I didn't always manage my temper as well as I should have. I was also the kind of person whose idea of a perfect day was one where everything went according to plan and stayed on schedule. The past few weeks had been a shitstorm, and today was threatening to push me over the edge. "Part of being the vice president of a company involves helping to make decisions that impact the overall direction of the company. In order to do that, I'd need to know what direction that is. And to do *that*, I'd need my boss to be open with me."

Once I stopped talking, I realized I'd been raising my voice slightly. I sat back in my chair and hoped it wasn't obvious that my heart was pounding. Nick was just staring at me. Why was he just staring like that?

He finally leaned forward, steepling his fingers. "Then I'm not obligated to be open with you until I become your boss, am I?"

I worked my lips to the side, biting back annoyance. "I didn't come to this interview with Dan—or you, for that matter—to beg for a job. I came to explain why I'm the best fit for it and why you'd be lucky to have me work for you. So if you want the privilege of having me work here, you'll be open with me. Starting now." I knew my face looked calm and collected, but my heart was pounding like crazy, and I could feel sweat beading across the bridge of my nose.

"You know? I have to admit," Nick said, "I was conflicted about this interview. I thought our past would make it hard to be objective in deciding whether to hire you. But I admire your backbone. Maybe you really do have what it takes for this job."

"I don't want to be rude, but you still haven't answered my question."

Nick's full lips flickered outward at the corners, just for a moment. His face barely showed it, but there was a lightness in his eyes now where there had been only hard, piercing evaluation a moment before. "I have some personal reasons for buying Bark Bites that won't impact you, but from a practical sense, I think there is a huge potential to grow the business model and restructure the company. That's where you can help me, assuming you still want the job, that is."

I felt like I was sweating more than a vegetarian at a barbecue, and I'd only had to endure a handful of minutes alone with Nick. My mouth was running on autopilot. I was in interview mode—kick ass and take no prisoners—but I hadn't even stopped to ask myself if I could really work for Nick King, of all people.

"Would you like some water?" Nick asked. "You look a little . . ."

"I'm fine," I said, except I thought I might be going through the five stages of grief at record speeds. None of this was real, I decided. It was all too far fetched, too absurd. I pinched my thigh and waited to be zapped from this nightmare to my bed. I closed my eyes in anticipation, but when I opened them again, he was still there. *And he was smiling.* I wanted to pull my shoe off and throw it at his smug, obnoxiously gorgeous face—even if it was going to take more than a black eye to ruin that kind of perfection.

"You really think hiring me would be wise?" I asked.

Nick mulled that over. "A few moments ago, you looked like you were going to punch me in the mouth for implying you might not get the job. Now you're trying to make sure I want to give it to you?"

I closed my eyes for a second and attempted to gather my thoughts. He was right, *annoyingly*. "I just mean, when you think about how— when you think about our . . . you know."

"Past?" he asked.

"Yes."

"Ahh, wow. I'm sorry. I feel like such an ass for not even thinking about that. You mean your feelings for me would make it uncomfortable for you to work under me?"

"No. *No.* That's not what I said." *Work under him.* Why was my mind so quick to twist that into its dirtiest possibility? And why did the mental image of Nick glaring down at me make my stomach twist with warm tendrils of heat?

"Of course. My mistake." But the look on Nick's face said he wasn't buying my story. The frustrating part was that he appeared so convinced I had feelings for him I was starting to wonder if he was right. "Forget I said anything," he continued. "But I am curious. Why are you here? Last I heard, you were planning to leapfrog your way to the top of Crawford Industries. A VP job at a failing small-scale company like this doesn't even come close."

"You weren't the only one who heard. The guys I was getting ready to leapfrog for a promotion decided it'd be better for everyone if it looked like I'd screwed up our biggest account. And maybe I wanted a chance to work somewhere that actually needed my help, for once."

For the briefest moment, Nick actually looked sympathetic, but his expression went back to amused so quickly I knew I must have imagined it. "Well, it's your lucky day, then. Isn't it?"

I felt my head sag forward, as if my forehead had suddenly developed a magnetic attraction to my knees. "That's one way to look at this," I said.

"And how do you look at it?"

"That there's no room in the business world for personal matters." I raised my eyes up and stared at him unflinchingly for the first time.

"And when you plan to get a job done, you do it, no matter what obstacles get put in your way."

Nick chuckled. "A bit dramatic, maybe. But I'll happily be your obstacle, especially if it means I get to enjoy watching you try to crawl over me."

I thought about objecting but realized I'd only make it worse if I acknowledged his implication. "Thank you," I said curtly.

"Well. Congratulations," he said. "The job is yours, if you want it."

I shook Nick's hand and left the room. As much as I wanted to portray calm, I couldn't help fast-walking my way toward the exit. I just needed space. *Air.*

I stared straight ahead. Confidence, confidence, confidence. It wasn't fair, but the business world expected an entirely different level of professionalism from women. Men could loosen their ties and joke around without losing the respect of their employees. Women didn't always have that luxury, so I knew I needed to keep my walls up. *Always.* The thought left a bitter taste in my mouth. Those same walls were part of the reason my "perfect" boyfriend was no longer in the picture. I'd made my choice, though. I'd been chasing my goals for too long to let anything get in the way. Even Robbie. And now I had a bad feeling if I didn't plow my way through Nick, he'd be the one doing the plowing.

I cringed. Why couldn't I stop accidentally turning my thoughts sexual when it came to him? I was supposed to want to punch him in the mouth, not kiss it. A few minutes alone with him was poisoning seven years of painstakingly maintained anger, and I needed to put an end to that before it got any worse. *Somehow.*

"Hey," Nick called from behind me. "Wait a sec."

I turned around and couldn't help drinking him in all over again. He was like a sweet wine with a bitter aftertaste. The first glimpse made jolts of excitement run through me, but then the past would bubble up and make my stomach turn.

Dark hair, dark-green eyes, glasses, and a heavy dose of brooding. His brothers could've been cast as the superheroes in any blockbuster movie, but Nick had a touch of the traits that would've made for the perfect sympathetic villain. He would've been the kind of villain audiences swooned over and rooted for, even as he was crushing the world under his boots.

Nick had always stood apart from his brothers in more ways than one. It had been what made me develop a hopeless crush on him back in high school. He usually wore an expression like he was trying to think through some impossible problem. The Nick I knew was always struggling to find something worthwhile for that bright mind of his, and whether anyone else wanted to admit it or not, I knew he was the backbone of Sion's multibillion-dollar success. Nick was the smartest man I'd ever met, and that was part of the reason I'd never forgiven him for dating Kira all those years ago. He was too smart to claim he didn't know how I'd felt about him back then. He'd also been too kind to let me write a poem like that for him and then pretend it had never happened.

But he'd changed, even in the last few months. It seemed like he was trying to date his way through every woman in West Valley before the end of the year. Except me, of course. Maybe watching his brothers pair off into relationships had him putting some kind of pressure on himself to compete.

He was standing now with that scrutinizing look. He wasn't the boy from high school anymore with the broad shoulders and the thin frame. He'd thickened up with a touch of muscle in the right places, and his face had matured in ways that made it hard not to gawk. Regardless, I would've had to dig very deep to find any warmth for him in my heart. I felt it in my skin and my stomach, but not where it counted. Seven years of holding a grudge did wonders for quenching flames, after all.

"Yes?" I asked. I made a monumental effort to be professional. I'd decided that was the final stage of this whirlwind. No matter how

I might feel about this, all I had to do was do my job and do it well. My feelings for Nick—or lack thereof—could sit in the back seat and get into as much trouble as they wanted so long as the car got where it needed to go.

"You dropped this." Nick held out a candy wrapper for me. The irritating twinkle in his eye made a wave of jittery panic run through me.

Calm, I reminded myself. *Be calm.* I reached out a steady hand and took it from him. "It must've fallen out of my purse."

"Since when do you eat candy?" Cade asked. He was still sitting in the lobby with his eyes glued to his phone. "I thought you were a green-smoothie-and-detox kind of person. You know, they make detoxing sound so clean and fancy. Nobody tells you it's just the process of blasting the contents of your stomach out in the form of liquid—"

"Cade," I said quickly. "If you would stay out of this, it'd be great."

"Stay out of this?" he asked. "Oh my. I hadn't realized you and Nick already graduated to *this* status. Well done, Nick. You've started to warm the heart of the ice queen, after all. Next, you'll just need to work that warmth down, and *down, and—*"

"It's just a"—I took a shaky breath, then regained my composure, which wasn't easy with two King brothers watching me and Cade spouting nonsense—"figure of speech. And unless I dropped some more trash, I should be going."

Nick licked his lips. "Actually, I was thinking we could grab something to eat. Break the ice and smooth over old wounds before your first day."

Cade looked up from his phone. "Are you barking mad? She swore an oath that she'd never date you. *An oath.*"

Nick and I both glared at him.

Cade looked between us, then sighed. "It was a pun. *Bark Bites.* Barking mad? Never mind. I don't need you to laugh to know I'm funny."

"Puns are only funny when they fit the context of a conversation," Nick said. "That's half of the art of a good pun."

Cade held up a finger to silence his brother while he tapped something into his phone and squinted at the screen. "Look," he said, still reading off his phone. "You're barking up the wrong tree. Today has been *ruff*, and . . ." Cade suddenly laughed. "Oh, wait, did I ever tell you about the time I went to the zoo and they only had one small dog? It was a shih tzu." He laughed again. "Shit zoo—you get it, right? Like the zoo was shit, but the dog was—"

"Are you just reading puns off a list online?" Nick asked.

Cade set his phone in his lap. "Uh, no? I was multitasking. Work emails, I shih tzu not."

"As much fun as it is to listen to my brain cells committing suicide one by one, I should really go," I said.

"Wait," Nick said. "You never gave me an answer."

"About lunch? I don't think that'd be a good idea."

Cade nodded. "She's right. You put that much chemistry in a small restaurant booth? *Boom.* Might as well jump into a swimming pool filled with soda while wearing a full bodysuit covered in Mentos. *Bad idea.* Trust me." He made an explosion noise and spread his fingers out. "Clothes everywhere. Just naked bodies. Sweat. Passion. Maybe a grilled cheese stuck on Nick's butt cheek." He put his hand to the side of his mouth and whisper-yelled the rest. "He's really into the whole food-mixed-with-sex thing. Also something about pegging? Pirate legs? I forgot the details, but really just anything pirate related would—"

"Could you . . . not?" Nick asked.

"I'll see you in the morning," I said.

"Oh," Nick said. "One more thing. Cade, can you go grab . . . *the package*?"

The evil twinkle in Cade's eyes immediately told me I wasn't going to like whatever the package was. He actually set off at a jog and disappeared into a room for a few seconds. When he emerged, he was holding a leash attached to the ugliest dog I'd ever seen.

It was some sort of mutt with short brown hair and an underbite so extreme that all its lower teeth were permanently visible. It was freakishly big, too, and it immediately jumped up on me and wagged its tail so hard that its butt was shaking.

I cringed, but the beast was unrelenting. It kept pawing at me until I finally gave in and gave it one grudging scratch on the top of its head.

"Meet Thug. He's kind of like the company mascot, and we apparently inherited him when we bought the business."

"*Thug?*" I asked. "What kind of name is that for a dog?"

"Well, his full legal name is actually Bone Thug. But Dan said he'll answer to Thug."

As if confirming this, Thug's head whipped toward Nick at the sound of his name. I was grateful to have what must've been all one hundred pounds of the creature off me. "Okay. Great to meet him, but I'm going to go."

"Well, that's the thing. I need you to find somebody at the company who can adopt him."

"Dan seriously just left his dog?"

"It's a mascot," Nick said. "Thug is part of the image, and we need him to be happy and healthy. So until you find a good home, I want you to keep him."

Nick stuck the leash out toward my hand. I stared at it.

"You want me to . . . I've never even owned a dog."

Nick shrugged. "It'll be good for you." He reached out and took my hand, peeling my fingers open before sticking the leash in my palm. "I think you two are going to make a great team."

I made the mistake of looking at Cade, who was practically giddy. The bastard was enjoying this. I considered finding out if Thug knew any attack commands but decided that'd be about as dangerous as pointing a gun at Cade and finding out whether it was loaded. I wasn't *quite* there yet.

"Okay. Fine. I'll find somebody to take him first thing tomorrow. How bad could one night be?"

"See?" Nick said. "That's the spirit."

I left as quickly as I could to avoid getting dragged any deeper into the madness that was the King brothers—except, I realized with a sinking kind of dread, escaping today was only delaying the inevitable.

The last ten minutes had made me feel like I was circling some kind of black hole, just barely resisting enough to be pulled any deeper, but caught in its orbit all the same. I knew I'd been spending too much time around Cade King, because I could practically hear his voice in my head. *You're circling Nick's black hole, huh? Some kind of fetish you want to tell us about?*

Despite everything, I grinned to myself.

This new chapter of my life was exactly the kind of thing I'd been avoiding for as long as I could remember. It was unpredictable. It stripped away control from me and put it in the hands of a man who had already proved he was capable of breaking my heart once.

I should've been terrified, but I had to admit there was a part of me that could hardly wait to see how this all went. It was either going to end in catastrophe, or it'd turn into the biggest challenge I'd ever overcome. At least there'd be fireworks either way.

I met Kira and Iris inside the West Valley High School gym for the annual pig-wrangling show. It was packed, just like every other town event in West Valley. Even the light snow outside and biting cold weren't going to stop anyone. We all met up in front of the little foldout table where high school kids were selling entrance tickets for two dollars apiece. Once we had our tickets, we headed inside the crowded gym.

I should've been feeling better, but my run-in with Nick King still had my brain spinning. I had a new job, but it had come with a sloppy side serving of complicated mess.

Kira nudged me. "You coming?"

I smiled and nodded. "Yeah, sorry."

"Actually," Iris said, "she probably isn't doing a whole lot of coming these days. Unless she busted that monster dildo back out again. What did you name it again, the ClamJammer?"

"I thought we agreed not to talk about that anymore. And, no, I called it the UpperCunter," I said tightly. I discreetly looked around to make sure nobody had overheard.

Iris and Kira both stifled laughter.

"Sometimes," Iris said wistfully, "I still see it when I close my eyes. Big. Black. Shiny. So imposing. I remember wondering how any woman could possibly fit such a beast ins—"

I pressed my palm to her mouth. My voice was wire tight. "I was going through a lot of stress in college. Okay?"

"I'd be stressed, too, if somebody tried to put that twenty-pound monster up my hoo-ha," Iris said.

Kira tried to hold back a smile but failed.

"What?" I asked. "You too?"

"I'm sorry," Kira said. "But I mean, come on. It was under your pillow. Unless you were planning to beat a home invader unconscious with that thing . . ."

"A change of subject would be great," I said. "Or maybe just two friends who are sympathetic after a breakup instead of teasing me about being single."

"Since when do you want sympathy?" Iris asked. "I got you a get-well-soon card once, and you lit it on fire because you refused to admit you were sick. Ten minutes later, I was holding your hair back while you blew chunks in the kitchen sink."

"Wait," Kira said. "I cooked you dinner that night. You threw up in the *sink*? Did you even sanitize it?"

"Could we all just agree to stop roasting me when I'm at a bit of a low point already?" I asked. "I thought best friends were supposed to help you out of the crappy parts, not smash your face farther into them."

Iris held up her fingers and turned them counterclockwise, making a clicking noise with her mouth.

"What was that?" I asked.

"Roasters are off," she said in a dull tone that meant I was stupid for needing it explained. "Oh, but speaking of monsters. How is the Thug life?"

I rolled my eyes. "Did Cade make you ask me that?"

She grinned. "No comment. But I have to admit the idea of some huge out-of-control dog in your perfect little life is kind of amazing."

"Who says he's out of control? I kind of assumed he was well trained."

Kira's eyes widened. "Did you put him in a cage or anything before you left?"

"A cage? Where am I supposed to get a cage big enough to hold a dog the size of a small horse?"

"Well," Kira said cheerily. "What's the worst that could happen?"

I felt a lump of anxiety the size of a basketball thump into my stomach. I put a lot of work into keeping my house pristine, and now my mind was racing with the possibilities of what Mr. Bone Thug could be doing to it while I was gone. "Maybe I should go back home and check."

"Nope," Iris said. "Your perfect little house will be fine. Poop cleans out of carpets, walls, and clothes. Just ask Kira."

"What the hell is that supposed to mean?" Kira asked.

Despite my nerves, I couldn't help laughing with Iris. "I'm not surprised the violent pooper herself decided to repress the memory."

Kira folded her arms. "I told you two a million times that it wasn't me."

"And that's exactly what you'd say if it *was* you," Iris said. "So forgive us if we're not entirely convinced. Besides, it's always the ones you least expect. Like serial killers."

I wiggled my eyebrows at Iris, just because it was fun to watch Kira get worked up. "You're right. But maybe Kira is a serial pooper. One bathroom after another. She devastates them and waits for somebody else to take the fall."

"I'm going to break up with both of you," Kira said. "I have perfectly normal bowel habits, and I can't believe you two just made me say that out loud."

Iris and I laughed. We finally decided to stop picking on Kira once we worked our way deeper into the building and more people were crowded in around us. It was one thing to tease her among the three of us, but we'd never risk letting something like that spin into a rumor. West Valley was worse than high school when it came to rumors.

"Wait," Kira said. She had her hair pulled back in a bun and her glasses on tonight. She had started dressing a little fancier since she'd reconnected with Rich, but she somehow still managed to look like she could fit right in restocking books at the local library. Of course, she was beautiful, too, but she was the wholesome sort of pretty that never seemed to bring out cattiness in other women. "I thought the event tonight was the apple cannon thing. Why are the criminals here?"

She was looking toward the center of the gym, which we could see now that we'd climbed up the bleachers a few rows. Three men in handcuffs were sitting inside a fenced-off area where a greased-up baby pig was snorting and sniffing around piles of hay. Seeing the pig explained the smell I'd noticed when we came in. I'd thought maybe it was just the collective sweat of a few hundred people, since everyone seemed to think the heat needed to get cranked up to sweltering whenever the temperature outside dipped below seventy-two.

"Uh, no," Iris said. She had started letting her short black hair grow out so that it now reached her shoulders. I wondered if that had been at Cade's request, or if Iris had just decided she was done trying so hard to look the way she thought a police officer should look. To me, she'd always been somebody who could kick my ass and look good doing it. For all Cade's negative qualities, he did seem to at least have a positive impact on Iris and her confidence. "The apple cannon thing is in July. How did you get that mixed up?"

Kira sighed. "I guess I just kind of show up most of the time. It's all some different version of crazy, anyway, right?"

"This one seems extra demented," I said.

"Why?" Iris asked. "Is it the criminal part?"

"There are kids here. What if one of them breaks loose and goes on a murderous rampage or something?" I asked.

Iris laughed. "Okay, see, you're forgetting we're in West Valley. Goat theft is about as criminal as things get around here. More often, we're looking at public drunkenness, disorderly conduct, and that kind of jazz. So, unless you brought a goat with you tonight, I don't think you need to be afraid of our criminals."

"I didn't bring a goat, but I did bring you. Is that close enough?" I asked.

Iris shot me an icy glare. "Careful. The roasters are still off, but I won't hesitate to flip you over and cook the other side if you test me."

I rolled my eyes and smiled.

"Why do they agree to try to catch the greased pig again?" Kira asked. "Isn't it kind of demeaning for them?"

"Because we give them a nice mattress and some other perks in their cell for a few weeks if they win," Iris said. "Oh, and don't look, but a certain ex-boyfriend is walking straight toward you, Miranda."

Robbie was shouldering his tall frame through the crowd and climbing up the bleachers. He *was* handsome. He'd been everything I'd thought I wanted in a partner when I'd met him at a company luncheon a few months ago. He was the kind of good looking that everybody could agree upon. There was nothing risky about him, from his safe, classical, and sensible features to the way he managed his life. Everything about him was always in order. After just a couple of months together, I'd been able to know almost for certain how our future would turn out. A few kids, a nice home, regular vacations.

We could've had all of it, and I knew it. But instead of comforting me, the thought had made me feel suffocated.

"Miranda," Robbie said. He shot Iris and Kira a look that clearly implied he'd prefer to speak to me in private. Kira started to stand up, but Iris grabbed her wrist with a sinister little grin and made sure she didn't go anywhere.

"Hey, Robbie," I said. It hadn't been an ugly breakup, so I gave a smile I hoped was friendly. I didn't have any reason to think we wouldn't be able to transition to being friends, but we also hadn't talked much since it had happened a couple of days ago. I'd explained my reasoning, and he'd done exactly what I'd expected. He'd understood. Robbie always understood.

"I've been doing a lot of thinking. About us."

"Robbie . . ." I blew out a long breath. "I know this is weird, but I think we—"

"She dumped you," Cade said. I hadn't even seen him coming, which was unusual, considering all the King brothers were ridiculously tall. He was standing on the bleachers below us now. "She's just too nice to say she never wants to see you again. She doesn't want you marinating in her friend zone. Because we all know you'd go home every night you thought she might've flirted with you and have a depressing little wank. Emphasis on *little*."

"Cade," I said. "Please, I can—"

Robbie's lips tightened into a thin line. He had never been the confrontational type, so I wasn't surprised when all he did was give me one subtle, questioning look.

39

"It's not like that," I said to Cade. "Since you don't really know anything about what is going on, it'd be best if you kept out of it."

"It would've also been best if nobody ever invented those big-ass spiders the size of your hand that hide under toilet seats," Cade said. "But take a look at Australia. It's hot as the world's butthole, and that steamy taint is chock full of huge spiders, giant snakes, and kangaroos. I mean, what is the point of a kangaroo, even? Why have arms at all? Didn't we learn anything from the T. rex, like—"

Iris gave me a quick smile and then pressed her palms into Cade's chest. She started leading him down the bleachers like she was trying to move a massive boulder, which wasn't too far from the truth—both in terms of the physical similarities and the mental deficiencies. Cade sighed and let the tiny woman move him away from us.

Kira looked like she didn't know what to do now that Iris was gone. She started walking backward so slowly I almost couldn't tell if she was moving.

I tried to mouth *"Don't you leave me too"* without letting Robbie see.

Kira hated awkward situations, and I could see from the look in her eyes that she didn't want to be witness to this. A moment later, she had scurried off too. *Great.*

I turned my attention back to Robbie and forced a smile. "So . . ."

"I was trying to say that I've been doing a lot of thinking, since . . ." His eyebrows creased together, as if the thought of the word *breakup* was causing him physical pain.

If I still needed reassurance that I'd done the right thing, all I needed to do was study that look on his face. I didn't feel any of the emotional sting of losing *him*. Staying in a relationship like that wouldn't have been fair, even if it seemed like everyone else thought we were so perfect for each other. "Robbie," I said as gently as I could, "I should've realized we had different goals earlier than I did. But that's all there is to it. I have a vision for where I want to be, and I can't let anything get in the way of that."

"Where you want to be?" Robbie asked. Anger flashed in his eyes. "Alone and sitting on the top floor of a skyscraper in New York? Is that it? Diving in your piles of gold coins at night and sleeping on megayachts?"

I shook my head. I knew he was only being cruel because he felt embarrassed, but it still stung. "I don't care about the money. You would know that if you'd really listened. I want to—" I stopped and pursed my lips. "You know what? No. I don't need to explain it to you again. Maybe if you'd cared more, this wouldn't be so confusing to you."

"There's nothing complicated about it. We're good together. Everybody thought so. And I don't want to sound crude, but what do you think will happen once the grace period is over?"

I frowned. "The grace period? Do I even want to know what that means?"

"I didn't really want to have to spell it out. But think about it. How long do you think women are going to wait now that I'm single?"

I couldn't help laughing out loud at that. Sure, he was right, but I was finally seeing just how much Robbie had been putting on a show while we dated. This was the real him. Nasty, ugly, and overconfident. "Well, don't let me stop you from putting out the memo. Actually, if you want, I can have some copies laminated for you. How do you want it worded exactly?"

"I'm not kidding, Miranda. I won't wait around for you to change your mind. So, what's it going to be?"

"I made up my mind. I'm sorry, but that's it."

Robbie's lips twitched, and for a moment I thought he might actually shout something. Instead, he released all his tension with a soft laugh. "No. It's fine. I'll give you a few more days to realize this is a mistake. We'll talk soon."

I watched him go, suspecting there was something threatening in his words.

"That seemed to go poorly," said a familiar voice from behind me.

I was still sitting, but I nearly toppled over when I saw Nick King was right behind me.

"Okay," I said suddenly. I turned completely around to face him and held up my palms. "What is going on with you? You've acted like I didn't exist ever since you and your brothers came back to West Valley, and now I can't seem to stop running into you?"

Nick watched me in that way I was surprised to remember so well—like a bomb could go off without shaking his focus. It was the kind of look that could undo a thousand cruel words—the kind of look that could even start chipping at seven years of built-up anger. I wondered what was going through that clever mind of his as he watched me.

"I haven't been avoiding you," Nick said. "I've been giving you space."

"Space," I said. "Yeah, in the sense that I might as well have been in orbit the past few months as far as you were concerned?"

He smirked. "That's an oddly appropriate metaphor, considering you've always felt way out of reach."

"If you were ever reaching for me, you weren't putting much effort into it."

"Or maybe you weren't looking hard enough. Like now."

Even though my chest was tight with nervous excitement, I didn't have to try hard to feel the old, familiar resentment bubble up. "Last time I looked, you were dating my best friend."

Nick's expression hardened. His eyes flicked to something behind me. "Cade," he said coldly.

The hairs on the back of my neck stood up. I turned and saw Iris and Cade both watching from a few feet away. Iris at least had the decency to look embarrassed to be caught eavesdropping.

"What the hell?" I asked. "Is it possible to have a conversation without somebody secretly leaning over my shoulder tonight?"

"I don't know," Cade said. "Maybe try not being such a source of drama, and it wouldn't be so fun to spy on you. Besides, I thoroughly enjoyed listening to you shut Nick down."

"For once, could you not?" Nick asked Cade.

"Sorry, my specialty is kind of doing. Not doing has never been a strong suit," Cade said. "Anyway, I was going to ask you what your plans were if Little Miss Perfect here hadn't turned you down? I mean, how did you expect to keep your head in the game when you were daydreaming about bumping uglies on the copier every chance you got?"

"I can't believe I'm agreeing with Nick on something, but, yeah, could you not?" I asked.

"Hey," Cade said, completely ignoring my question. He ran his thumb across Iris's jaw and grinned wickedly. "That actually sounds kind of fun. Want to go buy a copier and do a little role-play? I'll be your boss, except in our scenario, I didn't fail at seducing you, so we're absolutely blasting each other every chance we get."

"Seriously?" Nick asked. "You think you can just walk into a store and buy a commercial copier?"

"The practicality of buying a copier is the part of this you have a problem with?" I asked. I shot Iris an incredulous look, but she seemed above being ashamed.

Ugh. New love was disgusting. I'd had to watch Kira and Rich and how they were hardly able to keep their hands off each other when they'd finally gotten together, and now it was Cade and Iris. Somehow, it all made me more angry with Nick.

"Hey," Cade said. "You left the keys to the new biz in your car, right?"

"No," Nick snapped. "You will not—"

"Sorry!" Cade called. He was already pulling Iris by the hand and leading her away. "You know my policy. Never waste a good boner!"

Nick got up with a disgusted look. "See you in the morning, Collins. Oh, and it's nice to have you back from orbit."

Traitorous goose bumps tingled across my arms and legs. I had to clear my throat, but my voice still sounded quiet and a little scratchy. "I'll see you in the morning. *Yep.*"

Chapter 4

NICK

Today was Miranda's first day at Bark Bites, and I guessed it was mine too.

I fidgeted with a paperweight on what used to be Dan's desk while I waited for Miranda to arrive. The paperweight was shaped like a neat pile of dog poop, and once I realized I'd been idly running my fingers over it, I pulled them back and sighed.

I would normally be diving into the work by now. Instead, I was sitting here tapping my fingers because I was anxious to talk to her again.

She knocked softly at my door.

"Come in," I called.

As soon as Miranda looked at me, her back seemed to straighten, as if I could literally see the stick inserting itself up her ass. Distantly, I could hear the scratching paws of Thug scurrying around as he banged into things in Miranda's office across the hall.

I had become so used to seeing Miranda look like she was in control. The way her eyes slid uneasily from mine to the floor wasn't like her, and I couldn't help feeling responsible for it. Ever since she'd walked into the interview yesterday, she had seemed off balance. Sure, there had been flashes of the old Miranda, but it seemed like she was teetering. I admittedly knew I had something to do with that by giving her the job of taking care of Thug, but perfectionism was like a phobia. And what did you do to cure someone of a phobia? You exposed them to the thing they were most afraid of, little by little.

I'd felt an odd, hard-to-describe bubble in my throat from the moment Miranda had stepped back into my life. Until now, I'd assumed it was just anticipation. After all, she was the Mount Everest of challenges for me. But I was starting to realize the truth was something else. The strange feeling wasn't there because I wanted to sleep with her so badly—though, admittedly, *that* thought wasn't far from my mind.

For as long as I'd known her, Miranda had always been put into a box by everybody. They all saw how intelligent she was and how driven she could be, so they naturally assumed she'd basically conquer the world one day. In high school, it had driven her to study more and spread herself impossibly thin with extracurricular activities that would look good to colleges. Now I could see she still wasn't free of those expectations. They'd shaped her into the woman she was today, and I suspected there was only one way she could ever put it all to rest. She needed to "win." Somewhere along the line, she had clearly decided that conquering the business world was her definition of a win, and that was all that mattered.

She sat down, swallowed, and then looked up at me with those big blue eyes of hers. *God*, she was so distractingly beautiful.

"Tell me something," I said suddenly.

"Okay . . ."

"What is it you want out of this job?"

A few heartbeats passed before she responded. "Am I interviewing again?"

"No. I'm just trying to understand something." I shook my head. "To understand you, I mean."

"I want to be useful," she said slowly. "To be needed and to live up to expectations."

"And where does that desire come from?" I asked.

"Why does it have to come from somewhere? Can't that just be what I want?"

I studied her body language, noticing the way her fingertips had gone white on the armrests of the chair. Clearly, I was close to touching a nerve. It meant I was near the answer I wanted, but I'd need to tread carefully to get it. "You know, my parents expected my brothers and I to do something like this. Once they squandered the family fortune, I mean. They were so used to things just lining up perfectly to take care of them, so why wouldn't my brothers and I find a way to save their cushy lifestyle, right?"

"They must be proud of what you guys have accomplished, then," she said.

I chuckled. "No. I don't think so. Pride is for when people do things you thought they couldn't do. What happens when everybody already assumes you'll do it all?"

"Then all you have is the fear of letting everyone down," she said. She opened her mouth to say something, then shook her head and looked down with a sad little smile.

"Is that what this job is for you?" I asked.

"No. Maybe part of it, I guess. But it's important to me. Ever since high school, people figured I'd go on to do something important. My parents always joked about how I was going to be a doctor or a CEO. It was like a foregone conclusion. But all that matters to them is the title. That's their expectation. For me, I want more than that. I want to get the job they thought I'd get, but then I want to crush it. It's not just getting there. It's getting there and then doing it well." She looked down again and licked her lips. "And I'm oversharing," she said quietly.

"No," I said. "It's okay." I sounded calm, but my thoughts were racing through everything she'd just said. A slowly forming realization was settling around me like a cloud of icy air. Miranda's dream was in my hands. If I gave her the opportunity to earn the job I'd be leaving behind when I went back to Sion, she could have everything she ever wanted. If anyone so much as suspected we were romantically involved, on the other hand, I'd be destroying that same dream. It'd look like she got the job because of favoritism, and then everything she'd already accomplished would be called into question too.

If I cared about her, I had to make her think I didn't. I had to strictly be her boss.

I'd thought the Mount Everest challenge was winning Miranda over, but now I saw that it was going to be holding my real feelings in check. I wanted her to have her victory, and I wanted to give her the chance to earn it, because I knew that was the only way it would matter for her.

"Well," I said, letting out a big breath. I tried to inject some cheeriness into my voice. "I guess this is really the first day for both of us."

"Yeah," she said. "Sort of."

"I asked you to meet me this morning because I'm putting on a bit of a party tonight, and I'll need you to be there." As much as I tried, I couldn't stop my eyes from wandering across her smooth, tanned skin and trailing down her neck to the hint of cleavage her blouse showed. I gripped the armrest of my chair tighter and willed myself to focus.

Her eyebrows twitched up. "A party?"

"It's a professional event, and several key investors will be there. I've also invited all of the Bark Bites management because—"

Miranda leaned forward with slightly narrowed eyes. "You're looking for problems, aren't you?"

I laughed softly in surprise. I'd gone through this routine with dozens of companies, and nobody had ever seen through to my intentions so quickly, if at all. They'd always thought I just wanted to make a nice gesture and get familiar with the staff. I was instantly reminded of why I'd been so interested in Miranda all those years ago. I'd always felt like I moved through life on a different frequency than everyone else. It made it nearly impossible to connect with anyone, but Miranda was different.

"Yeah," she said, nodding her confirmation after something she must've seen in my face. "I was trying to puzzle out how you must do what you do. I bet you start with the most likely problems and work your way down to the least likely. So people problems are the most common causes of a failing business, huh? Or maybe they are just the easiest ones to rule out first."

I had to make an effort not to smile like a teacher who had just witnessed their student pass a test with flying colors. Miranda wasn't my student, but I felt alive just talking to somebody who thought about these things the way I did. *Again.* I remembered bitterly that it had always been like this between us. Only now I had seven years of experience to show me that I couldn't find that kind of connection with anyone else, no matter how hard I might try.

I made sure my voice didn't betray any of what was going on in my head when I finally spoke. I needed to draw a line in the sand now, before it got too tempting to let things between us develop. "Interesting theory, but maybe you should leave the planning to me. Your role as my VP is to execute my orders, not to analyze or understand them."

Miranda sat back in her chair. The small spark of something I'd seen in her face vanished, and all that was left was the same cold neutral I'd seen when she'd first arrived.

Sitting there and watching the tentative trust she'd been building with me melt away was one of the hardest things I'd ever done. It felt like the air itself was thickening between us, like her walls were coming back up.

I gripped the armrest of my chair until my knuckles cracked. This would get easier. Any mutual feelings she might have for me were surely going to dry up soon.

Seven years ago, I'd broken her heart. Now I finally had a chance to make amends for what I'd done. I just wished there was a way to do the right thing *and* tell her the truth. Unfortunately, the truth involved the part where I realized I still cared about her. *A lot.* The kindest thing I could do was suck it up and let this lie play out, no matter how much it stung.

Chapter 5

MIRANDA

I closed the door to my office at Bark Bites and sank down with my back against the wall. I fished through my purse until I found some chocolate and an old, half-eaten bag of chips.

At the sound of crinkling wrappers, Thug came bumbling toward me with his ridiculous underbite.

"Don't even talk to me right now," I said to him. He hadn't pooped in my house, but he'd knocked over the trash can and transported the contents to the corner of my bedroom, where he'd built a stinking, half-rotten little nest. I'd found him happily snoring in the center of it when I'd come home. He'd even had the nerve to look smug when I'd had to give him three baths to get all the smell out of his fur. "We're fighting," I added.

Thug didn't seem to share my hostility. He nosed—and *teethed*—his silly lopsided snout into my hands and tried to get my chocolate.

"No," I said. "Chocolate kills you things. And if you keep begging for it, I'm going to be tempted to let you off yourself."

Thug sat down and made a pathetic grunting sound.

"Don't even try to look cute. You look like a hairy gremlin. And, *no*, that's not a compliment."

He tilted his head at me. I sighed. "Here," I said. "You can probably eat a chip without dying." I tossed one to him, and he snapped it out of the air, swallowing it without chewing.

Even chocolate and salt couldn't stop me from wanting to headbutt my new boss slash ex-crush in the balls.

I crunched into a chip and chased it with a square of chocolate, but the sweet-and-salty blend didn't do anything to clear my head. I could still feel the bottled-up emotions threatening to crack through to the surface. I had just been starting to think I was wrong about Nick—that maybe he had grown. But I guessed that was his signature move. He'd let you start to develop feelings for him, and then he'd do something inexplicably horrible and rude to crush all of it and make you feel like an absolute moron for imagining he liked you.

My door opened, and I jumped to my feet, half throwing the bag of chips behind me. In a blind moment of panic, I shoved the rest of the chocolate in my mouth and tucked the wrapper into my bra. Thug took the opportunity to walk over to the corner and start nosing his way into the bag of chips.

Nick paused, looking toward my desk, then flinched back when he saw me standing in the corner of the room instead of sitting at my desk.

I wasn't surprised when he seemed content to stand there and wait for me to speak first, even though he was the one barging into *my* office. He carried silence as comfortably as a child carried their favorite blanket. Where most people felt the need to punctuate every moment with words, no matter how senseless, Nick had always been the kind of man who said only things that were worth saying.

So, in a silent game of verbal chicken, we both stood there while Thug noisily chomped down the remains of my chips.

"Yes?" I asked, after lasting a whopping four seconds and change.

"This was left on my desk." He produced my phone, which, I cringed to remember, was currently inside a cat-themed phone case, complete with pink, rubbery ears. I could've explained that it was mostly a joke—mostly, because I really did think the case was cute, but I'd only let myself buy it because I knew my friends would think I was kidding and laugh—but I just snatched it from him and tried not to meet his eyes.

"Thanks."

Nick's eyes sank down to my chest.

I could hardly believe he had the nerve to come in here and gawk at me, so I yanked up on my blouse, and I didn't try to be subtle about the gesture, except . . . I felt the crinkly edge of my candy wrapper when I reached down. Apparently, I hadn't actually tucked it far enough into my bra to conceal it.

"I just hope you're chewing before you swallow this time," he said.

"It's not mine." I reflexively pressed the wrapper deeper into my bra. It wasn't until I was knuckles deep that it occurred to me how inappropriate this all was. My cheeks must've been bright red as I pulled my hand out and cleared my throat. "I was just holding it for a friend."

"In your bra . . . ," Nick said.

"Maybe it'd be best if my boss didn't talk about my underwear," I said.

Nick's nostrils flared, but I thought I saw a glimmer of amusement behind his eyes. "You're right. Well, there's a vending machine in the lobby if your friend likes uneaten candy bars. Were those for your friend too?" He nodded toward the chips spilled in the corner. "Because I don't think Thug was planning on leaving any for them."

"I need to get to work." I muttered the words half-heartedly and went to sit at my desk. I expected Nick to leave, but he just leaned in the doorway and watched me with an interested expression.

Shit.

I found myself sitting behind my desk with absolutely no work to do. Meanwhile, Nick was just watching me expectantly. I cleared my throat daintily, scooted my chair in, and shook the mouse around to wake up my computer. I was greeted by a log-in prompt, which reminded me that I didn't know my password yet.

I rested my chin on my knuckles and scrunched my forehead like I was reading something particularly troubling. *Maybe some numbers from finance that didn't add up.* I reached for my coffee cup, because these imaginary numbers were so problematic that I needed a dose of caffeine to tackle them.

Except I saw my mug was still empty. I'd been planning on filling it as soon as I finished my little stress binge, but Nick had interrupted me. I pretended to take a sip anyway, then pretended to swallow as I set it back down.

I was too scared to look up and see if Nick had noticed the cup was empty, so I kept glaring at my screen. I finally looked back up at him and did my best to appear impatient. "Is there something else? Or were you going to just watch me work all day?"

"I was just curious how long you'd be able to keep it up."

"Keep what up?" I asked. If my cheeks had been red and hot before, they were molten now.

"Oh," Nick said. "Before I forget . . ." He fished out a note card from his pocket and set it on my desk. "That's your log-in info and password. And did you want me to fill this up so you don't have to stop whatever you're in the middle of?" He put his fingertips on the handle of my empty mug.

"I'm good," I said through a tight throat. "Thank you."

Nick took two steps backward while still wearing that obnoxiously cute smirk. All the indifference I'd seen in his office was apparently forgotten, at least momentarily. It was like I could see straight back to seven years ago when we'd flirted almost every day in AP Chemistry class. Back then, he'd been the only guy who ever seemed interested in me for my intelligence and not because of how I looked. But the smirk on his face suddenly melted away. He looked startled, even. "Sorry to interrupt," he said quickly, then shut the door behind him.

I glared at Thug, if for no other reason than because the real person I felt like glaring at had just left. All I'd done so far was show him that I was a bumbling idiot. He'd walked in on me stress-bingeing twice and had just watched me make a fool of myself pretending to work and drinking from an empty coffee mug.

All I needed to do was remember that this was good. Even if it was painful to make a fool out of myself again and again in front of him, at least it was helping to simplify the situation. After all, I wouldn't need to worry about developing feelings for him if he didn't want anything to do with me in the first place.

Except there had been something in his eyes that didn't quite add up. In his office, it had seemed like he was actively trying to put distance between us. Then, just minutes later, I'd sensed something else.

Thug came up to me and headbutted my thigh until I relented and scratched his ears. He sat down contentedly, apparently assuming the scratches would continue.

"You're a manipulator," I said to him. "Aren't you? Can't get by on your good looks, so you have to resort to psychological warfare. Well, don't get used to it. I'm going to find somebody to take you off my hands as soon as I can."

Unsurprisingly, Thug was not impressed by my tough-guy act.

When my thoughts went back to Nick—which seemed an inevitability lately—I wanted to groan with frustration. Why couldn't he just make it simple? Either he was interested, or he wasn't. Either I'd landed this job because he thought I was qualified, or it was because he was trying to get into my pants.

Nick was painfully attractive, but the idea of him giving me a job just to try to sleep with me made my stomach turn over. For more reasons than one, I desperately hoped that wasn't the case. Then again, with the way he'd shut me down in his office, it felt more like he was trying very hard to keep out of my pants.

"Why are men so complicated?" I asked Bone Thug.

He tilted his goofy protruding teeth up at me and then sloppily licked his lips.

♥ ♥ ♥

Nick was hosting the party at his house, but calling the place a house felt as inadequate as calling a gunshot wound a "boo-boo."

It was a mansion in every sense of the word. The driveway sloped and curved down toward what appeared to be a massive garage below. Huge, perfectly squared-off hedges stretched out from either side but didn't completely conceal the watery glow of a pool in the back. And the building itself was a glass-and-steel masterpiece with so many architectural flourishes that I probably could've spent hours just admiring the outside. It all looked sparkling and new, because it was. Houses like this hadn't existed in West Valley before the King brothers brought Sion here. He must've paid a fortune to have the construction fast-tracked, because I would've thought something this massive would take years to complete.

As much as I didn't want to admit it, seeing Nick's house in person made him feel even more like some larger-than-life figure. On one hand, I couldn't help realizing he was exactly what most guys would be if they had a magic genie lamp and unlimited wishes. He was shockingly handsome, rich, and intelligent. I played pretend at being perfect, but Nick was nearly the real thing. So why should I have been so surprised that he passed on me all those years ago?

I'd still spent seven years brooding over the way it had all happened. Seven years of unintentionally elevating him to supervillain status. A few months of being ignored by him while watching him gallivant around town with his brothers had only helped push him even farther up the evil totem pole. And now he was adding emotional whiplash to his bad track record with me to round it all out.

The only problem was that obsessively thinking about Nick for seven years had apparently had some unintended side effects on my brain. Instead of doing what normal people did and moving on long enough for the flame to grow cold, I found it still raged inside me. I liked to think it was an angry kind of raging, but I was starting to see the danger of feeling *any* emotion so powerfully for so long.

It felt like all that energy could just as easily get redirected if I wasn't careful. One wrong look, one flirtatious comment, or one innocent touch could be enough to set me down a dangerous path with him. I was already feeling it in how much unwarranted focus I was putting on a few interactions with him, how I was endlessly turning the conversations over in my head and trying to read his intentions.

I took a steadying breath and tried to focus my thoughts elsewhere. I was here for business. Maybe that was all I needed to do. Focusing on my career had always been enough for me before. I just needed to get my head back to that place and stop seeing the other side of Nick. For now, he was my boss. He wasn't the boy I used to daydream about, and if his recent behavior was any indication, he wasn't interested in me as anything but an employee, anyway.

Inside his house, I found a relatively tame party. I was halfway prepared for some playboy billionaire–style engagement. I'd thought I might find scantily clad women dancing in giant glass tubes filled with smoke and aggressive techno music.

Instead, the party had the vibe of a business Christmas party before anybody had gotten drunk enough to risk looking bad in front of their bosses. People chatted in small groups with drinks and appetizer plates in their hands, tastefully professional music slid from unseen speakers throughout the house, and waitstaff circulated throughout. It was all very prim and proper.

Since I hadn't seen Nick after my initial sweep of the main area of the party, I decided to do a little exploring before I introduced myself to anyone. I found a hallway lined with windows and art displays that seemed to take me away from the hub of activity and music. It led to a sort of theater room, where Cade King was reclining on a daybed with a metal plate of grapes beside him.

He was so deep in thought that he didn't even look up as I approached.

"Cade?" I asked slowly. "Is everything okay?"

"Hmm?" he said. He seemed to notice me for the first time, then smiled. "Oh, hey, Miranda. I was just trying to sort through some issues."

I leaned against the wall and folded my arms. I didn't see Iris anywhere, and my thoughts immediately went to the worst. Were they fighting? "I know we've had our differences in the past, but if you need to talk, I'm listening."

"It's just . . ." Cade frowned, then popped a grape in his mouth and chewed it before speaking again. "I mean, where the fuck are snails even going? Like where would you be trying to go in that situation? You look like a wet booger, you move at the speed of drying paint, and, I mean, let's be honest—if sex is on your mind, you can't seriously be too excited about getting your snail dick anywhere near some snail booty, can you? Do you think that's it? Maybe they're all just slurping around, looking for love? Do snails even know what love is, or is it just about the sex to them?"

I sighed, pushing off the wall. "Do you know where Nick is?"

"What does that have to do with snails? Were you even listening to me?"

"Just answer the question."

"Nick is probably avoiding everybody, if I had to guess. Maybe upstairs in his sex dungeon, or something."

"Nick has a sex dungeon?" I asked.

Cade smirked, popping another grape in his mouth. "All right, all right. I was just messing with you on that. I mean, who knows if he's got a secret door somewhere, but no. As much as he'd like to be avoiding everyone, he's probably convincing somebody they should invest their life savings in our newest business. He can get you thinking the most logical thing in the world is to give half your money to a bunch of billionaires if you give him a few minutes. It's kind of scary."

"Right. Thanks." I started to leave but stopped, putting my hand on the wall and then looking back toward Cade. "If I ask you a question, can I trust that you won't ever tell Nick I asked?"

"You can trust that nobody believes half the things I say."

I grinned. "I guess that works. Does Nick ever talk about me?"

Cade sat up suddenly with a mischievous look in his eyes. "*Oh*. Oh my. I didn't see it until now, but it's so clear." He walked over and started circling me with this goofy expression on his face. "I think I smell infatuation on you. Well, that and dandruff shampoo." He took a pinch of my hair and held it up to his nose, but I pulled it away before he could sniff again. "No shame in a little bit of dry scalp, though. I'm not judging."

"What kind of person can detect that by smell alone?" I said.

"The kind of person who knows when somebody is thinking about doing the nasty to his little brother."

"I'm not thinking about 'doing the nasty.' I just . . . I wanted to get a better handle on what's going on in his head. One minute, I think he hates me. The next, I'm not so sure anymore."

"If you want my professional opinion, Nick is lonely. He's too smart for his own good, and he gets bored with every woman I've ever seen him date. Let me put it in the simplest terms I can think of: Some men like a nice, big, luscious ass. Others want boobs they could fall into from a ten-story building and live to tell about it. But Nick? He's got a boner for big brains. Not literally, obviously. Wait . . . what if that's what the snails are really after? An intellectual connection. Do you think that could be it?"

"You really are an idiot," I said with a grin. "And thank you."

Cade did a little flourish of a bow and nodded. "Anytime you need my expertise, just ask. You're also a shitty listener, for the record."

I found Nick just as he was walking away from a group of smiling businessmen. I was about to approach him, but I noticed he seemed to be heading somewhere with a purpose. Curiosity got the better of me, so I decided to follow him at a distance.

Nick wove through the crowd, smiling and exchanging a quick greeting with people as he passed. He eventually headed up the twisting staircase that led from the main room to the series of balconies that made up the second floor.

Within a few steps, the sounds of the party had faded away. Following Nick suddenly felt much more stalkerish and a lot less innocent, but I persisted. He disappeared into a room near the end of the hallway a few moments later.

I paused, taking a deep breath and trying to think hard about the smart thing to do. None of my usual single-mindedness for work was compelling me back down to the party. I knew I would typically dive into the task Nick had given me, aiming to blow him away by how many investors I'd be able to bring to our cause, but then again, I hadn't really felt normal lately.

My heart was pounding as I reached for the door handle. I didn't know why I should expect to find anything but him grabbing something from a closet or anything equally innocuous, but my skin was prickling with anticipation. Maybe a stupid, hopeless part of me was hoping he'd turn around, lock those bright eyes of his on me, and confess that he'd had feelings for me his whole life—that he just never knew how to tell me.

I shook my head. *Stupid.* Wild, childish fantasies were not going to help me do the job I needed to do. And neither was peeking inside this door, but I found myself pushing the handle down and moving my head to peer inside all the same.

Inside, I saw Nick and a young, beautiful woman standing together with their lips locked. As soon as I saw them, my eyes widened, and I clicked the door shut, forgetting to be quiet in my hurry to get back downstairs.

Chapter 6

NICK

I pulled back and fought the urge to wipe my lips with the back of my hand. I couldn't believe she'd kissed me.

I heard the door open a moment after the kiss and turned my head just in time to see Miranda's wide eyes. She pulled the door shut without a word.

Shit. I wanted a line in the sand, and I guessed I couldn't have asked for a sharper stick to draw it with than this, could I? But that didn't help push back any of the overwhelming guilt I felt.

"Laine . . . ," I said slowly. "I'm sorry—"

She was breathing heavily as she looked up at me. She let her eyes fall and sighed. "God. I'm an idiot."

"Hey," I said. I awkwardly reached out to touch her shoulder but thought better of it. I'd apparently sent enough mixed messages already and didn't want to make it any worse. She was pretty, with shoulder-length black hair and a freckle-specked nose. I pulled my hand back and let it flop to my leg. "It's okay. I'm just not . . . interested in you that way."

I had dated her briefly a few weeks back. I hadn't heard from her until a few minutes ago when she'd sent a text telling me she'd come and needed to talk to me about something important upstairs. I'd assumed she was going to ask for a favor, but when I'd come in here, she'd confessed that she hadn't been able to stop thinking about me and kissed me before I knew what was happening.

I think part of me had suspected something like this was going to happen, and maybe I'd even wanted it to. Getting back in a relationship with Laine would've simplified my Miranda problem immensely. I was a lot of things, but disloyal wasn't one of them. Dating somebody else would put Miranda from my mind, but it would've also been an extremely shitty thing to do to the woman I'd decided to date as a distraction. Once Laine kissed me, I knew I couldn't go through with it.

"*God*," she said. "I thought maybe the reason it didn't work was that you were testing me somehow. Like you were waiting for me to be brave enough to do something physical. I had this grand plan for how that would play out, but as soon as I saw the look on your face, I knew I royally fucked it up."

I smiled and spent the next few minutes trying to easily let her down. I gave her a quick hug that included a couple of awkward, brotherly back slaps—just to be sure there were no more mixed messages—and said goodbye.

Once she was gone, I sat down in an armchair and breathed out a heavy sigh. Something had to be wrong with me. There was nothing objectively wrong with Laine. She was kind and attractive, and she also had a respectable job. She had never even seemed like she was interested in me for my money. But when I thought about dating her again, all I felt was emptiness. When I thought about dating Miranda, my skin got hot, and my pulse quickened. Even the idea was a thrill, but the electricity didn't come without an oily, sick undercurrent. I'd be just as shitty for trying to date Miranda as I would be for using another woman to distract myself.

I laughed bitterly. I'd gotten myself in one hell of a situation that apparently meant the only path for me going forward was celibacy. I was an asshole if I dated somebody other than Miranda, and I was an asshole if I dated Miranda. *Perfect.* But maybe this would all pass. Maybe it was just the natural human tendency to want the things we couldn't have most. After all, the moment I'd decided she was off limits, it was like my desire for her had gone through the roof. I'd gone from being aware of how attractive she was to having to run my shower cold to stop from actively imagining what she'd look like standing across from me with water running between her breasts and her wet hair sticking to her body.

I pressed my palms into my eyes and made a frustrated sound. *Jesus.* This was absolutely ridiculous. In the span of two days, I'd become unhinged. I wasn't thinking about work. I was only thinking about her and about the things I wanted to do to her—the things I wanted her to do to *me.*

I tried to steer my thoughts down a more innocent, business-focused path.

I wondered if Miranda had stayed at the party after what she'd seen. Knowing her, she was probably down there landing us more funding than we'd know what to do with. I smiled a little at that.

She really was an impressive woman. Determined. Hardworking. More driven than anyone I'd ever met. On the other hand, I'd seen a new side to her since the interview. Miranda the robot warrior was showing some signs of weakness, and instead of disappointing me, those chinks in her armor were only making me more drawn to her. I wanted to help mend her and get her life back on track.

I just wished the best way to do that didn't feel like breaking her heart all over again.

♥ ♥ ♥

I spent most of my morning sorting through Bark Bites' financial accounts. So far, I hadn't spotted anything that felt like a smoking gun to point toward the imminent failure of the business. Then again, I was hardly surprised. Every few minutes, I went back to turning over the

Miranda issue. I had to hope that things would simmer back down to normal in a few days, or this takeover was going to turn into a failure.

There was a knock at the door to my office.

"Come in," I said. "Oh. Miranda, hey. I'm sorry we didn't get a chance to talk at the party last night."

She smiled briefly. Cold. Professional. As usual, she was dressed impeccably. A nicely fitting pantsuit that she still managed to make feminine and—no, the word that almost came to mind was *sexy*. I didn't need to be throwing words like that around.

"It's fine," Miranda said. "We were both busy. I actually just wanted to tell you that I found something I thought you should know about."

I raised my eyebrows. I hadn't given her any tasks yet, partly because I was curious to see how long it'd take her to come ask me for something to do. I wasn't sure what she could've found on her own, but I was curious. I was also wondering if she was really going to pretend she hadn't seen anything last night. But maybe that was for the best too. "Is that right?"

"I wanted to make myself useful, and, well, here." She set a folder on my desk and left without another word.

I picked up the folder. A neat stack of papers was bound inside and marked with highlighter and color-coded sticky tabs. I thumbed through and quickly realized it was a financial report on Bark Bites. I nearly flipped through the section covering business expenditures, since I'd just finished looking through those myself, but I noticed a highlighted summary of her findings.

Apparently, Dan had been representing the business expenses under the wrong tax code, which, according to Miranda's math, was an extremely costly mistake. A costly mistake that I'd completely missed.

I sat back in my chair and stared at the folder. *Damn.* Miranda hadn't just found a mistake I'd overlooked, but she'd also compiled it into a neat and organized little package to drop on my desk? And she'd done it all before lunch, to boot.

I got up suddenly and headed to her office.

I half expected to find her hiding in the corner with some random assortment of junk food strewn around her again, but she was sitting behind her desk with perfect posture.

"Hey," I said.

She jerked even more upright, and something thudded under her desk. Miranda winced, reaching down and rubbing at what I assumed was a bumped knee. "Do you have to come flying in here like Kramer?"

"Who?"

"Never mind. Is everything okay?" she asked.

"Sorry. I just—" I held up the folder. "I was skimming this, and I can already tell this is amazing work. Maybe we can grab lunch, and you can go over it all with me in detail?" What the hell was I doing? I'd never been the impulsive type, and my brain was just now playing catch-up with my actions. It was like I'd moved so quickly that my logic hadn't been able to keep pace, and now I was neck deep in what was undeniably a bad plan.

"Lunch?" she asked. "I don't want to sound rude, but it's color-coded and should be pretty easy to follow. That was kind of the idea."

"Maybe I should try brutal honesty for a change?"

Miranda gave me a hint of the first real smile I'd seen from her since coming back to West Valley. "That might be an effective strategy."

"Strategy . . ." I couldn't help grinning back at her. "Usually strategies involve systematic approaches to overcoming a challenge. Achieving a goal. Winning a prize, even. Are you trying to imply that I'd need a strategy when it comes to you? That you're a prize I'm trying to win?" I wanted to kick myself in the shin. *Stop it, Nick.* I'd only just tried to start doing the right thing, and I was already testing the boundaries of my own rules.

I couldn't be sure, but I thought a hint of red had crept into Miranda's cheeks. "Those are some relatively self-serving examples of when a strategy could be effective. I would've said they are also helpful when you come across as an ass to your newest employee and want to mend fences."

I smiled. "Fair point. Let me start over. I feel awkward around you, and I'm not used to feeling awkward around people. One minute, I'm trying too hard to pretend we don't have a history; the next, I'm having to force myself to remember you probably hate me. But maybe we can do this again. Colleagues now. Not enemies. Not friends, unless you want to be. Just colleagues." *That was better.* All I had to do was force the words out, even if I wanted far more than friendship from her.

"I could live with that," she said. "Especially if you keep saying nice things about my color-coded folders."

"Oh, absolutely." I held up the folder. "If you keep color-coding, I'll keep you around forever." My stomach sank when I heard my own words. There wasn't any scenario where this lasted forever. Either I'd make her my replacement and we'd go our separate ways at the end of all this, or I'd be forced to do the unthinkable and let her go if she wasn't right for the position. I couldn't do anything else if I cared about her. Putting her in charge of a company she wasn't ready for would screw over every employee under her, and it would cheat the dream she had for herself. But I couldn't help wondering if I'd really have it in me to fire her. Thankfully, she seemed to be more than capable, and I didn't believe it would come to that.

Miranda tapped her fingers on the desk thoughtfully. "Forever . . . as nice as that sounds, I've always been the type to keep my eye on the chair above me."

"If there's a chair above you, I'd suggest doing more than just keeping an eye on it. I'd consider moving out of the way before it falls on your head."

She rolled her eyes. "Sometimes I forget you and Cade are related."

I winced. "Please. Next time, just tell me it was the dumbest joke you've ever heard and spare my feelings."

It was good to see Miranda looking more loose for a change. She was giving me a devious half smile that said she was enjoying the conversation. "So," she said. "Do you still want to go get lunch?"

Chapter 7

MIRANDA

Nick and I grabbed some greasy gyros from a little collection of street vendors and sat down on a bench. We had a quaint view of the distant hills and the river that wound its way through town.

"You know," I said. I blew on my gyro and waited for it to cool a little more. "All these vendors would've never survived here before you guys brought Sion to town. Can you imagine trying to convince a bunch of homebody locals to eat Greek food?"

Nick nodded, then did his best impression of the slight country drawl some of the older residents of West Valley tended to have. "If it doesn't have *bacon*, *barbecue*, or *homestyle* in the name, we're not interested."

I laughed. "I almost forget you're from here too. It's weird. But that impression is spot-on."

"You're not alone. Being back is weird too. Everybody treats us like we're outsiders now. I guess I can't blame them. When I think about how we must seem to you all—to y'all," he added with a grin, "I understand why you wanted nothing to do with me."

I lowered my eyes. I wanted to say the polite thing—that he was wrong. Except he wasn't. The problem was that he was right for the wrong reasons. I didn't want anything to do with him, but it wasn't because I saw him as an outsider.

Then I thought about the girl I'd walked in on him kissing at the party. Rich and Cade had a bit of a reputation as playboys before they'd settled down with Kira and Iris, respectively, but Nick never seemed like that kind of guy. Recently, he'd been seen around town with a new woman every week, so I shouldn't have even been surprised when I walked in on him kissing that girl at the party. Maybe some stupidly innocent part of me was hurt because he'd told me he was single— almost like he was hinting that he wanted to try to make something happen between us.

Whether I wanted that something to happen or not, I didn't know how to feel about being misled. For all I knew, he'd met the girl after he told me he was single, but even that felt strange. Was it that easy for him? And if it was, why had I been putting the idea of dating him on some forbidden pedestal for so long? I guessed kissing one woman didn't make him a playboy, either, but it made it harder to believe the rumors that he wasn't actually sleeping with any of the women he dated.

"Well, not everybody wants to avoid you." I hoped I didn't sound too bitter. I wanted to kick myself for saying something I knew was motivated by pettiness, but at least Nick had no way of knowing what I really meant.

"Yeah," he said. He flashed a genuine smile that told me he'd completely misread what I'd said. "And thank you for that. I know it's probably not easy."

"You're not the worst King brother, at least," I said.

Nick laughed. "Cade doesn't set the bar very high, but thank you."

"And sometimes you can be kind of nice, when you're not actively trying to be an asshole, at least."

Nick lowered his eyes. It looked like he wanted to say something but was stopping himself. "And your reputation as a business badass is well deserved." He patted the report on the bench beside us. "If this is what I can expect from you, I think I'll need to consider a raise."

I smiled, and in an instant his innocent compliment felt like much more as we met each other's eyes. I could see that same desire I thought I'd seen back in my office just after he'd pissed me off.

"You know," Nick said softly. "I think—"

"Maybe we should jump into the financial report I made for you?" I suggested quickly.

Nick pushed his glasses up his nose. He was too perceptive to miss anything, and I knew he was looking straight through me. But he nodded and smiled politely all the same. "Of course. Can we start with this quarterly report? I wanted to know how you—" Nick's eyes focused on something behind me.

I turned, following his gaze, and saw Bear approaching us. Bear was Cade's five-year-old son, but because of a complicated series of events, he'd only been living with Cade, and now Iris, for a few months.

"Bear?" I asked. "What are you doing by yourself?"

"I'm not. Daddy is playing hide-and-seek with me. He gets sad if I find him too fast." Bear pointed matter-of-factly toward a bush about ten yards away, where I could now clearly see Cade's huge body curled up and barely concealed. "He thinks he's good at hiding."

Nick nodded. "Cade thinks he's good at everything."

"Mm-hmm," Bear said. He was an adorable kid, if you were into the whole children thing, at least. I'd always had a hard time wrapping my head around it, personally. It wasn't easy for me to grasp why people would willingly bring small people into the world before they'd achieved all their goals. Chasing a dream was hard enough when you had to think about only yourself. Doing it while trying to balance cooking dinosaur chicken nuggets and managing tantrums seemed like it might as well be impossible.

Still, he was cute, and he did occasionally say things that made me get a strange, pulsing kind of longing in my chest. But that was just biology, and I was perfectly capable of ignoring that, just like I could ignore the way my belly got warm, swimming feelings every time I was around Nick.

"Daddy says you two are *in like*," Bear said.

"We just work together," I said. I held up the folder to show him. "See? This is work. Sometimes grown-ups have to talk about work."

"Daddy said you'd say that. But he said that's a 'prop.'" Bear even paused to use air quotes. "He said you're using it to pretend this isn't a date. And he said Uncle Nick is pretending he doesn't want to hold your hand."

"Cade!" Nick said loudly. "Come out of there."

Cade straightened and brushed some debris from his clothes. "Iris," he said. "We've been made. Come on."

Iris, with a mischievous glint in her eyes, popped up from behind a small hill.

"What the hell is this?" I asked.

"Well," Cade said as he plopped down and sat cross-legged in front of our bench. Iris sat down beside him, and Bear distracted himself by chasing after a little bug that was scuttling on the sidewalk. "When I was in the service, we called it reconnaissance. Hear, but don't be heard. See, but—"

"You were never in the military," Nick said dryly. "And we could both see and hear you the whole time. You breathe louder than a pug when you're excited."

"Okay," Cade said. "I haven't *been* in the service physically, but I've watched *Band of Brothers* at least three times. And *Saving Private Ryan*. I also had to do jury duty once because those bastards wouldn't accept a generous bribe. I could go on, but I don't want this to get embarrassing for you."

Iris cleared her throat. "What he's trying to say is we were curious. So we decided to do a little digging. We were getting Bear ice cream when we saw you two lovebirds strolling around."

"We weren't 'strolling,'" I said tightly.

"Frolicking. Gallivanting. Call it what you want," Iris said. "We saw you and decided to take action."

"By hiding in a bush?" Nick asked.

"Behind the bush," Cade said. "Technically."

"This is not a 'prop,' by the way." I held up the folder and pointed to it. "We came here to discuss work."

"Oh, I'm sure that's what you told yourselves," Cade said. "I like to leave our multimillion-dollar, top-of-the-line headquarters when I have to talk about work too. Because, you know, the office is really just for walking around and looking busy."

"Look," Nick said to me softly. "I know Cade well enough to know he's not going to leave us alone unless he gets what he wants. Just cross your fingers behind your back and follow my lead."

"Cross my fingers? What are we, three years old?"

"I can still hear you two," Cade said. "But he's right. I want Miranda to look Nick in the eyes and say, hmm . . ." He tapped his chin thoughtfully. "'You are my moon and stars.' And then tuck a lock of hair behind Nick's ear. Slowly."

"This is ridiculous. I'm not doing that."

"Then we're not leaving. Unfortunately for you, Iris is the only one of us who has somewhere to be. I can pester you all day."

"Or we could just leave," I said.

"Miranda," Nick said. "It's harmless. He's just a child in the body of an adult. If we humor him, he'll leave. But for the record, I don't have 'locks' of hair."

Cade rolled his eyes. "I didn't ask for excuses. Just make it happen, people."

I looked at Nick and fought the urge to sigh dramatically. "You are my moon and stars," I said in a dull monotone. Then I pantomimed tucking a hair behind his ear. My fingers brushed his temple, and I didn't fail to notice the wave of goose bumps that sprouted on his neck.

"Good," Cade said.

"You're just letting this happen?" I asked Iris.

She grinned. "It's about time you mounted another horse. So, yes."

"Actually, I think the idea would be for the horse to mount her, in this case," Cade said.

"What's 'mounting'?" Bear asked.

"It's when—" Cade started.

"It's time for you to leave us in peace so we can actually get work done," Nick said. "Now."

Cade and Iris looked like two scolded children, but they finally left.

"Maybe one day we'll be able to go somewhere in public without my brother sneaking up on us," Nick said.

"He's . . . persistent."

Nick chuckled. "That's putting it lightly. He just worries about me. I think he's convinced that all the dating I've been doing is some kind of sign that I'm going off the rails."

I tried not to look too interested. I counted to three—albeit a little quickly—before responding. "Why the sudden change, anyway?"

"Hmm?"

"I just mean the whole speed dating thing. It's not like I was cataloging your personal life, but, I mean, one minute you seem content being single, and the next you're with a new woman every week."

"That's a bit of an exaggeration."

"Well, if you want to get technical. Three weeks ago you were dating that redhead—the one with the blog. Then two weeks ago it was that sporty girl who always had her hair in a ponytail. And last week it was Mary. I mean, we all knew Mary from back in high school, and I hardly ever thought . . ." I trailed off when I saw the look on his face. My cheeks suddenly felt very hot. "God. I sound like a complete stalker."

He smirked. "Just a little bit. But your point is taken. I guess I've been a little more active lately. It's mostly that my parents start trying to set me up with random women from wealthy families if they think I'm not currently dating."

"And you have to date as frequently as you have been to keep them off your back? Wouldn't it make sense to just stick with somebody for a little while?"

"Theoretically," he said. "I just feel guilty when I know it's not going to work. Stringing them along, I mean."

I did my best casual voice, staring off into the distance as I spoke. "People around town are saying you don't even sleep with any of these women, so I guess you find out it's not going to work pretty quickly, huh? What gives it away?" *God.* That did *not* sound casual, at all.

Nick watched me for a few seconds, and if I didn't know better, I'd think he was biting back a smile. But he reached down and picked up the folder suddenly. "Can you walk me through how you broke down those July expenses?"

I forced a smile and made an effort to look unbothered. Great. I'd freaked him out. "Yes. Of course," I said.

♥ ♥ ♥

I met Kira and Iris at Bradley's for dinner. For the longest time, we'd only ever meet at Bradley's for coffee in the morning, but our evolving schedules meant it was becoming more normal to have our get-togethers whenever our schedules allowed. None of us complained. Bradley's was the heart of West Valley for us in so many ways. It was where Iris had told us about her first kissing experience in middle school—the now-infamous "vacuum cleaner with teeth" incident that happened after she fell asleep on Bobby Sullivan's couch while watching *Buffy the Vampire Slayer.* It was also where we'd convinced Kira not to shave her head after she'd gotten lice freshman year. It was where we'd met to celebrate when I'd gotten my first grown-up job at Crawford and all the promotions that had come shortly after.

Just being in the dimly lit and busily decorated building always made me feel a little better, no matter what was happening.

Kira and Iris were already waiting at our table by the windows when I arrived. They both stopped talking and watched me with an uncomfortable level of focus as I came in to sit down.

I smiled nervously, shifting my eyes between them. Iris was still in her police uniform, and Kira was dressed like she'd come straight from the classroom. "What?" I asked.

"Well," Kira said. "New job, huh? We didn't even know you'd lost your job at Crawford. And then we find out from Cade that you're working for Nick. It has been two days, and you haven't said a word to us about it."

Iris was nodding, arms crossed. "Not a word."

"Oh, *you* stop," I said to Iris. "You and your little husband have been stalking us. I didn't need to say anything because you creeps have spied it all for yourselves by now."

"It's the principle that counts," Iris said. "I shouldn't have to spy on my best friend to get the dirt. You should be shoveling it into my eager ears."

I grinned. "There is no *dirt*. Okay? I got let go at Crawford, and I should've told you guys, but I was already getting a sympathy overdose after the breakup and didn't want you guys to worry. Besides, I knew I could find another job and figured it'd be easier to talk about once I did."

"We're not just here for the good times," Kira said. "You're *supposed* to lean on us when things are shitty. It's part of the job description."

"It's also in the job description that you are allowed to spy if your bullheaded friends are too stubborn to talk about their problems," Iris added.

"I should've told you guys, and I'm sorry. But, seriously, there's no dirt. Yes, the whole Nick-as-my-boss thing was a surprise. And, *yes*, I might've had to sort through my feelings about that for, like, *an hour*.

But I'm good now. He's my boss, and we knew each other forever ago, but that's all in the past now."

"Mm-hmm," Iris said.

Both of them watched me until the silence hanging between us felt accusatory.

"It's complicated," I said. "But I've got it handled."

They still wouldn't say anything.

"Okay, so I still have some feelings for him," I said. "But I care more about doing the job right."

"Oh, Miranda," Iris said wistfully. "I still remember how easy you made it sound when you were on the other side of the fence. Just stay away from them, you said. Just be strong, you said. Most importantly, *remember the oath*. I won't lie; it's nice to see even the great Miranda Collins is going to fold under the same pressure we did. Those King cocks are just striking us down, one by one, like three beautiful dominoes—one a little more beautiful and combat ready than the others, but beautiful nonetheless."

Kira tilted her head. "Am I the combat-ready domino?"

Iris glared. "What's the best way to stop somebody who has both their hands on your neck?"

Kira thought about that. "Blow a rape whistle?"

Iris reached across the table and gripped Kira by the neck. Kira's eyes bulged, even though I could see Iris wasn't squeezing.

"You bring your hands up inside my wrists and then push out. Most people try to pull at the wrists from the outside, but you've got to get inside and then explode out—yeah, like that."

I waited while my friends went from choking countermeasures to the best way to flex your fingers for gouging out eyeballs. I decided to go grab a coffee when they transitioned to how to blind somebody by whacking them with their ponytails—a technique I was pretty sure Iris was completely making up.

When I came back, they were both waiting for me with folded hands. "What?" I asked.

"Trying to escape the interrogation, are you?"

"Uh, no," I said. "I was just giving you two time to play."

"Self-defense is no game," Kira said. She paused, then looked toward Iris, who nodded her approval.

I grinned. "You two are idiots."

"Two idiots who will survive a choking attempt," Iris said. "And you can try to change the subject all you want, but admit it. You're going to fold when that King cock comes a-knockin' at your door."

"Nobody is folding," I said. "Sometimes I feel like taking my bra off by lunchtime and slinging it out the window, but I don't, just like I'm not going to let any feelings I may or may not have for Nick mean anything. I have a job to do, and that's what is going to happen."

Kira rolled her eyes as she did a half-assed job of repeating what I'd said in a robotic voice. "Must do job. Must ignore feelings. Must not have fun. Ever."

"Kira's right," Iris said. "You've seen *The Shining*, right? You remember what happens to the dad when he gets too obsessed with his work? Because I'll tell you right now, if you try to break through my bathroom door with an ax, I won't just cower in the corner and scream. I'll Tase your ass." She whipped a Taser out from her belt and tried to twirl it on her finger, but it fell to the ground. Both prongs discharged into the wall the moment it hit the ground.

Iris scooped it back up and cleared her throat. "Just like that. You'd be the wall."

"Don't even pretend that was on purpose," Kira said, laughing.

Iris blushed while she quietly reset the thing and put it back on her belt.

"I have the rest of my life to worry about fun," I said. I was starting to feel exasperated. They really just didn't get it, and Iris had the attention span of a poorly trained monkey. "If I keep my head down a little longer and focus on my career, I'll be able to have *so* much more fun for the rest of my life."

"Because money equals fun?" Kira asked.

"Hey. Neither of you get to pull that line on me. You married billionaires."

Iris sighed. "Coincidentally, the guy you have all these feelings for is a billionaire. If you wound up marrying him, you'd get to have all that fun you are talking about."

"I'm not going to pursue a guy because I want his money. I just want to . . ." I looked down. For some reason, it felt too personal to just blurt out, even though I'd basically explained it all to Nick yesterday. "It's not about the money," I said simply. "And what if this is my last chance at this kind of career and I throw it away because I'm chasing some guy who will end up breaking my heart?"

"Well," Kira said, "what if this is your last chance to fix things with Nick too? If you had to choose between your career and your heart, which one are you willing to risk?"

"That's a little dramatic," Iris said. "She's not going to *lose* her heart if it turns out Nick was actually the right guy all along. It'll just kind of fester and get smelly, like that pack of chicken breasts you bought on the weekend because you were totally going to eat healthier this week, but every time dinner rolls around, you end up coming home with tacos and pizza, so by Friday it smells like death took a dump in your kitchen. For the rest of her life, no guy will ever want to get close because they'll be able to smell it from a mile away. *So tragic.*"

I gave both my friends a level stare. "Sometimes, I wonder why I bother asking you two for advice at all."

"That's simple," Iris said. "Because underneath that stony exterior, you're like a fragile, delicate little flower who just wants to be cuddled."

"Uh," I said. "No. That's definitely not it."

Iris held her fingers close together and squinted. "Isn't it, though? Just this much?"

I sighed.

Chapter 8

NICK

I was leaning on the kitchen island while Rich clanked his way around my cabinets. He had something sizzling in a skillet and a tray of veggies roasting in the oven.

"You said you do have basil?" he asked.

"Yeah. On the windowsill. It's fresh. You use the clippers in the knife rack to trim whatever amount you need."

"Fancy," he said.

I grinned. "Not really. Even Cade could keep a basil plant alive, and it means I don't have to remember to buy more when I run out. It's self-refilling."

Rich paused long enough to give me an incredulous look. "Cade couldn't even keep the artificial plants I got him for his birthday alive. This basil plant would be in flames within a day."

I chuckled. "Okay. You're right. But you get my point."

"So, how is the Bark Bites acquisition going? I'd been meaning to ask you about it."

"Fine," I said.

Rich paused with a handful of basil in one hand and the tiny clippers in the other. "Fine?" he asked. "What happened to the Nick I know? The one who would usually have exact figures and projections memorized by now? *I estimate that—*"

"Point taken," I said. "And I don't have an estimate I'm confident in yet. This one is . . . complicated."

"They're all complicated." Rich had completely stopped what he was doing to watch me. I could feel that obnoxiously perceptive mind of his putting the pieces together already. I knew him well enough to know there was no point in trying to hide it now. Keeping something off Rich's radar was possible, but once he'd set his sights on it, it was only a matter of time before he would figure it all out for himself.

"Working with Miranda is complicated," I said.

He nodded, as if he'd already figured that out. "Cade told me about that. When you failed to mention it to me after a couple days, I wondered."

"I didn't mention it because I already decided how to handle it. I'm not going to get attached, because I don't want my feelings impacting my business sense." *And I'm not good for her. She needs me out of her mind and out of her life.*

Rich folded his arms.

"Shouldn't you stir that?" I asked.

He didn't budge. "It can wait."

I wanted to groan.

"Do you want me to step in and run this one?" he asked. "Remove yourself from the situation if you can't trust your judgment?"

"No," I said. "I don't run from things when they get hard. This is my problem to solve."

Rich watched me through narrowed eyes before laughing and turning to stir the food. "Damn. Nothing gets you riled up. You must really like her."

"I've barely talked to her in seven years. If I really liked her already, I'd be as worried about my judgment as you seem to be."

Rich spoke now with his back to me as he moved around the kitchen, tending to the meal. "Love isn't like a cake, Nick. There's no set recipe and no required cooking time. It's more like cookies. You can eat that shit raw, if you want, or you can pop it in the oven and wait to see how it turns out. You can do both. You can leave it in the oven *too* long, and it still tastes good. But from the moment you mix up the dough, you know if you like it or not. Time isn't really going to change that."

I couldn't help laughing. "Advice on love from Martha Stewart, brought to you by Richard King."

He turned to smirk at me. "I'm serious, though."

"I know you are. That's why it's funny. But being able to restate something in the form of an analogy doesn't mean it's true. That's your idea of love, not mine."

"You ever been in love?" Rich asked.

"No," I said.

"Exactly. Then your opinion on love doesn't get to overrule mine. Love is like cookie dough. Case closed."

I shook my head and began checking emails on my phone. "Then I'm choosing not to taste the cookie dough, because it'll be better for everyone involved. I'm also pretty sure there's an increased risk of getting foodborne illnesses from eating raw cookie dough. Haven't you ever read the packaging?"

"I don't read packages, and I cook it from scratch. Besides, the purpose of a cookie is to be eaten. Not eating a cookie means it existed for nothing. How could that possibly be the best for the cookie? It sounds like you're just choosing what's best for you."

"I refuse to take this seriously anymore. I'm not going to get into a philosophical debate on whether a cookie's purpose is to be eaten and pretend it has any bearing on my love life."

"It doesn't, because you don't have a love life," Rich said. "And you never will, at this rate."

"Good. Then I'll be able to stay focused on work."

He gave me an obnoxious look, like a grandma who was planning to patiently hold her tongue so I could learn a lesson for myself.

"You know what? Why don't you save me some leftovers? Tell everybody I couldn't make dinner tonight."

Rich raised an eyebrow. "You couldn't make it to dinner. At your own house."

"Yes. I need to head to Bark Bites and look into something."

"Miranda's eyes?"

I gave him a dry look. "She has been off work for a few hours now. It's just going to be me there."

"All right. Whatever. I'll throw some of this in Tupperware, but my pasta isn't as good left over. Just warning you."

"It's not that great fresh either."

"Asshole."

Chapter 9
MIRANDA

I rubbed my throbbing temples and let my forehead thump down on my desk. I wasn't sure what I was trying so hard to prove by coming in late. Well, that wasn't entirely true. I was here because when everything felt complicated and confusing, I could always count on work to be simple. I could come in, find something meaningful to do, and do it.

Except I was hitting dead end after dead end. I didn't have access to the complete financial records of Bark Bites. I had the publicly reported data as well as what their accountants *officially* compiled. I didn't have the unofficial data, which was what grabbed my interest the more I looked into the numbers.

I was almost certain those would be in Nick's office, just like I was almost certain the security guard who had let me in was still watching a movie on his phone at the front desk. I doubted he'd even think to come back to this wing of the office.

I scooped a paperclip from my desk and headed across the hall to Nick's door. I tried the handle, but it was locked. *Of course it was locked.* That was why I'd grabbed a paperclip.

For a few moments, I stared down at the innocent little scrap of aluminum. Was I seriously considering this? *Yes.* Was I seriously going to do this? *Yes.*

With a sigh, I carefully unbent the clip and started my amateur attempts at unlocking the door. I slid the long end of the clip with the tiny hook I'd fashioned into the hole on the doorknob. After a little fishing around, I thought I felt the groove I was looking for. When I turned it, I felt the lock slide open.

A cold thrill ran through me. I knew how to unlock doors like that only because the bathroom in my house sometimes locked itself and had the same kind of lock. Picking the lock to a door I wasn't supposed to open was an entirely different experience.

It would be fine, though. I was just trying to do my job, and my boss happened to not be in the office to give me the documents I needed.

I walked behind his desk and couldn't help feeling the sense of fore-boding wash over me. I had to be imagining it, but I thought I could smell the faint scent of his cologne behind his desk, like some kind of stupid, sexy ghost lurking over my shoulder.

I convinced myself that I didn't need to feel guilty for snooping through Nick's desk. I doubted he had even bothered to move anything personal inside yet. I was basically snooping through Dan Snyder's desk. Besides, I was pretty sure if I looked up the definition of snooping, there would be some specific language about trying to find personal items. I was just looking for some boring old financial papers. If I saw anything weird, I'd . . .

I frowned at what appeared to be a massive stash of some kind of trading cards in his desk. I flipped a few over and saw pictures of fantasy creatures with a bunch of statistics on how much damage they would do and how many "mana" they cost to summon. I grinned. I wondered if they were Nick's or Dan's.

I had to blindly reach toward the back corner of his drawer because of the awkward angle. I felt around and was about to give up when my fingers touched a small folded piece of paper. When I pulled it out, I couldn't help feeling the strangest pang of familiarity. It looked old and well worn, like it had been folded and unfolded so many times that the creases were as soft as cloth.

When I opened it, my breath caught. I recognized every word. It was a poem. A sappy, embarrassing, loaded-with-clichés poem written by the hand of a teenage girl. Even as full of cringe as it was, I couldn't help feeling a deep sadness as I read through it. The vocabulary was definitely from a young girl, but there was no denying the emotion practically bleeding from the page.

At some point, the paper had apparently gotten soaked by something—maybe a drink spill in his locker or any number of things that could've happened afterward. But the part that made me frown was when I noticed the bottom of the page. The combination of spilled liquid and the paper being folded over had left a ghostlike imprint of random letters at the bottom, almost like a signature.

I'd written the note anonymously, but when I squinted down at the fuzzy, water-smeared letters, they seemed to say *ira*. When I folded the paper a few times, I realized it had come from part of a sentence: "I ran from my feelings for long enough."

My frown deepened when everything clicked together. I'd known Nick was smart enough to figure out who had written him the note from context. But I hadn't planned for what would happen if he thought somebody had signed it.

I was so absorbed in the note that I didn't even realize he'd been standing in the doorway.

"This is a surprise," Nick said. "Not exactly what I was thinking when we set the boundaries, though."

In a moment of rare hand-eye coordination, I discreetly tucked the note into my palm and turned my wrist to conceal it. I knew I'd need to find a way to replace it soon, or he'd likely put two and two together, but I could worry about that later. "Oh God. This looks so much worse than it is. Seriously, I can explain."

82

He walked into the room and planted his palms on the desk. He leaned forward, eyes boring into me. *God.* I'd never known a man with eyes that carried so much weight. I thought Nick could've likely carried a conversation without ever uttering a single word. All he'd need were the various stages of his glares.

"I was just looking for some documents I thought Dan would have in his desk."

"Yeah? Well, this isn't Dan's desk anymore."

"I realize that. I just thought you might not have had time to move his things out yet, and—"

"And you didn't think it would be a good idea to ask me in the morning. So you broke into my office instead?"

I opened my mouth to object, but he held up his palm, silencing me.

"Miranda. If I can't trust my vice president, then she's useless to me. What would you do if you were in my position? Give you a slap on the wrist?"

I had to resist the urge to let my head hang. Getting lectured by Nick like this was mortifying, but I couldn't let that show. I knew I'd cry if I admitted how this made me feel, and crying in front of Nick was *not* going to happen.

"I would," I said, then I had to stop to swallow hard. *Get it together, Miranda.* "I would give my vice president a chance to show me what she thought was important enough to break into my office for. And then I'd decide what to do with her."

"What to do with her," Nick mused. His voice sounded deeper than usual, *darker.*

Chills raced across my skin. Why was it so hard to focus? My job was on the line, yet my stupid brain was trying to twist his words into some pathetic fantasy. "Yes," I said. "What to do with her."

"All right." He stood up and crossed his arms. "What documents did you need?"

"The internal financial reports. The ones that came straight to the accountants before they filed their reports."

Nick walked calmly to a cabinet on the wall, pulled it open, and scooped out a folder. "This is last year's report. Good enough?"

"Yes," I said shakily.

He handed me the folder. "You have twenty-four hours. Show me something important, and we'll forget about this. Fail to do that, and we'll have a conversation."

A day. Why did people always think it was more intimidating to set ominous deadlines by the hour? I nodded. "Can I go?"

He stuck his arm toward the door and dipped his chin, never taking his eyes from mine.

I wish I could say I walked from his office in a calm, controlled way—that I showed my spirit by holding my head high and keeping it together. But it took everything I had to hold back tears. I walked out of there as fast as I could and shut the door to my office as soon as I was inside. I sank down on the ground and buried my head in my hands.

I was an idiot to think I could work for Nick and pretend it was a normal job. Even as driven as I was, I'd never have been so desperate to prove myself that I would've broken into my boss's office to do it. I'd also never take a little scolding so personally. My past with him was clouding my judgment. And now . . .

My fingertips ran over the note in my hand. Now I didn't even have a reason to hate the old Nick. After all this time, I'd been the idiot. I'd given him the note and waited for him to come talk to me about it. Instead, he'd avoided me for three days and eventually asked out Kira. The poem was full of references that he would've known had to be from me if he had half a brain, so I'd assumed the worst. I'd thought he was asking Kira out to shut me down in some cowardly, nonconfrontational way. Then I'd decided it was even more sinister than that. I'd thought he was laughing about the poem behind my back, and asking Kira out had been a calculated stab in the back.

I shook my head as I turned the folded-up paper over in my hands. It was hard to believe that I'd wound up sitting right where I was today because of a childish decision to write him an anonymous poem instead of simply talking to him about the way I felt. Things might have been different if I'd just had the guts to sign the thing, but I'd told myself I was making it so obvious that I didn't have to.

Idiot.

There was a soft knock at my door.

I stood and rubbed at my eyes, trying to clear any evidence of the tears that had been welling up without ruining my makeup. I opened the door and did my best to look annoyed. "Has it already been twenty-four hours?"

"I wanted to . . ." Nick blew out a long breath. He looked uncharacteristically uncomfortable with his hands in his pockets and his eyes down. "Can I come in?"

"You own the building. I'm pretty sure you can do what you want in here."

His eyes flickered up at that. The moment I saw his face, I knew his mind had taken my comment to a dirty place. I blushed, even though I hadn't been trying to imply anything.

"Within reason," I added.

Nick didn't say anything as he slid past me, crop-dusting me with that intoxicating smell of his. He planted his hands on the chair in front of my desk and hung his head. "I'm trying my best to keep things professional. If it ever seems like I'm being more of a dick to you because we have a past, I want you to say something."

That was what this was about? I almost felt disappointed. "I think getting pissed that I broke into your office was a reasonable reaction, if that's what you're worried about."

He nodded but still didn't turn to look at me. "Actually, what I wanted to say was that I booked cabins for the entire company at a resort out west called Julian Ridge." He finally stood up, straightened, and regained his ability to look me in the eyes. "It's an all-inclusive kind of thing. Racquetball courts, tennis courts, an indoor and outdoor pool, horseback riding, bowling, shopping, a free movie theater, and even buses that'll shuttle you around the grounds, running all day and night."

"Uh . . . okay."

"I got us neighboring cabins so it'll be easier to go over our findings during the trip."

"Our findings?" I asked. Why was my stupid heart beating so fast? Logically, I already understood what he was getting at. He'd mentioned that people were often the reason a company failed. It was why he'd thrown the party before. This must mean he still suspected there was something to be found from getting to know the staff better. I knew all of that, but I needed to hear him say it so my stupid heart would stop jumping to conclusions.

"Everybody else will be there to have fun. You and I are going to be discreetly investigating our employees. I've seen some numbers in the records that have me convinced somebody was embezzling money from under Dan Snyder's nose when he ran this place."

I nodded. It was the same trail I'd been hoping to look into. "How likely do you think it will be for somebody to admit they're embezzling money from the company to their bosses?"

"To me? Probably not very likely. But to somebody new to the company who is looking for a way to pad her pockets, maybe not so unlikely."

I scoffed. "No way. You want me to go around implying that I'm looking to get in on something illegal to a bunch of people I barely know?"

"I want you to be the Miranda Collins I thought I was hiring. The one who does what it takes to get the job done. So, tell me. Did I hire the woman I thought I did?"

Chapter 10

NICK

Julian Ridge was as beautiful as the pictures had made it out to be. The drive from the airport was loaded with mountain views, glimpses of pristine lakes, and winding forest roads. Once we'd driven through the gates, we were in the middle of hundreds of acres of the perfectly maintained resort grounds.

I found a handful of employees already checking in and making themselves at home in the lobby of the main building—a massive thing that looked like a distant relative of the White House. Inside, all the decor seemed to be aimed at an eighteen hundreds aesthetic with checkered floor tiles, lavishly carved wood furniture, and gold-flecked wallpaper as far as the eye could see.

Two young women I didn't recognize rushed over to me when I stepped inside. I tried to suppress my annoyance at the distraction. The truth was I just wanted to see Miranda and make sure she'd found her way here okay. I had arranged for a car to bring her after debating whether having her share a car with me would send the wrong message. Now I was just imagining all the ways a vehicle could've lost control on the winding mountain roads we'd taken from the airport to get here.

"Mr. King!" said the blonde one. She was pretty. Both of the women were, I noticed.

"Yes?" I asked.

The woman exchanged a giddy glance with her friend—a brunette.

"The guy at the desk said our cabin is going to be on the same row as yours. So"—she shrugged and bit her lip—"we just thought that was such a coincidence. And if you—"

"Yeah," I said. "I hope you two enjoy this place. It's supposed to be really nice. Sorry to be rude, but I've really got to go check on something." I trailed off as I walked away from them and headed back outside. She wasn't in the lobby, it seemed.

I wandered through the gardens and past the stables, where at least a dozen horses were walking beneath the shade of huge oak trees, and I even checked the bowling alley and arcade. I wasn't sure what I thought I was going to find. Miranda Collins was hardly the type to show up at a work retreat and throw on her bathing suit immediately. If anything, she would probably sneak into her room and start working right away.

All I found were more and more Bark Bites employees, along with their dogs, starting to fill out the amenities. Some were already making use of the outdoor and indoor pools, and a couple were skill-lessly whacking tennis balls around while a little bulldog chased after them. One pair was even getting geared up for a horse ride. Everyone seemed extremely grateful and wanted to stop me to say thanks, but I found myself increasingly impatient with it all. I knew how it would look if I called Miranda to check and make sure she'd arrived safely, but it had been almost an hour since I got here, and I knew she should've made it by now. We'd come in on the same flight and left at roughly the same time.

I sat down on a bench overlooking a playground in the middle of a sloping, green expanse of grass. A guy in his twenties and two women were goofing around on the swing sets, spinning each other until the chains were wound tight and letting go.

I called Miranda's cell phone. It occurred to me that this was the first time I'd actually called her. She'd listed her number on her résumé but had never officially given it to me.

"This is Miranda Collins." She sounded so businesslike and professional. She also didn't sound like she was trapped in a crushed car or in the process of being abducted, or any of the other hundred things my idiotic brain had decided to wander to. If I was smart, I would simply hang up and let her write it off as a spam caller. I'd already gotten the information I needed.

"It's Nick," I said.

Pause.

"Oh, wow. Hey," she said.

"Who is that?" a man's voice asked from the background.

My throat tightened, and I felt my fingers clench around the phone. "Was that the driver?" I asked. *Remind me to fire the nosy bastard.*

"Uh, no," she said. "Just—hey, would it be okay if I catch up with you when I get there?"

What the hell? I took a deep, calming breath. I needed to remember what I'd said. If I wanted to believe I cared about Miranda and not just about sleeping with her, then I needed to also remember to keep out of her personal life. Getting romantically involved with her, or even implying I wanted to, would tarnish everything she'd worked for and everything she cared about. She'd think she got the job only because I liked her, and what kind of asshole would I be to put my dick before her dream? "Sure," I said. "Later is fine."

"Thanks. Bye," she said, then disconnected.

I hung my head and blew out a shuddering sigh. *Damn it.* This was going to be harder than I thought, and I already expected it to be hard. I guessed I just needed to think of this as the new challenge. I'd thought winning Miranda over was the Mount Everest for so long, but the real Everest was setting aside my feelings for her best interests.

I decided to head to the outdoor pool in hopes of relaxing some of my stress away. The view really was beautiful. A hill behind the pool sloped away to give breathtaking views of mountains that went so far back I couldn't tell where the clouds started and the mountains ended.

I ordered a plate of french fries from the little restaurant attached to the pool and kicked off my shoes to lounge and admire the view.

"Beautiful, isn't it?" a familiar voice asked.

Cade sat down in the chair beside me and grabbed a fry, popping it into his mouth. "Did you know there are *two* helipads here? Pretty badass. Although I wouldn't have had to crash your party via helicopter if you'd booked me a room like a normal, loving brother might have."

I groaned. "Please tell me you're just visiting."

"What? This is a company retreat, right? I'm part of the company."

"It's a Bark Bites retreat."

"And you invited people from the corporate office as well as the chain locations. I'm a corporate employee. Deal with it, *bitch*."

I chuckled. "Will you at least try to avoid sowing mayhem and carnage while you're here?"

"I will do what I always do. I'll be myself as aggressively as possible."

I couldn't stop from grinning a little. To be honest, I would've been worried if he'd said anything else. "Then maybe just aggressively be yourself out of my way, whenever possible. And if you see Miranda around, just—" I shook my head. "No. Forget I said that."

"Oh my." Cade sat up straighter. Somehow, he'd taken his shirt off without me noticing. He also produced a bottle of sunscreen and was liberally applying it to his chest and abs. He winked at me as he ran a finger down his stomach and made a sizzling noise.

"You're such an idiot," I said.

"And even an idiot can see through your little game, Nicholas."

"Don't call me that."

"Saint Nick, it's clear as day. You want to play hide the hot dog with Miranda. If you bottle something like that up, it's going to explode on you. It's like blue balls for your brain. *Like . . .*" He paused, obviously thinking very deeply. "It's like balls brain."

"Balls brain . . . wouldn't blue brain make more sense?"

"See?" He punched my shoulder. "That's why you're the smart one. So, anyway. You're going to give yourself brain balls if you keep holding this back. It's going to build up and build up, and before you know it, you'll be a hopeless mess around her. All you'll be able to think about is how badly you want to do the deed with her."

"Your problem is you can't understand that not everybody operates with the same mental deficiencies you do. Even if you were right about how I feel—which you're not—I could control my emotions. I can be an adult and put the business first."

"Right. Because being an adult is so great. Except, wait a second! I almost forgot that having billions of dollars practically exempts us from needing to be adults. You know what an adult is? It's a slave to the system. It's those poor people who have to spend more time working than they do sleeping, eating, fucking, and enjoying life. And you know why they do that? Because they have to. Because adults have responsibilities, but responsibilities are just code for bills."

"You don't think your child counts as a responsibility?"

"Bear is a privilege. And he's a well-trained privilege. You train them right, and they practically operate themselves. He can wipe his own ass now," Cade added, as if that was a completely reasonable and interesting bit of knowledge I'd need.

"Okay, but you do realize I enjoy the work. Right? We obviously don't need the money anymore, but I still work because it's important to me."

Cade blew a raspberry and flopped back into his chair. "To be young again," he said wistfully. "So young and so innocent to the world. It's cute, really. But you know, when you grow older and wiser, you'll realize that people don't exist to work. We exist to make a minimum of one baby. But really two is ideal. And if you have genetics as good as mine—and yours, to a lesser extent—you're honestly obligated to make as many babies as you can. *That* is your divine purpose. Not feeding dogs under the table."

I shook my head as I stared off toward the mountains. "You do know the world is heading toward overpopulation, right? If everybody keeps making babies like there's no tomorrow, we're all going to starve in a century."

"I plan to be happily dead in a century, thank you very much. And I didn't say everybody should make babies. I said people like me who won the genetic lottery are obligated to."

"Sometimes, I can't tell if you're actually being serious or if you're just trying to get a rise out of me."

"Why can't it be both?" Cade asked.

Once I realized relaxation was not going to happen with my brother within fifty yards, I headed back to my cabin. It was situated on top of one of the many rolling, grassy hills in the resort and part of a line of maybe twenty other nearly identical cabins in a row. I stopped at the foot of the hill when I saw who was getting out of a car beside the row of cabins up above. Miranda carried a small handbag down the path to her cabin. An athletic-looking guy, maybe in his thirties, followed behind her. He was pulling a big cream-and-gold suitcase I had to imagine wasn't his own.

I clenched my fists. I thought back to the voice I'd heard in the background when I called her and how short she'd been with me. I didn't get it, though. Miranda had hardly left the office since I'd hired her a few days ago. I couldn't figure out how she would've had time to meet somebody. I also couldn't figure out how she'd managed to get him in, considering I'd paid a great deal of money to keep the resort exclusive to only Bark Bites employees.

Logistics aside, I didn't understand *why*. The timing made no sense. Yeah, sure I'd let her go on thinking what she'd seen between Laine and me was whatever she'd assumed, but . . . *shit*. I had to stop letting myself go down that line of thinking. What was I going to hope for? That she'd been secretly saving herself for me, even while I was busy going out of my way to make her think I wasn't interested?

If I was strictly following the whole boss first, friend second, boyfriend never plan, I would've patiently waited for her and the guy to go inside. I'd stay right where I was and keep my mouth shut.

But there was another angle to this whole thing, and it was one I planned to exploit. "Hey!" I shouted. I started climbing up the hill but immediately regretted not walking the short distance to the side, where there were perfectly good stairs cutting up the steep incline. Instead, I was forced to duckwalk upward with both Miranda and the mystery guy staring down at me. "This is an employee-only retreat," I said. I'd made it halfway up the hill and was starting to breathe heavily.

Miranda and the guy waited patiently until I got to the top. I fought the urge to rest my hands on my knees. I was in perfectly good shape, but that was a steep-ass hill, and I was too pissed to be breathing properly.

"This is Max Frost," Miranda said.

I tried and failed not to laugh out loud. I calmed myself, closed my eyes, and straightened my features. Then I broke into another burst of laughter.

Max watched me with a look that said I wasn't the first person to laugh at his name.

"Sorry. *Sorry,*" I said again. "It's just that I was pretty sure there was an old Arnold Schwarzenegger movie with a bad guy who shared your name. But he wore spandex and shot ice out of his hands." I felt my lips quivering and threatening to break into another smile, but I finally held it back.

Miranda was glaring openly at me. "Max is a news anchor. He heard about Sion's acquisition of Bark Bites and thought I'd be a great starting point to research the story."

"The story?" I asked.

Max stepped forward and reached to shake my hand. I took his hand in mine, and we both tried to squeeze as hard as we could. I locked eyes with him and squeezed a little harder. He squeezed back until I was sure either my knuckles or his were going to pop out of our hands any second. His thick black eyebrows drew together as we locked eyes.

Miranda cleared her throat. Max's eyes darted to her, and then he let go of my hand.

I stood a little straighter. *That's right, dick.* Then I felt like a child a moment later. Since when did I get into masculine pissing matches? *Since you started trying to deny your feelings for Miranda Collins.*

Max Frost—I still could hardly even *think* the name without wanting to laugh—looked exactly like a news anchor. He had a thick, well-groomed beard, masculine features, and bright-blue eyes. He looked like he probably liked to wear turtlenecks and drink eggnog when it got cold out, and he was also probably the type of guy who could get into a passionate argument about the merits of charcoal grilling versus propane or natural gas. I immediately hated him, and I didn't think it was just because he was obviously trying to move in on Miranda.

"The story," Max said. He had a deep, ridiculous voice too. "Like it or not, when a billion-dollar company headed by three of the country's most well-known faces does something out of the ordinary, it's a story."

"This is hardly out of the ordinary," I said, even though I knew exactly what made him curious about this. I wanted to disagree with him just because agreeing with him would've left a sour taste in my mouth.

"Bark Bites was valued at just over a million when you acquired it," Max said. "Prior to Bark Bites, the smallest company Sion has acquired in the past four years was valued at more than fifty million."

"That's all very interesting," I said in a bored voice. "But this is also an employee-only retreat. So if you don't mind, you could drop off my vice president's bags, collect your tip, and head back to wherever you came from, because there are no available rooms for you here."

Miranda's glare was practically molten now, and it took a serious effort not to flinch away from the heat of it. "Do you mind giving us just a second, Max?" she asked.

Even the sweet way she spoke to him made me want to break something.

"Sure," he said, smiling.

Miranda took me by the arm and pulled me a few feet away from him. I was painfully aware of how good she looked and even smelled standing this close. "Why did you give me this job?"

"What?" I asked.

"Did you give me the job because we have a past, or because you believe I can help you turn this company around? And don't give me some bullshit answer. Tell the truth."

I stared right back at her. The full truth was complicated, but I knew the truth I had decided on—the one I was going to operate based on moving forward. That truth was going to have to be good enough, because I did believe it, even if my feelings for her might have influenced my decision too. "I believe in what you can do," I said.

"Then let me be helpful. Max is going to give us publicity. He brought a drone and a camera crew. This whole thing is going to be a great look for Bark Bites, okay? All you have to do is stop looking at him like you want to kill him. Can you do that?"

"Yes," I said through gritted teeth. "But I can't promise I'll stop *thinking* about killing him."

Miranda looked incredulous. "What is your problem, anyway?"

"My problem is that I went out of my way to make this an employee-only event, and you brought some reporter. I also don't trust the way he went about this. What did he do, flag you down on your way out of the airport?"

"Sometimes you have to make the best of unexpected circumstances."

"Did you read that on a fortune cookie?"

"No. I learned it firsthand. So, do you want to trust me on this or not?"

I sighed. "Fine. But if he does anything creepy, you—"

"I am a big girl, Nick. And I certainly don't need my boss trying to police my personal life."

"Wait. Personal life? When did *Max Frost* and his stupid-ass name stop being a business opportunity and start being part of your personal life?"

Miranda took a step back and raised her voice again so Max could hear. "You said my cabin actually had two bedrooms, didn't you?"

"No," I said quickly. "Completely out of the question. As an employee, you—"

"You can crash in the other bedroom." She was ignoring me now and talking to Max like I'd spontaneously puffed out of existence. "I think it's the kind that is separated by doors with locks, so we can each have our own space."

I was going to kill him, especially when I saw the brief, smug glance he threw my way. He thought he was winning. I wondered how smug he'd look if I accidentally knocked him down the hill.

Calm. Down.

I was losing my goddamn mind over this. Max Frost was a distraction—a stupid one with an appropriately stupid name. He'd caught me off guard, but I still knew my plan, and he wasn't going to change it. That was all I needed to focus on.

"You're both adults," I said, inserting calm into my words that I didn't feel. "If you don't mind cutting the size of your cabin in half, then go for it."

Miranda shot me a look I couldn't quite decipher before heading into her cabin with Max right behind her. A few moments later, the driver I'd assigned her was doing his best to keep hold of the leash as Bone Thug half dragged him down the path toward Miranda's cabin.

"Did anything happen in the car between the two of them?" I asked the driver.

"Sorry, sir. I was just looking at the road."

I sighed.

This was fine. No, it was *good*. It was all completely great, as long as I looked at it from the right perspective. Max Frost might have been a joke of a news anchor who had to change his last name—I assumed—to make himself sound like a video game character, but he was also going to make it easier for me to do what I'd set out to do. Forget about my feelings for Miranda. Let her live her life. Get the hell out of her way, and above all stop acting like a jealous child.

It was the out I'd been looking for. I may not have felt like I was able to date anyone without being an asshole, but this was the solution. All I'd needed was to wait for Miranda to get in a relationship of her own. It was the perfect solution I'd always been looking for. The catch was this one tasted entirely bitter and not the least bit sweet.

Chapter 11
MIRANDA

To his credit, Max was a gentleman about our living arrangement. I'd been bracing myself for the potential of a few awkward minutes of boundary definition, but he'd just smiled and taken his things through the partition separating our halves of the cabin, leaving the door open a hair. It probably helped that we'd both just finished a long day of traveling and wanted nothing more than a shower and a night's rest.

Thug set to the task of investigating the cabin, and for once, I didn't have to stress about him destroying anything. If he did, it would be on Nick's dime. Maybe that was petty of me, but I could live with the guilt, just like I was sure Mr. Billionaire could live with the financial burden of the bullheaded dog he'd forced on me.

In what I was coming to realize was typical Bone Thug fashion, he found his way into the weirdest spot in the room to curl up and take a nap. In this case, it was the bathtub, and his entry was far from graceful. Once he was done slipping his awkward, long legs into the tub and circling while grunting for several minutes, he finally curled up and fell asleep almost instantly.

Idiot dog. At least he was almost cute when he was sleeping. Actually, cute was pushing it too far. He was less hideous and a little less annoying, but that was all I was willing to give the brute.

I stuck my head in Max's room to let him know I was going to lock up for the night a few minutes later.

Max was standing in front of his TV with his shirt off and a muscular torso on display. I covered my eyes and backed out, slamming the door behind me. "God, sorry!" I shouted through the door. "I was just going to let you know I was locking up and getting ready for bed," I said, resting my forehead on the wall and squeezing my eyes shut.

"No worries," he called through the door. I couldn't be sure, but I thought I could hear the smug smile in his voice.

I sat down on the edge of my bed and stared at the wall. Why was this so confusing? Nick had made himself about as clear as he could. We were colleagues. Nothing more, nothing less. Our past was where it belonged—seven years behind us—and we were both going to do the adult thing: move on.

So why was there an oily little ball of guilt rolling around in my stomach? I should've been giddy at this made-for-television setup between Max and me. He was the handsome reporter, and I was the young, successful businesswoman. I could already imagine TV audiences rooting for us to hook up, especially if they got to see how Nick had turned me down before I'd even decided if I wanted to make something of my feelings with him.

Max Frost, who admittedly did have an incredibly stupid name, seemed like a great guy. He was handsome and successful, and he had made no secret of the fact that he was interested in me.

I should've been biting my lip and letting my mind wander to all the dirty little scenarios that might follow after walking in on Max with his shirt off. He'd knock on my door and confess that he didn't think it was fair to have such a one-sided exchange. He'd say he was going to need to see mine, too, in the interest of fair-and-balanced journalism.

Except I was forcing it. And every scenario I imagined ended with Nick King kicking down the door and carrying me away like a misbehaving child. The worst part was that I felt the strongest emotional response to the idea of Nick carrying me off, even if half of it was outrage.

Max was making it unfortunately clear for me. I wasn't done harboring feelings for Nick. Worse, those feelings I'd been telling myself were anger for so long had miraculously turned into something a lot more like longing, especially when I'd learned the truth about my dumb poem.

Maybe all I needed was some sleep. A few good hours of rest and everything would be more clear in the morning. *I hoped.*

♥ ♥ ♥

I woke to a gentle tapping at my door. Groggily, I got out of bed and threw on one of the complimentary robes to cover myself up. It was comfy, so I tugged it a little tighter around myself and let out a soft, happy little noise. Thug must've heard me getting up, because I could hear his stupid, toothy self scrabbling around in the bathtub as he tried to get out. I smiled. I'd never admit it to anyone, but I was starting to enjoy seeing all the varieties of dumb that Thug could get himself into.

A short man with a silly hat was waiting outside my door. He had a cart with silver domed plate covers and an assortment of condiments and small drinks. "Breakfast?" he asked.

"Uh, sure," I said.

He wheeled his cart into the room and started opening everything up. What I'd assumed was an array of choices for other guests to choose from turned out to be all for me. He set up everything on the table in my cabin on a combination of heated plates for the warm food and chilled plates for the fruits and sweets. When he was done, it looked like a meal big enough to feed four people, complete with eggs, hash browns, bacon, pancakes, fruit with some kind of syrupy drizzle, and endless packets of fancy-looking butter and little glass bottles of condiments.

I raised my eyebrows at the haul once he'd left. "Well then," I said to myself. I held up the tiniest ketchup bottle I'd ever seen and marveled at how adorable it was. "I'm totally keeping you," I whispered.

Thug was sitting close to the table, licking his lips.

"Calm down," I said. "I'll look up what stuff on here is safe for you to eat and share. But I get to eat first."

As if he understood me, Thug let out a pitiful little groan. I sighed and tossed him a pancake, which he caught and smacked down without chewing.

I looked toward Max's door and wondered if they had brought him breakfast as well, or if they were assuming I was the only one in the cabin. I raised my hand to knock on the door separating my partition of the cabin from his and paused.

Max seemed like a nice-enough guy, and I didn't want him to go hungry. I could invite him over to share some food without it having to have any kind of romantic implications, couldn't I?

I knocked on his door twice and waited.

I heard him unlocking it, then the door swung open. He was thankfully fully clothed this time and apparently already set to start his day. He looked freshly showered, and he was wearing a navy-blue polo. "Morning," he said.

"Hey, they brought me enough food to feed a small army. I was making sure they brought you some too."

"No such luck," he said, gesturing to the empty table in his room.

"Well, come grab yourself whatever you like. I'm not a huge breakfast person, so you can take your pick."

Ten minutes later, I was sitting across from Max, who had misunderstood my offer and seated himself at the table in my room to eat. Even though our conversation was completely innocent, I kept feeling a pulsing wrongness about the whole thing. Nick was right next door, and I'd stubbornly insisted on bringing Max here. I just had to keep telling myself how clear Nick seemed to make our situation. He was my boss, and I was his employee. Whether he felt something for me or not, he seemed to have decided not to act on it. So if I was going to be worried about having a man in my room, it should have been only the natural worry of my boss thinking I was behaving inappropriately on a company-sponsored trip.

"How long have you known him?" Max asked. He ate a forkful of eggs before looking up and waiting for my answer.

"Who, Nick?" I asked. His question had come out of the blue. A second ago, he had been talking about why he liked golf so much.

Max nodded.

"A pretty long time, actually. We met back in high school and were really good friends for a while. Rich and Cade were always kind of the untouchable jock overlord types, but Nick was more approachable back then. I don't think he knew how cute he was." I awkwardly swallowed, realizing how weird this was to talk about with Max. As far as I could tell, Max seemed to believe he was charming his way into my life, and he probably wasn't interested in hearing how cute I thought my boss used to be. "I just mean a lot of girls liked him, and I don't think he realized he was friend-zoning everybody. He was more innocent back then, I guess. It seems like he has figured out what he has going on lately, though." The thought was more than a little bitter. I didn't like knowing that Nick had become so fast and loose with relationships recently, even if I did at least know it was mostly just to keep his parents off his back.

"Wait," Max said. He set his fork down for the first time since he'd joined me at the table and leaned in. "You mean your boss was your friend back in high school? How long ago was that, if you don't mind me asking?"

Suddenly, I felt less like I was having a quasi date and more like I was being interviewed. "Uh, seven years, give or take."

Max leaned back and wiped his mouth. From the way his eyebrows were pressed together, he clearly had some kind of deep thoughts about all of this, even if I couldn't quite imagine what they'd be.

Someone knocked at my door. Thug barked one time, and lazily at that. I think he was more interested in waiting to see if Max, who appeared to be a human garbage disposal, was going to leave a single scrap of food for him.

I opened the door, expecting the guy with the little hat, but I saw Nick standing on the porch like a dark cloud. His hair was still wet—I assumed from a shower—and he wore a dark collared shirt with even darker pants, which looked scandalously good on him. In typical Nick fashion, he didn't seem to think he needed to explain why he had knocked on my door or why he was just standing there, glaring at me.

It felt like every bit of moisture in my mouth had evaporated until my tongue was just a stupid, useless blob of dry sandpaper. I wanted to say a dozen things. I wanted to tell him to stop glaring at me like he owned me. But I also wanted to explain why Max was sitting at the table behind me with a stupid look on his face.

Instead, I just motioned to the table. "Hungry? There's still some left," I said.

I didn't think Nick could glare any harder, but I was wrong. "Can I have a word?" he asked.

I nodded and followed him out to the porch. He pushed the door shut behind us—it wasn't quite a slam, but it was close.

Nick licked his lips and paced a few steps in a small circle, then ran his hand through his hair. If I wasn't so on edge, I could've laughed out loud to see how at war he seemed to be. I would've given anything to know what was going through his head, because I knew whatever came out of his mouth was going to be a half truth, at best.

"Do I even want to know?" he finally asked.

I raised my eyebrows and shook my head. "How am I supposed to know what you do or do not want to know? Have you even been honest with me one time since our interview?"

"Wait. *What?*" Nick asked. He stopped pacing now and fixed those heavy eyes of his on me. "How did this become about me?"

"This? Maybe I could help you figure it out if I even knew what *this* was."

Nick scowled, then started to laugh humorlessly. "Fine. If you want me to say it, I'll say it. As your boss, I'm not impressed to see that my vice president has so little self-control—that she couldn't even make it one night without letting some doofus with an idiotic name into her bedroom."

I pulled my head back, and my mouth hung open. *Oh, hell no.* He was going to just assume I'd slept with Max? "Jealousy is not a good look on you," I said tightly. I walked back to the door and put my hand on the handle. "And you know what?" I turned. I was about to say more, but I bit my tongue. I didn't need to debate him or try to plead my case. He was acting like a child, and if he wanted to act that way, I was happy to treat him like one. I went back into my cabin without so much as glancing his way.

Chapter 12
NICK

I didn't see Miranda all day, but it wasn't for lack of trying. Ever since she stormed off on me in the morning, I'd been hoping to catch her out somewhere. I didn't dare call her or knock on her door, and I tried to tell myself it wasn't just because I couldn't stand seeing that guy in her room again. It had taken everything in my power not to walk in there and do a little sloppy dental work on him.

Thankfully, I had never been the type of man to let my desires rule over my actions. No matter how fiercely I might be at war in my head, I could keep my eyes forward and do what needed to be done.

The unfortunate twist to this whole resort situation was that what needed to be done was people watch. It meant I could convince myself I was working while I was probably just hoping to find Miranda somewhere on the resort grounds.

I didn't have a fully formed plan for what I'd do when I did find her. I'm sure some of it was just wanting assurance that she wasn't in her room having wild sex with Max Frost at this very moment. I clenched my teeth at the thought. Another part of my need to find her was to apologize, though.

While I stood by my right to expect professionalism from my vice president, I knew I'd been a total ass earlier. I should've let her explain instead of shoving assumptions down her throat. But it was hard to be reasonable and calm when it felt like my blood was boiling.

I had taken lunch by the pool. I hadn't been able to relax because I'd kept expecting Cade to literally jump out of a bush the whole time. When not thinking about Cade, my mind had gone to the idea of her fingers digging into Max's stupid back. The idea of her sleeping with other men hadn't occurred to me when I'd thought up this grand scheme of mine, and I was worried it was going to break what little was left of my resolve.

I had also been constantly licked, sniffed, and prodded by dogs. Apparently, everybody had decided their dogs would like to swim as well, which the resort staff hadn't seemed pleased by. By the time I had headed back to my room from lunch, I had been soaked from the waist down from canine attention—and numb from the shoulders up after several conversations with women who hadn't bothered to hide their intentions.

It was just past seven when I gave up for the night and went back to my room, feeling oddly defeated. I wasn't used to letting go of control, but that was exactly what I'd done with Miranda. The right thing to do was to keep my nose out of her business, so that was exactly what I was going to do, even if it killed me.

I heard muted laughter about half an hour later. I half tossed my laptop on the bed and moved to the door, pressing my ear against the wood. I stepped out onto the porch of my cabin and looked toward Miranda's. She was heading out in a little black number and looked dressed to kill.

Jealousy spiked through me. Who was she trying so hard to impress, and why did I want to strangle them so badly?

"Hey," I called out. Our cabins were separated by only a dozen feet of space, and I barely had to raise my voice to catch her attention.

"Oh," she said. "Hey."

"Got plans?" I asked.

She busied herself looking for something in her purse but apparently had no plans to answer me.

"If you are trying to look for a chocolate bar in there, no thanks. I've seen where you stash them for your friends. I can only imagine where one for me would come from."

She gave me an odd look. "What?"

I blew out a breath and rubbed the back of my neck. *What the hell?* I never had trouble talking to women, but now I was trying so hard to walk some blurry line between professional and personal that I was failing at both. "I was trying to make a joke. Since you had stuffed the candy wrapper 'for your friend' in your bra the other day. At the office," I added awkwardly. I was suddenly wishing I'd been smart enough to stay in my goddamn cabin. I was doing about as well here as a hormonal teenager who was trying to hide a boner behind his calculus book—not that I'd ever had any personal experience with that technique.

"I was looking for my phone, actually," she said. There was a cold flatness to her voice that made my stomach feel empty.

For the millionth time, I reminded myself that I was only getting what I wanted. I had been the one to decide I was going to push her away, and, go figure, she was thoroughly pushed. "You enjoying yourself so far?"

"Ready?" asked a deep voice from inside her cabin.

Miranda turned, nodded quickly, and gave me a tight-lipped smile. "Gotta go," she said.

Max Frost stepped outside wearing a button-down shirt and so much cologne I caught a whiff from where I was standing. I bet the dickbag was wearing his favorite underwear too. He probably thought he was going to score tonight. *Maybe he was. Maybe he already had, and tonight would just be the extra-point attempt.*

A strange, stifled groan came from my throat. I coughed, cleared my throat, and waved back. "We'll catch up later," I said.

Then I went back in my room and tried to clear my mind. There were a few ways I could handle this. The least productive, but most satisfying, would be to grab a heavy object and go give Max Frost and his stupid name a concussion so he couldn't try to worm his way into my vice president's pants. The most pathetic would be to skulk around and try to spy on them so I wouldn't have to sit here and imagine the worst. And the smartest thing to do—the thing I was going to do—was to sit my ass down and go to sleep.

The hardest things to do were usually the ones that were the most worth doing. And if that saying held any truth, then staying inside my cabin was going to be one of the most worthwhile things any human being had ever done since the beginning of time.

Except I didn't sleep. I flicked on the TV and tried to find something to watch. It took me several minutes to find a channel that wasn't on commercial break, which meant I was stuck watching some sort of dog beauty contest. I leaned against the headboard and watched with glazed eyes. At least it meant I could take my mind off what Miranda and that jackass were probably doing right now.

Chapter 13

MIRANDA

Max and I sat down at one of the many bars throughout the resort. This particular bar was a beautiful outdoor space strewn with dangling white lights and a stone patio that overlooked the mountains in the distance. There was a pleasant chill to the air, and it should've been a perfect night. No, it *was* a perfect night.

I'd been doing some soul-searching and decided that I needed to do more than just shove Nick to the back burner in my brain. I needed to aggressively get over him, or it was never going to happen. That meant I had to do something, like say yes when Max asked me if I wanted to go grab a drink with him. Maybe I hadn't felt any spark between us, but that was the whole point of going on a date, right?

So here I was. A handsome man was sitting at the bar beside me, the view was breathtaking, and I was basically on a free vacation.

"I'm glad you agreed to come," Max said once the bartender set our drinks down. We had both been pleased to learn that even the alcohol was covered under the company tab. I was never much of a drinker, but tonight, a little liquid courage sounded like a good plan.

"Me too," I said. I sipped the wine I'd ordered and made an appreciative noise.

"Your boss is kind of an asshole, isn't he?" Max asked.

I took another sip of my wine that was admittedly more of a gulp at his question. "Sort of," I said. "I mean, it depends on how you look at it."

"Then tell me how *you* look at it, then."

I sighed. I'd come out here tonight to get Nick off my mind, not talk through my feelings for him. "I don't know, exactly. Like he has always sent me extremely frustratingly mixed signals? One minute I think he's romantically interested, and the next he's actively trying to make me not like him."

Max looked at his drink thoughtfully, then smiled in a way that made me think he hadn't really cared about my answer, after all. "You deserve better than that," he said.

I smiled, but it felt forced. I drained the last of my glass. I could already feel a slight buzzing in my head that told me I was right about where I should stop drinking if I wanted to keep my mind sharp. I hadn't really eaten since that huge breakfast, and I was already a light-weight to begin with.

"She'll have another," Max said.

I shook my head. "No, it's okay. I think I need to eat something before I drink any more."

"Hey," he said, leaning in. "What are you worried about? That asshole reprimanding you for having too much fun? If he's going to be a dick either way, why stop yourself from having fun at his expense?"

I thought about that. There was a certain satisfaction in the idea of doing something to spite Nick, even if it was petty. "Just one more glass," I said.

An hour later, my head was thoroughly spinning. Max was about ten minutes deep in a story about some locker room confrontation that had led to a fistfight back in his high school days. He had stood up and was acting out the story, punching, ducking, and weaving to the side.

My phone buzzed from inside my purse. "Hey," I said, stopping Max. "I've got to run to the bathroom for a sec, sorry."

"Oh," he said, deflating a bit. "Okay. I'll order you another drink for when you get back."

I stood, nearly fell sideways, and then tried to not look as drunk as I felt on my way to the bathroom. I checked my phone once I was inside and alone in a stall.

Nick: You two planning to stay out all night? Do I need to remind you this is a work event, not a personal vacation?

I glared down at my phone and thought up a response that would be witty and biting—and teach him to stop trying to control me. In my drunken haze, I pulled up the camera app and snapped a shot of my ass in the black dress I was wearing and captioned it, Drinks are on the company tab! Kiss this! I added a bunch of random emojis and fired off the text before I had time to think it over.

I stumbled back to the bar and looked at the drink Max had ordered me. With uncharacteristic abandon, I threw back a long gulp. I almost immediately regretted it, as even the motion of tilting my head back sent everything spinning.

Closing my eyes only made it worse. It felt like I was in a washing machine, and even with all the nausea-inducing dizziness, I *still* couldn't stop thinking about how silly I felt for doing all this to spite Nick. Even behind wine goggles, it had become clear that I wasn't romantically interested in Max after five minutes of listening to him talk tonight. If I was honest with myself, I think I'd known it from the moment he got in the car with me at the airport. Deep down, I knew I was just using the excuse of his story helping our business because I wanted to put Nick's feelings to the test.

Ugh. When had I become so pathetic? I distantly wondered if it was less of a bitchy move when the plan hadn't been premeditated. And how could it have been? I'd been off balance from the moment Nick had walked back into my life. Everything I did was just a desperate grab for stability—one wild, scrabbling grasp after another. And tonight was a new low, even by my recent standards.

I thought I might pass out any minute, and I felt deep, terrifying pangs of panic at the idea of Max being responsible for taking me back to our cabin. I almost sent another text to Nick asking him to come rescue me, but there was no way to do it without Max seeing.

I tried to will myself to sobriety, but I was too far gone, so I resolved to stare glassy eyed at the bar and refuse to drink another drop of alcohol. I was not going to pass out.

Chapter 14

NICK

I commandeered a golf cart to get to the bar faster. I'd covered Miranda's ass in the picture she'd sent me while I showed every employee I could find. I needed to know which bar had a bathroom that looked like the one in the image. I tore through the quaint little pathways, dodging more than a few pairs of Bark Bites employees who were drunkenly staggering home, jogging with their dogs, or just out enjoying a night-time stroll.

When I arrived at the bar, I found Max Frost and Miranda on their way out. Max was holding Miranda, who looked like she was on the verge of passing out. He had her arm slung around his neck and his hand around her waist as he half dragged her.

I stopped the golf cart directly in front of them and stepped out. I knew rolling up in a golf cart was probably the least intimidating way on earth to make an entrance, but I didn't care. "Miranda, are you okay?" I asked.

She looked at me, and for a brief moment, I thought I saw relief in her face. The expression passed and was replaced by a look like she was about to throw up, but I knew what I'd seen, and that was all it took to make my decision clear.

"I'll take her from here," I said.

"Like hell you will," Max said. "I know all about you. Miranda told me what an asshole you are. About how you are always leading her on. Besides," he said, shooting a curious look toward Miranda. He'd apparently decided she was drunk enough that he could speak freely. "I'm the one who spent all night getting her drunk. You think I'm just going to hand her over to you?"

"Set her in the golf cart," I said in a cold, barely controlled voice.

"No."

"You can either put her down carefully and walk away, or I'm going to make you. If I have to make you, I'll do everything in my power to make sure the news station you work for knows what a fucking creep you are too. It's your choice."

He stared at me, jaw flexing and unflexing. I sensed what he was about to do just before he did it, lunging forward to catch Miranda as he roughly let her go.

As she slipped from his arms, she drunkenly whooped like she was on a thrill ride. When I dipped to my knees and caught her, she fist pumped and cheered, eyes rolling back in her head. "And Nick steals the home run!" she whisper-yelled. "The crowd goes wild!" She made a hissing noise and did some strange gesture with her hands.

I really had never been the fighting type, but I knew if I hadn't had to worry about Miranda's safety, I would've already gone off on the man. I wanted nothing more than to hurt him. The intensity of my anger scared me, though. Burying my feelings for Miranda to do what was best for her career had seemed like the right choice, but I don't think I realized she could stir up emotions this strong in me. It made me wonder if keeping these kinds of feelings from her was really the right thing to do.

"Happy?" Max asked.

"Every second I have to look at you pisses me off more."

"Try closing your eyes," Max suggested.

"Walk. Away," I warned.

Max sniffed dismissively. "Having money doesn't make you invincible, you know. This isn't the last you'll hear from me, and you're going to wish you hadn't fucked with me." He spit on the ground before stalking off.

I picked her up carefully and sat her down in the golf cart. I wasn't afraid of his threats. He was just trying to save face. I was almost certain.

As much as I wanted to go after him and start a fight, I wasn't willing to leave Miranda alone for long enough to do it. So I turned the wheel on the cart and headed back to our cabins.

When I took the first turn to the right, Miranda slumped into my shoulder and made no sign of wanting to straighten back up.

"You schmell yummy," she slurred in a drunken approximation of Sean Connery's accent.

I pressed my lips together. *Do not engage.* She was beyond drunk, and, unlike Max, my plan was to take her to her room, set her on the bed, and leave.

"I've always wanted to take a nibble out of you," she said, clamping her teeth together a few times for emphasis. "Did you know that? Nope. You didn't, 'cause you asked out the wrong girl."

I swallowed hard. *Ignore all of this.* I had to resist the overwhelming urge to tell her the truth, even if she was hardly likely to remember any of this tomorrow.

I stopped the golf cart in front of our cabins and unbuckled her carefully. I had to tug her black dress down her thighs to avoid getting a pervert's view as I did so, and I couldn't help picturing the image she'd sent me on her phone a little while ago. *The image I knew I had no plans of deleting.*

I offered her my hand, but she shook her head, closed her eyes, and leaned back against the seat. "Sorry. This one is all out of walksies. You'll have to carry me with those big, strong, juicy muscles." She opened her eyes then and tried to give me what I took for a seductive look, except one eye was squinting far more than the other, and her smile was crooked.

I could've laughed if I were seeing this under any other circumstance. Instead, I sighed and scooped her up. "Where's your key?" I asked when we got to the door.

"Probably in my purse. Right next to the dildos," she added with a snort. "Just kidding. My dildos are way too big to fit in there."

I couldn't help grinning a little. I set her down and propped her against the wall as I looked in her purse. I frowned when I saw a familiar piece of paper folded into a small square. When I pulled it out, I knew exactly what it was.

"Why did you take this?" I asked. My heart was in my throat at the thought of her reading it. Things with Kira had never worked out, but it didn't mean I wanted to embarrass her. I also didn't want to have to explain why I'd kept the thing for so long. "Was this why you really snuck into my office? To snoop and steal my shit?"

She raised her eyebrows, then squinted, like she could barely see what I was holding a few inches in front of her face. "Oh. No. I took that because I was the one who wrote the damn thing in the first place. Your dumb ass got it wet. Then you thought some smears of ink were a signature. It was supposed to be an anonymous letter, *Nick*." She said my name in a comically deep voice, then shook her head and rolled her eyes. "Anonymous, but obvious."

My knees felt weak, so I crouched down beside her and tried to wrap my head around what she'd just said. The *ira* I'd assumed to be Kira's name, minus the *K* for reasons I could never puzzle out, had been from Miranda. *Shit.*

One of the most satisfying things about overcoming a complex challenge in just the right way had always been the sensation of things falling into place. It was like a domino effect. Once the right action was taken, it trickled down, sometimes in unexpected but gratifying ways. This was similar, but deeply unsettling.

It was a puzzle I'd had wrong my whole life, and now I knew it was because it had all been based on one single faulty piece of information. The poem hadn't been from Kira. I could still see the shock on Kira's face when I'd asked her out a few days after I got the note in my locker. It explained why Miranda had acted so utterly betrayed. She'd been waiting for me to tell her what I thought of the poem—the damn poem that was so obviously from her if it hadn't been for the name I'd thought had been given at the bottom.

Anonymous, but obvious. She was right. It would've been, and what would've happened if I'd asked her out instead of Kira back then? Would Miranda and her friends have even made their stupid oath in the first place? God only knew, but one thing was certain. Nothing I'd thought I knew made sense anymore. All the decisions I was making had been based on a flawed foundation of understanding, and I'd need to take the time to sort through all this.

"I can't find the key," I said a few minutes later when I had dug through her purse thoroughly enough to be sure. "I also didn't see any dildos."

"That's fine. We can share your bed. And I've always preferred the real thing, anyway."

I picked her up again, carried her to my room, and laid her on my bed. I had zero intention of getting in that bed with her, so all I did was slip off her shoes and pull the comforter up over her. I thought she had fallen asleep, and I was just admiring how heartbreakingly beautiful she was when she made a soft moaning sound, then smiled.

"One stupid poem cost us seven years." She muttered the words so softly I wondered if I had imagined them.

I leaned closer, straining my ears—waiting for more. The only answer she gave was a delicate little burp before she rolled over and seemed to fall asleep.

I made myself comfortable in the chair on the other side of the room and tried to sleep, but with everything running through my mind,

I was almost certain I wasn't going to find any rest. Nothing was going to be the same between us after tonight. Miranda might care about her career, and it might be the cornerstone of her identity, but if she was really holding back thoughts like *that*? Then I couldn't lie to myself anymore.

I'd been doing everything in my power to bury my feelings for her. The only thing giving me the willpower had been the belief that I was doing the right thing. Now, though? I wasn't so sure it was right, after all.

Chapter 15

MIRANDA

I would say I opened my eyes, but that would imply there was no struggle in the act. The reality was that I had to pry my eyes open with what little power my eyelids had. They felt crusty and dry. The faint light streaming through the window wasn't helping my pounding head, and I had the worst case of morning breath I'd ever had. I breathed against the back of my hand, sniffed, and reeled back. "Jesus," I muttered.

"Just Nick, unfortunately."

I jerked my head toward the sound of his voice. "What the hell are you doing in my room?" I spotted a small bottle of mouthwash on his nightstand and drained the whole thing, swishing aggressively, and then realized I had nowhere to spit, so I swallowed it and winced against the burn.

"I take it you don't remember last night?" Nick asked.

Oh no. I lifted the covers and peeked under. I silently thanked God that I was still fully clothed. I'd done a lot of things in life that I regretted, but blackout drunken sex had never been one of them.

Last night started to come back to me out of order. I remembered nearly throwing up while riding a golf cart. I remembered sending some kind of text to . . . "Did I . . . happen to text you something? Because I was not completely in the right state of mind, and I hope you'll cut me some slack if I said anything out of line."

Nick licked his lips. There was something different in his face. The coldness I had seen come and go from him didn't feel like it was momentarily gone this time. It felt like it was *completely* gone. "You might have sent me something. And it probably could've been considered out of line, but I enjoyed it."

I reached for my purse and pulled my phone out. I needed to know what I'd sent, and, from the look of amusement in his eyes, Nick was looking forward to the moment when I saw it. I pulled up my texts. *God.* There was a picture of me smiling with half-lidded eyes and my dress pulled tight against my ass. I'd even sent an obnoxious caption to him. "Wait," I said. I suddenly remembered Max and his stupid high school war stories. I'd gone to get drinks with him, but ended up in Nick's room? "What happened last night?"

"Your date seemed pretty intent on getting you sloppy drunk. When I found you two, he was practically dragging you back to the cabin. I took the liberty of telling him to fuck off, but I couldn't find your key, so you got to crash in my bed for the night."

"It wasn't really a date," I said. I groaned when I tried to sit up and pushed my palms into my eyes.

"Do you remember anything you told me last night?" he asked. He was openly smiling. My gut told me that was a very bad sign.

"Do I want to?" I asked carefully.

Nick produced the folded-up square of paper from his pocket and raised his eyebrows. "You told me the truth about this."

My eyes bulged. "I didn't—I . . ." Despite the fact that I considered myself to be a fully grown adult, I was so embarrassed that I yanked the comforter up and covered my head with it. Maybe hot guys and monsters had the same limitations about not being able to penetrate the defenses of a blanket over the head.

"I can still see you," Nick said.

"What exactly did I say?"

"Enough to convince me of something."

"What?" I asked impatiently. I was still hiding under the comforter, but I didn't want him to see how red my cheeks were. I guessed burying myself under a blanket was arguably more embarrassing than blushing, but I wasn't going to worry about that.

"I'm tired of pushing you away."

I peeled the comforter back. *Jesus.* Now I really wanted to know what I'd said. Before last night, it had felt like Nick was using a cattle prod to urge me as far out of his life as possible. Now he was saying this?

Nick moved from the chair and sat on the bed beside me. He spent long enough gathering his thoughts and raking a hand through his dark hair that I couldn't help admiring him. He was the kind of good looking most people could go a lifetime without ever seeing in person. It was the unquestionable kind—the sort of good looking that made complete strangers stare without worrying what anyone thought. It was like seeing a natural phenomenon, except this one had dreamy eyes with long eyelashes you could get lost in; full, playful lips; and an easy smirk that made me want to melt into a puddle.

Despite all that, I think I would've still been intrigued by him if he'd looked like a gargoyle. Every other guy I'd entertained interest in since Nick had felt like settling. Worse, it had felt empty. I had started to accept that it was silly and immature to think I deserved to find somebody who made me feel the way I'd felt back then. Except now I wasn't so sure. He was sitting right here, and even if he wasn't making it easy, I didn't know if I'd forgive myself for not at least taking the chance.

"I've lied to myself for a long time," Nick said finally. "About you. About how I felt." He shook his head, eyes fixed on something outside the window. "I've made it into such a complicated mess in my head. It's like some puzzle where I keep thinking I'm almost finished, then I realize the first pieces I placed were all wrong—that I need to wipe the board clean and start over. I just can't—"

His face was so close that I had to lean forward only a few inches to find his lips with mine. It all happened in an instant. The buzzing of my thoughts was silenced the moment my mouth met his, like a window slamming shut on a noisy night. At first, he didn't respond, and I had enough time to wonder if I'd made what would go down as the most embarrassing mistake of my life.

I pulled back from the kiss, eyes closed. "I'm sorry," I said. "I just wanted to show you that it didn't have to be so complic—"

Nick's hands swallowed me up, and his mouth was on mine again, hungrier this time. There was no air in my lungs, no time to think. All I could do was let myself get pulled along with his wave, to kiss him back and marvel at the silky warmth of his tongue against mine, at the way I could feel passion radiating between us like heat.

Before I knew what was happening, I was falling backward to my pillow, and Nick was propped above me. I couldn't catch my breath. I couldn't even *think*. Every train of thought went off the rails, like Nick's presence was a tsunami-force event, demanding every available ounce of my focus.

"W-Wait," I stammered between kisses.

Nick stopped, and the surprise I saw in his eyes told me he'd been feeling exactly as I'd been. Pulling back from his touch felt like waking from a pleasant dream only to remember you were staying in a dingy motel across from the fast-food chicken place with a neon red sign. Except all I would've needed to do to fall back into that dream was reach out. It would've taken only a single word. *More. Please.* It would've been so easy, but it had happened too fast.

"You're right," he said. He pushed himself off me and stood up. He shook his head slightly.

Someone knocked at his door.

"Room service," called a voice with a heavy French accent.

Nick pointed at me and motioned for me to hide.

"Hide?" I mouthed.

122

He nodded quickly and made some face and expression I couldn't figure out. I decided to take his word for it and rolled off the bed, slipping underneath.

I could see his shoes from where I was lying, so when he opened the door, I saw the expensive leather shoes of somebody who was definitely not room service step inside.

"Somehow, I knew," Nick said.

"Whoa," the man said. I immediately knew the voice. *Cade.* But I had no idea how he would've found his way here. "Is that a boner? You watching that cheap hotel porn again, or were you j—"

"Would you get your eyes off my dick, please?"

"I'd love to, but your dick is kind of demanding attention right now. I feel like it's reaching out to me, like it wants me to—"

"Why are you here?"

"I was checking on you and that griefcase you like to carry around."

"What?"

"Emotional baggage. Your griefcase. Don't look at me like I'm crazy either. You know whoever decided to call it emotional baggage was missing a major opportunity."

"I don't have emotional baggage."

"No? What about Miranda? I'd say the way you pine after her but keep denying yourself qualifies. You know she wants it as badly as you do. All you'd need to do is extend the olive branch." Cade paused. "Well, or you could extend *that*. Either one would probably get the message across."

"Could you stop looking at it?"

"I'm just impressed that it is still full mast. I mean, I'm starting to wonder if it's *me* that arouses you. The thing is like a bloodhound that has the scent."

"Trust me, it has nothing to do with you."

Cade was quiet for a few seconds, then I saw his feet approaching the bed.

"What are you doing?" Nick asked.

"I didn't make it where I am in life by being an idiot, Nick. Boners don't just make themselves, and they don't stick around that long *unless* . . ."

I was suddenly staring face-to-face with Cade, who had flopped down on his stomach beside the bed. "As I suspected. Ladies, gentlemen, and erection—we have the source of the arousal right here. Did anyone tell you it's much comfier to sleep on top of the bed, Miranda?"

I awkwardly wiggled out from under the bed and stood up. "This isn't what it looks like at all," I said.

"Classic." Cade was smiling between the two of us like a proud teacher. "Let me give you whippersnappers a piece of universal advice. When something isn't what it looks like, that just means the people involved don't understand what it actually is. Things always look like what they are. And this," he said, motioning to the clearly visible bulge in Nick's pants, "looks like two consenting adults who were getting ready to fulfill their biblical duty."

I tried to avert my eyes from Nick's pants, but I felt a devious little tug of temptation that made me want to look again. It was flattering to know a few kisses had him that excited, but it was also confusing. "Nick is my boss," I said.

"Hey." Cade held up his palms. "I'm not here to judge you two on your kinks. Nick can be your kitty cat, for all I care. All I'm saying is you two lovebirds don't need to hide it from me. Think of me like your big brother, too, Miranda. I mean, I guess I will be once you two make this whole thing official, right?"

Nick put his hands on Cade's arm and started pushing him to the door. "Why don't you get back on your helicopter and go spend some time with your family instead of creeping around our business trip."

"Hey, if I knew business trips were just sex-fueled kink parties, I wouldn't have been avoiding them for so long. But Iris and Bear are here, actually. I flew them in last night. We're going to play some croquet once I'm done here. I don't know the rules, but how hard can it be, right? Well, probably not as hard as *that*, at least." He nodded to Nick's erection again.

"Can you just—" Nick started.

"Say no more." Cade stepped out of the door, then popped his head in one more time. "Oh, and don't use protection. I want nieces and nephews." He winked, then left.

"I should get back to my cabin," I said.

Nick looked like he was about to say something, but then he nodded. "Yeah, sure. Should we—"

"Later," I said. "We can talk about it later. I just need a little space to think this all through."

"Hey," Nick said, touching my arm before I reached the door. "You sure you want to go?"

"We'll talk later," I said. I practically ran out the door. I felt suffocated, but not in an entirely unpleasant way. The frightening thing was how badly I seemed to want to embrace that lack of oxygen—to let myself drift away to wherever he wanted to take me.

As soon as I stepped outside, I knew it wouldn't be that simple. I remembered how Cade said Iris was here, and I decided I needed a serious dose of girl talk.

I found Iris after a quick exchange of texts. She met me beside the indoor pool. The echoey room smelled like chlorine, and a pair of men were swimming around the shallow end with a big German shepherd. I found the splashing sounds and smells oddly nostalgic. Something about that smell specific to indoor public pools reminded me of late nights at motels on family vacations as a kid. It was like I could close my eyes and go back to simpler times, except I wasn't sure I would've traded simple for where I was anymore.

Things had become almost unbearably complicated, but I was starting to sense that if I could find my way through the tangle of choices ahead, happiness was waiting for me.

Iris and I took up two lounge chairs. She sank back comfortably into hers, but I perched on the end of mine, legs vibrating on their own.

"You look like a drug addict jonesing for your next fix, by the way," Iris said.

"The hardest drug I've ever done were the painkillers they gave me after my tonsils got taken out. So, no. Guess again."

"I don't need to guess." Iris rolled her head to look at me with an obnoxious little smirk. "Cade told me about the boner."

I rolled my eyes. "We just kissed, and it was only for, like, a minute. Maybe."

"Who kissed who?"

"I kind of started it, technically. He was talking circles around it, and I just kind of . . . went for the kill."

She reached out her fist toward me and waited.

"I'm not going to fist-bump you over this," I said.

"Suit yourself. Still though. *Nice.*"

I laughed, shaking my head. "Not really. I kissed my boss and managed to turn an already complicated situation nuclear."

"Hardly. The whole *no dating your boss* thing is really only a big deal when your boss is way above you on the company ladder. If you and Nick were on a company ladder, your nose would practically be in his ass—which you'd love, I'm sure."

"I don't follow."

"It's not weird when you two are practically in the same position. I mean, think about it. It's weird if you're his secretary, because then he could promote you like twenty times before you're right beneath him—pun intended. But if you're his VP, it's not like he's going to just step down and give you his job because you're greasing his pole."

"Ew," I said.

"So," she continued, "if he did decide to give you his job, he wouldn't be your boss anymore. If he doesn't, then he's not playing favorites. Get it? It's a win-win situation. He literally can't abuse his position because of his feelings for you."

"In a stupid kind of way, I guess that does make sense. I mean, assuming I ignore the fact that everybody I've ever known would think I only got the job in the first place because we were already together, but just hiding it. And then they'd wonder about every job and promotion I've landed in the past."

"That would be their opinion, and opinions are like assholes, anyway."

"Everyone has one, and most of them stink?" I asked.

"What? No. And what kind of person goes around sniffing assholes? I was going to say everybody acts like they're so great, but if you look at them up close, they're usually all gross and puckered little gremlin holes."

I stared at her. "I don't even want to acknowledge that with a response."

"I'm just saying that you'd be shocked by how good it feels to stop giving a shit what people say about you. Maybe do what you want for once instead of what people think you should want."

I sighed. "It's not that easy."

"You're right. I can only imagine what I'd do if Larry the goat farmer thought I had slept my way to the top in my career. Or God forbid Mary Stevens, the world's foremost expert on daytime-television game shows, thinks you've been too promiscuous. How would you even go on living without their approval?"

"West Valley is home. How am I supposed to just say, 'Screw it—I don't care what everybody I've ever known thinks about me'?"

"You find something you care about more than their opinions, I guess."

I nodded. "Maybe you're right. *For once.*"

"Good. So now you can stop fighting your primal instincts and go jump his bones."

"Not exactly. Even if I wipe away the whole boss thing, I've still got issues."

"Yeah, no kidding."

I glared. "I mean with the idea of dating Nick."

"Right. And those issues are?"

"I don't know . . . the oath? That I found out he didn't ask Kira out because he was an idiot seven years ago. It was only because, well—" I cleared my throat. I'd never told Iris or Kira about the poem, and I wasn't sure I wanted to go down that path. The poem itself was riddled with horrible teenage clichés and sappy language. Iris and Kira would have enough material to make fun of me until we were wheelchair bound if they ever got their hands on it.

"Because . . . ," Iris said.

"I recently learned that the whole reason I hated him all this time was based on a misunderstanding. And even though I know that now, it's hard to rewire my brain. I still have these conflicting feelings when I'm around him. Like part of me just wants to enjoy the moment, and the other part can't stop feeling ashamed for wanting that."

Iris worked her lips to the side thoughtfully. She could be a complete goofball and seem like she didn't have a serious bone in her body, but I could tell she was finally giving this legitimate consideration. "Okay," she said finally. "Why do you feel ashamed?"

"Because, I don't know . . ." I sighed. "Maybe I know it would distract me from my work? I've spent my whole life trying to succeed, so the idea of putting that on the back burner, even for a little while—it's just scary."

"And does success have to mean advancement in your career? Look, I get that you and I are totally different animals, but I thought I wanted to prove something to my dad for the longest time. I wanted to show him that I could still be a real cop, even in a little town like this. I wanted that from such a young age that it started just being a given that I never questioned. Then Cade came along, and I finally questioned it. Turns out it didn't hold up when I looked closer. I didn't care about that anymore, and all it had been doing was sitting in the background, shitting on everything that would've made me happy. It sounds like you've got to take a look at yourself and ask what you really want. What's important." .

I nodded. "That actually makes sense. Thank you."

"*Actually* makes sense? You say that like I don't normally."

"I mean, no. Normally, you don't."

She laughed. "It doesn't take a blind person to see what's going on here. I'm just stating the obvious."

"It doesn't take a—" I put the back of my hand to my mouth to cover my smile. "I feel like that's offensive, and it doesn't even make sense."

"All I'm trying to say is that sometimes your friends know you better than you know yourself. And as your friend, I think you should stop worrying so much about it. Just act like a normal adult and go on a date with the man."

"He hasn't asked me on a date yet."

"Yet. Maybe he just needs to see a little more confidence from you. Send some signals. Think of it like this. You and Nick are a pair of walkie-talkies, but every message you send to him is coming out all garbled and distorted because he's an idiot."

"He's not an idiot," I said.

Iris held up her finger. "When it comes to this, he is. So what do you do when the walkie-talkie messages aren't getting through to him? You throw your walkie-talkie at his head. Send him a message he can't misinterpret."

"What message is throwing a walkie-talkie at his head supposed to send?"

"It's called a metaphor, Miranda. You're not supposed to take it literally. *Jesus.*"

Chapter 16

NICK

I asked Miranda to meet me that evening in the Scarlet Lounge, which was an aptly named room in the lower level of the main hotel grounds. The walls were patterned with dark wood paneling and red satin accents. There were also several small dogs napping while a group of employees chatted at a large table in the corner over drinks.

I'd put on my favorite suit for the meeting. There was a buzzing need in my bones that I couldn't ignore anymore. Finding out the poem had been from her was an open door to an entirely new set of thrilling possibilities, and I had no interest in letting the opportunity pass me by.

Making up my mind to pursue Miranda again brought a new set of challenges. Chief of which was the fact that I still respected her drive to have a successful career. Yes, I had been dreaming about the indescribable taste of her mouth all day, but I also had to be careful how I went about this.

I knew the way she dressed would be my first real indication of what she was thinking. A conservative outfit probably meant she was trying to reestablish the boundary we'd kissed our way through.

I saw her legs first as she came down the stairs to the lounge. They were long, but seeing them come down one step at a time had a seductive, almost hypnotic effect on me. First, there was a black shoe. Then the tanned skin of her leg, followed by another. I could feel my stomach in my throat while I watched more and more leg before finally seeing the hem of her white dress. *Midthigh, maybe a little longer,* I noted. It was right between conservative and seductive.

She paused at the bottom of the stairs and looked my way. I couldn't help thinking how badly I wanted to pull her into me and whisper something dark and possessive in her ear—to tell her if she so much as thought about seeing Max again, I'd bend her over my lap and remind her who her boss was.

I could've laughed at myself. If she only knew what perverted thoughts were running through my head, she would run.

"If the goal was to wear something I'd want to take off, you succeeded," I said.

Miranda's eyes bulged. "What? Is it that bad?"

I laughed. "No, as in—you know what, never mind. I shouldn't have even said that."

She looked down at her feet as her cheeks went red. "Yeah, well, it's not like you could get it off without a pair of scissors, anyway. I think I broke the zipper when I was putting this thing on."

"Let me see," I said.

"The zipper?" she asked.

I motioned for her to turn around. The zipper was at her waist, just above the roundness of her ass. I put one hand on her hip and gave the zipper a little tug with the other. It resisted. "Oh damn. It really is stuck pretty good."

"Nick, I think this probably looks—"

I tugged again, and the zipper jerked down about three inches. Miranda jumped and quickly reached back to zip it up.

When she turned to look at me with bulging, surprised eyes, I had to cover my mouth to stop from laughing.

"I'm sorry," I said. "But, hey, at least you won't have to ruin a good dress to get it off now. Right?"

She looked around to make sure nobody had seen and then sat down next to me. "So is that how it works with you, Nicholas? One kiss and suddenly you think you can go stripping off my clothes in public?"

I chewed my lip, grinning. "No, but if you keep calling me Nicholas like that? I can't promise that's not how it's going to work."

"In all seriousness, I kind of need to know where we go from here. I don't really do improvisation very well."

"You want me to draw up an agenda for you? Maybe a four-phase plan? Phase one, you aggressively maul me on the bed this morning. Phase two, I return the favor the first chance I get. Phase thr—"

"Not like that," she said, shaking her head. "What has gotten into you, anyway?"

"I'm done lying to myself. That's what. No more running from you. No more convincing myself it'd be better for you if I acted like I wasn't interested. *No more excuses.*"

She frowned as she studied my face. "There's a big difference between what feels good and what *is* good. I know Bark Bites is just the next business in a long line of businesses you've turned around, so maybe it's not that important to you. But to me, this is all I have right now. It matters to me, okay? I mean, how am I supposed to live with myself if I throw away my career because I'm attracted to you?"

"So you *are* attracted to me," I said with a smirk.

She glared. "Of course I'm attracted to you. You look like Batman with a side of Clark Kent."

"Wait, with or without the mask?"

She finally cracked a smile. "Without the mask. I just forgot the guy's name. The one who is actually Batman."

"Bruce Wayne?"

"Yeah. Being attracted to you or not isn't the point, though."

"I know," I said. As much as I wanted to talk about something else, I couldn't ignore the facts. "And I get it. Being with me would call into question everything you've ever accomplished in your career, and maybe everything in the future too."

"Yeah," she said slowly. "And it's not only about what everyone else would think. How could I not start to wonder if I really earned this job, or if you just gave it to me?"

"Hey," I said, taking her hand. "I planned to tell you to get lost when you walked into that interview. Seriously. But when you started talking, I realized you have the reputation you do for a reason. And I was right. When I haven't been distracting you, all the work you've done already is top notch. You deserve this job, okay? The way I feel about you has nothing to do with that."

Miranda swallowed hard, then looked away. She was frowning as she toyed with one of the rings on her fingers. "How do you feel, exactly?"

"Like I'm getting a chance to fix the biggest mistake of my life, and I'm going to do everything in my power to avoid fucking it up again."

"What mistake was that?"

I chuckled. "Play your cards right tonight, and maybe you'll get to find out."

"I don't know if that's entirely fair. From the sound of it, I drunkenly spilled my guts to you last night. You should even the playing field."

"I kind of like being on top. And, yes, I seem to recall something about you confessing your undying love for me."

She swatted at my arm, but it was at least with a smile. "Please tell me I didn't say that."

"Not precisely."

Miranda folded her arms. "I'm going to need you to tell me exactly what I *did* say so you can stop dangling vague comments like that in front of me. It's not fair."

"I think I enjoy watching you squirm too much."

"Why does everything sound so sexual when it comes from you?" she asked.

"Because we tend to see what we want."

She didn't speak for a few moments, and when she finally did, her voice was soft. "Tell me, Mr. King. When you look at me, do you see what you want too?"

"Very much," I said. "And since you beat me to making the move this morning, I think it should be my turn."

"What would be your first move?"

"Well," I said. "I was thinking I'd invite you to a business meeting but leave things open to turn it into a date if things went well."

Miranda smirked. "Bold. Your move includes an escape plan?"

I laughed. "I hadn't thought of it that way, but, yeah, I guess it does."

"Then you might as well throw away the key to that escape door."

I grinned. "Why would I lock an escape door? I'm pretty sure that's illegal, not to mention impractical. Do you think I'd want to be fumbling for keys if the room caught on fire?"

Miranda glared. "Keep making fun of me and maybe you will need that plan B, after all."

♥ ♥ ♥

I took Miranda back to her room so she could change into a pair of pants. When I mentioned horseback riding, she actually jumped up and down while making a little, barely restrained squealing noise. It was probably the most excited I'd ever seen her, and I wasn't shocked. Back in high school, she had mentioned once how she always dreamed of being one of those kids whose family owned a stable of horses. She'd thought it would've been amazing to get to ride every weekend and have a horse of her own to bond with.

I was happy to see her love of horses apparently hadn't dimmed with time.

She took almost a full minute to stop happy dancing. When she was finished, she bent to pet Thug. She even rubbed him behind the ears, muttered a few things to him, threw his toy so he could chase it, and then finally got up to come with me.

"So," I said as we walked toward the golf cart. "How is finding a new home for Thug coming?"

"Fine," she said. She hopped on the seat beside me, and we drove toward the gardens, where the horses would be waiting. "I mean, I've been pretty busy since we got here. But once things calm down, I'm sure I'll be able to find someone for him."

"You're not getting attached?"

"What? No. I've never been a dog person."

I grinned. "What is your animal of choice, then?"

"Elephants. If somebody genetically modified an elephant to stay baby size forever, I would sell everything I've ever owned to have it. No hesitation."

I laughed. "Maybe that can be our next business venture together. Genetically modified animals. We can branch out to other animals too. Miniature giraffes, gorillas, cows . . ."

"Don't tease me with that. It makes my heart hurt just to think about them. Imagine coming home to a little elephant sleeping on the couch."

"Or taking your tiny giraffe for a walk."

We arrived at the gardens. A woman was standing with two horses that were already saddled up and ready to go.

"You excited?" I asked.

"I've never ridden a horse before," she said. "You think it's okay?"

The woman with the horses overheard and smiled. "You'll be fine. I'll take a few minutes going over the basics, and then I'll let you and Mr. King take them around the grounds."

"By ourselves?" she asked. "Is that safe?"

"Mr. King is an experienced rider. These horses are also extremely well trained. You'll be absolutely safe."

Miranda looked at me with a raised eyebrow. "I never took you for a horse rider."

"Yeah, well, I went through a little bit of an equestrian phase after high school. I don't like to talk about it."

"Do your brothers know?"

"Of course they don't," I snapped. I blew out a breath and shook my head. "Sorry, it's just . . . yeah, please never breathe a word of that to them. Especially Cade. He'd never let me live it down."

She was smiling wide now. "Did you wear those tight beige horse-riding pants and the little hat?"

"It's a helmet. And I wore the equipment you're supposed to wear. Sometimes the pants were beige," I added.

She clapped her hands and laughed. "Oh my God. I can't even picture it, but I want to. Is it some sort of requirement that all men in the King family have to have a weird hobby?"

"What do you mean?"

"Well, Rich has the dinosaur thing. You have horses, apparently."

"*Had*," Nick corrected. "I mean, don't get me wrong. I still enjoy riding, but I don't compete or anything like that."

"Actually," Miranda said, "does Cade have a weird thing, other than, well, being weird in general?"

"Yeah. Never ask him about bugs or snails. He will talk for hours about them."

She smirked. "I think I caught the tail end of one of his snail talks, come to think of it. But what made you get into horses in the first place?"

I shrugged. "This girl I liked talked about how she always wanted to ride. I guess I imagined I'd get the chance to sweep her off her feet and ride into the sunset someday."

She gave me a funny look. "Did you?"

"Not yet," I said.

Her eyebrows twitched together, but I didn't think she understood exactly what I meant, which was probably for the best. Holding in the way I felt about her, even just for a few days, was making it feel like it all wanted to come exploding out of me now. If she knew how fast my heart was pounding just from going on an innocent little ride together, I thought she'd probably run for the hills and never come back.

"You ready?" I asked.

Half an hour later, Miranda had the basics down. We thanked the trainer and set off at a slow trot down the horse trail. We could see most of the Julian Ridge grounds once we led our horses up a hill, and it was quite the view. Streetlamps dotted the hills, and a few cabins with their warm yellow lights were visible as well. If I squinted, I could see the occasional movement of pairs or groups of people, some with dogs on leashes, as they moved from place to place.

"This is incredible," Miranda said. "I feel like we're in our own little world up here."

"Yeah. I always enjoyed riding like this. It's pure."

As if on cue, Miranda's horse lifted its tail and took a giant, thudding shit into the mud.

Miranda looked back, horrified. "Did it just . . ."

"Yeah," I said slowly. "Mostly pure, I guess."

She laughed. "When we genetically modify miniature horses for our business of the future, we'll have to figure out how to potty train them too. Maybe there's a gene for that."

"Hey, wait," I whispered. I motioned for her to stop her horse and pointed through a patch of trees, where we could see a road. "Is that who I think it is?"

There was a bright-orange sports car parked on the shoulder with smoke hissing out from under the hood. And I'd be damned if Max Frost himself wasn't on his cell phone, leaning against the car.

"Oh my God," Miranda said. "That is him."

"Is it just me, or would this be the perfect opportunity to get some childish payback?"

"Like what?"

"Follow me." Miranda and I jumped off our horses and then started carefully picking our way down the sloping path toward the road. As we got closer, we could hear bits of Max's conversation, but the trees were thankfully thick enough that there wasn't much risk of him seeing us.

"Okay," I whispered once we were close enough. "You have his phone number, right?"

Miranda nodded. She pulled out her phone and scrolled through the contacts list, then pointed to his name. "Why?"

"Call him and say you still think he's an ass, but you wanted to warn him that there have been reports all over the news about a pack of rabid bears roaming the forest. Say you knew he was probably headed that way and wanted to give him a warning or something."

Miranda grinned. "Seriously?"

I shrugged. "The guy tried to get you drunk and drag you back to his room. The least we can do is make him piss himself a little."

With a sigh and a half smile, she tapped his number.

"Hold on," Max said into his phone. "That's her calling right now. I told you she would."

"Hey," Miranda whispered.

"Why are you whispering?" Max asked.

"Because . . . I'm out in the woods with some guys looking for you. The front desk said you left by yourself. I figured you hadn't seen the news about the rabid bears."

There was a short pause. "Rabid bears? Miranda, what is this about? Do you want me to come back to our cabin?"

"I just wanted to make sure you knew to be careful. Don't get out of your car until you're clear of the woods. Not for any reason. Seventeen people have already been killed."

138

"*Seventeen?*" I mouthed to her.

She bulged her eyes and shrugged.

"What the hell," Max said quietly.

I didn't have a great view of him, but I could tell he was pacing around now.

"Where are you?" Miranda asked.

"I see what this is," he said, and all the fear had left his voice. "You want to screw with me because Nick has had all day to tell you lies about what happened last night. You realize he just wants you for himself, right? And he'd do anything to sleep with you, including telling you whatever lies about me suit him."

"I remember enough," she said. "And, sure, this was just a dumb joke. Actually, you should go as deep as you can into the trees and enjoy nature a little bit. Have a great life." She hung up the phone and gave me a look that said, *Now what?*

I picked up a big rock and heaved it as far as I could. It thumped and rustled into a bush, rolling downhill a little until it got caught against the base of a tree.

Max turned suddenly. He had his phone in his hand as he rapidly tapped through to call someone. "Hey," he said quickly. "Can you go online and search rabid bears near Julian Ridge Resort for me?"

There was a short pause.

"Robbie," he growled. "Just fucking do it."

Miranda and I both shared a curious look. *Robbie?* Obviously, it could've been a coincidence. After all, there had to be at least two sets of parents in the world who were cruel enough to make a grown man have to introduce himself as "Robbie." Except everything about Max had already seemed just a little too *off* and a little too inconveniently convenient. Something made me sure it was Miranda's ex, Robbie Goldman, on the other line.

"You're sure?" he asked.

I'd been planning on doing my best bear impression, but right now I just wanted to eavesdrop instead.

"Thought so," Max said with an irritated sigh. "But, yeah, I got everything I'll need. We're good, man."

I frowned at that. What had he needed? Miranda and I both knelt down, listening intently for another few minutes until Max eventually hung up and got back in his car, presumably to wait for the tow truck.

We headed back up to the path together and stopped once we'd reached our horses.

"You heard that, too, right?" Miranda asked.

"Yeah. Robbie. For some reason, I don't think it was a coincidence."

"Me either. I just don't get what it means."

"Maybe . . . what if Robbie was the one who put Max up to getting you drunk. He might've been planning to take compromising pictures and blackmail you or something. He said he got what he needed, though. He couldn't have already—"

"No. The door between our rooms was locked. And nothing ever happened. The only time he was in my room was when you barged in during breakfast."

I grinned at that. "I didn't *barge* in."

"You totally barged. You were so jealous I could practically see steam coming out of your ass."

I laughed. "I don't think ass steam is a symptom of jealousy, but okay. I was jealous. Max wasn't good enough for you either. If you were going to be with some other guy, I at least wanted it to be somebody who deserved you."

She watched me, biting her lip. "And what makes Nick King deserve me?"

I put my hand on the horse beside me and thought about that. "What about the fact that I only ever learned how to ride horses to impress you?"

She smiled. "I was hoping I was the girl you were talking about earlier. What else?"

"A glutton for flattery, huh?"

She shrugged. "I spent seven years thinking you were an asshole. Forgive me if I enjoy seeing the nice side of you a little too much."

"Okay, I think I deserve you because I wanted you badly enough that I was willing to let you go, but I also wanted you badly enough that I couldn't actually do it."

She laughed. "Okay, I feel like there's a nugget of sweet in there somewhere, but I also don't think that actually made sense."

"I deserve you because you ruined women for me. I dated my way through half of West Valley, and nobody ever came close to the way you made me feel."

"Pretty good reasons," she said in a thick voice.

I took her by the hand and pulled her closer. "I'd kiss you, but I think your horse just took another dump, and I think I also deserve a better second kiss than that."

We rode together for nearly two hours, looping Julian Ridge once and then eventually meandering through less-established paths in the forest. Our conversation was flowing so easily that neither of us seemed ready to call it a day and head back to the stables. We eventually found our way to a clearing that was so picturesque we both laughed out loud when we saw it. It looked too perfect to be real.

"This is ridiculous," she said.

"There's even a trickling stream," I said, pointing to where crystal-clear water studded with smooth stones cut through the grass. "All we're missing are some baby deer and bunnies."

I helped Miranda off her horse, and we wandered toward the water. The grass looked so soft I almost wanted to kick off my shoes.

"Is it normal for my ass to hurt this much?" she asked.

"It'll be worse tomorrow." I nearly commented that I'd be happy to massage away the soreness in the morning, but I didn't want to spoil the moment.

We both sat down beside the stream and watched the satisfying way little bits of debris were carried along with the flowing water. Then I heard the sound of hooves, and my stomach sank. I stupidly hadn't tied up the horses, and when I looked, I saw them both galloping back the way we'd come.

"Is that bad?" Miranda asked.

"Only if you mind walking five or so miles back to the nearest road."

"We're totally going to get eaten by rabid bears."

"They'll get Max Frost and his stupid name first, for sure."

She narrowed her eyes. "Why does this feel like some kind of elaborate setup? A romantic horse ride through the hills and we end up at this impossibly perfect little clearing. Moonlight is streaming through the trees, and the stars are shining. And then our horses just happen to run off? Nicholas King, did you plan this?" she asked.

Something about the way she said *Nicholas* made me want to push her back into the grass and kiss the sass from her mouth. "If I pretended I did, would you be impressed, or mad?"

"I guess that depends where the night takes us. But would it ruin your scheme if I pointed out that we could always just call for somebody to come get us?"

"Maybe. Except I think we'd still be stuck here for at least a few hours until they could find their way through the backwoods. But, look, I'll text Cade and let him know we need to be rescued. How about that?"

"Or we could make an adventure out of it. A midnight hike to freedom." Miranda's eyes lit up, making her look painfully gorgeous in the moonlight.

"An adventure . . . ," I said slowly.

Chapter 17
MIRANDA

"Feeling adventurous yet?" Nick asked. His formerly pristine button-down shirt was torn in a few places, and his normally perfect hair was in disarray.

The forest path had seemed tame when we were riding high up on our horses, but on foot it was another story. The bushes and branches were thick, forcing us to push our bodies through scratchy tangles of leaves at times. Nick was taking the brunt of the abuse, because he was clearing the path, but I'd still managed to whack my head on a couple of branches. I'd even tripped over a tree root and fallen hard on my knee shortly after we'd left the clearing. I could still feel the dull throb.

The worst moment had come when a thick caterpillar had fallen from a tree branch onto my neck. I'd let out a bloodcurdling scream, fallen to the ground, and flailed uselessly around until Nick had picked it off my neck and laughed at me. Apparently, I was not suited for the forest life.

"A little," I said. "I'll admit, I was picturing more like a nice night-time hike through the forest. I guess it turns out that I don't know what hiking through the forest is really like. There are a lot less paths and a lot more piles of scratchy things to squeeze through than I thought."

Nick smirked. He had tucked his glasses in his pocket, and his face was smeared with dirt. The rugged look was different on him, but I found myself enjoying it. "We can still text Cade, if you want."

"No," I said, sighing. "Can we just sit for a little bit to catch our breath?"

Nick hopped up on a fallen tree log, and I sat down on a mossy rock across from him, not even caring that I was probably smearing a nice green stain on my ass. We'd been walking for close to an hour, and my legs and calves felt as stiff as rocks.

"So," I said. "We've been here two days. What insights has the retreat given you on the status of our employees?"

"Unfortunately, I have only been watching one employee."

I smiled. "Which one?"

"Hmm, I wonder."

I licked my lips. "Do you remember when I was student council president back in high school, and you helped me plan the prom at the last minute?"

"Of course. Christina was supposed to help you do it, but she bailed on you. I was actually really excited when you asked me to help."

"You were? I never took you for the prom-planning-enthusiast type."

He chuckled. "I wasn't. I was more of a Miranda Collins enthusiast."

I felt my mood sour slightly.

"Sorry, did I say something wrong?" Nick asked.

"No, it's just . . . *hard*. Thinking about it, I mean. If you were interested in me when we planned the prom together, that means we were both interested at the same time."

"Maybe the way it worked out was the only way that would bring us here."

"Sweaty, scratched to hell, and three miles of walking from civilization?"

"Together," he said.

My throat went tight. I tried to swallow, but it made an embarrassingly loud noise. "Technically or figuratively?" I asked.

"Call me traditional, but when you jumped my bones on the bed in my room, I thought that was a decent step toward technical. That and the part where I basically poured my heart out and told you how much I want to be with you."

"Okay. Clarification. That was a mutual kiss. I actually lost my balance and kind of fell toward you. The way I remember it, you closed those last few inches on your own, *and* you're the one who pushed me backward and climbed on top." My voice grew quieter and less confident as I spoke. Just talking about it was doing all sorts of things to my body. I had been trying not to think about how good it had felt or how long it had taken my heart to stop racing afterward. Now I was retelling it to Nick's face, and it felt somehow dirty and exciting all at the same time.

"You fell into me?" Nick was still smirking. "Then why did your eyes go all lovey-dovey right before you fell? I think it might be more accurate to say you became so aroused that you lost control of your body. So the 'fall' was still a result of your inability to control your attraction."

I folded my arms. "At least you're not lacking confidence."

"It'd be hard to with the way you've been looking at me."

I knew I was blushing but hoped it was too dark for him to notice. He was seeing straight through my bullshit, and I wasn't even sure why I was trying to play games and stretch the truth. He and I both knew what had happened. Maybe it was time to accept it.

"So, let me get this straight," Nick said. "We aren't technically together, because you didn't technically kiss me on purpose, right? Does that mean if we share an intentional kiss, we'd be together?"

"I wouldn't call myself an expert or anything. But I think that would hold up in a court of law."

Nick stood up and walked over to me. In an ideal world, we would've still been in the grassy meadow. He would've eased me backward onto the soft grass, and little forest fairies would've started playing harps from the treetops. Instead, I was pretty sure there were armies of spiders and ants ready to devour me whole if I lay down in the forsaken underbrush, but it apparently didn't matter. Nick took my face in his hands, bent down slightly, and kissed me so tenderly I thought I'd melt.

His lips were warm velvet against mine. There wasn't the same passionate, out-of-control hunger from before. This kiss was different. The first had made me want to strip my clothes off and do something reckless. This one made me want to throw away what remained of my emotional armor and let him in. All the years of resistance I'd been putting up to cover my fear of getting hurt again were breaking down with each tender kiss.

"How's that?" Nick asked when he pulled back.

"I want you to text Cade." I made no secret of what was going through my mind when I looked up into Nick's eyes. I wanted him. I was done running from him, and seven years of desire were threatening to explode out of me. As badly as I wanted to let the moment carry us both away, we were in the middle of a scary forest, and I could barely see his face a few inches in front of me.

Nick pulled out his phone.

♥ ♥ ♥

We eventually heard the distant sounds of Cade calling out for us. I also heard some sort of engine running.

Cade barreled through a patch of bushes on a four-wheeler with ridiculously big wheels. I wasn't even sure how he'd navigated some of the tighter patches of trees, but I'd learned that Cade always found a way. Especially if that way was stupid with a touch of absurd.

"Didn't I suggest a horse?" Nick asked.

"I don't trust horses, especially those two bucktoothed bastards that left you two out here with your dick in your hands. Well, I guess it's just Nick's dick, and it'd be in Miranda's hands—but you get the point."

"They probably got spooked by something," Nick said. "It's not an issue of trust. We should've tied them up."

"That's what you think," Cade said. "If you took me out of green pastures where I could shag any stallion I wanted, slapped a saddle on my back, and tried to ride me while wearing stupid hats . . . I'd murder you the first chance I got."

"Stallions are male horses," Nick said dryly. "You know that, right?"

"Didn't ask for trivia night. Do you two want out of here, or do you want to talk more about horse cocks?"

"How are we supposed to all fit on that thing?" I asked.

"Nick gets to cozy up to my firm ass, and you get to kind of cling on to his back like a scared baby monkey. If we all get real tight, I think you'll have a little bit of something to sit on."

Hanging on like a scared baby monkey was an unfortunately accurate description of my ride back to the resort. There was about an inch of seat for me to sort of take the weight off my arms, but it meant I was constantly having to push myself into Nick's back—and coincidentally, his ass—as well as clutching my arms around any part of him that allowed me to hold on. All in all, the experience was equal parts arousing and terrifying.

Cade dropped us off in front of our cabin and stood there with an expectant look. "Okay, so I'm just going to say it. You two went on a romantic horse ride together into the moonlight? Then you tried to hike halfway back before giving up and texting me. Either you got in a big fight, or you got really horny, and you needed a bed. Which one is it? *Oh shit.* Wait. Or maybe you went skinny-dipping, and one of those jungle fish I read about climbed inside your dick hole. Do you—do you need me to take a look?"

Nick took Cade by the shoulders and guided him back to his four-wheeler. "It's the one where I thank you for helping us, but ask you to leave so we can get some sleep."

"Together?" he asked with a shit-eating grin.

"Not if you keep this up," Nick said.

Cade reluctantly hopped on the four-wheeler and gave us one last smirk, then rode off.

My phone buzzed several times in my purse. I hadn't realized I was out of service range, but I must've been, because I could tell a barrage of texts had come in. I glanced down at the display and saw unread messages from Kira and Iris—and two from Robbie. *Why would Robbie be texting me?*

"Everything okay?" Nick asked.

"Yes," I said, shoving my phone back in my purse. "Sorry." I wasn't sure where to go from here. In the forest, it had felt natural. I'd wanted to take things a step further, even just to kiss him again. But our little intermission with Cade felt like it had broken the spell. All the old, familiar doubts had been given time to creep back into my thoughts.

Nick and I were skirting around the very real idea of openly dating. When I was in the moment, it was as easy as breathing to let one thing lead to another. But could I really just throw caution to the wind and forget about what everyone would think? Dating him would almost certainly mean putting my career in a coffin. If that wasn't bad enough, it'd mean putting my heart in his hands again. Last time I'd done that, he had taken the first excuse to practically run away from me at full speed. What was to say the same thing wouldn't happen again?

"Hey," he said. He stepped closer and took my hands in his. "If you're having doubts about this, I can wait. I'll wait as long as you need, okay?"

I felt slightly embarrassed that he could see straight through me so easily, but I was also reassured. He wasn't going to make me rush into things before I was ready, and that meant I would at least have time to sort through my feelings if I needed to.

"Would it be crazy to ask if I can sleep in your room tonight? I don't know if I'm ready for . . . *that*, but I'm not ready for tonight to be over either."

He nodded, and the way his eyes were locked on mine might've been the sexiest thing I'd ever seen. It was like I could see something primal at war within him, but he was keeping it in check. I loved both parts—that he wanted me so badly *and* that he was able to control it.

"I need a shower before bed, though. We can take turns," he added.

I insisted on letting Nick shower first. I sat on the edge of his bed while I listened to the running water and the occasional splashing as he cleaned himself. I tried not to dwell too long on the image of his naked, powerful body and his hands running soapy water across his muscled torso. I didn't know why it felt like I was having so much trouble with the idea of having sex with Nick. It felt like I was putting the idea on some pedestal, as if the act was going to bind us together permanently and mean we'd wind up married.

It was only a few weeks ago that I broke off my relationship with Robbie because I felt like it was heading downhill toward marriage, white picket fences, and kids. The thought of that with Robbie had scared the living crap out of me. It went against everything I thought I'd wanted.

So why wasn't the idea of the same things with Nick as terrifying? I didn't know, but I knew I needed to wait—at least a little longer. I needed to understand what the hell was going on in my head before I risked getting whisked away on his wave. Because I made no mistake about it. Nick was very much like an impossibly strong, slow-moving wave. I could walk away from it, maybe forever, but I'd feel it looming behind me, just like I had for the last seven years. Only now I'd turned and put my hand in the waters. I'd felt the irresistible tug of its power, and I knew that all it would take was one moment of surrender. I just had to stop running from it, and it would swallow me up. There was a mysterious allure in the idea of getting absorbed into that wave, but it wasn't something to take lightly. I needed to be sure. Absolutely sure.

I remembered the texts when I glanced over at my purse. I picked my phone out and checked Iris's and Kira's texts first.

Iris: Cade told me everything. OMG!!! I need details. Measurements. The play by play. Gimme Gimme!

I grinned. She was such an idiot sometimes. Most times, actually. I guessed that was what made her and Cade so perfect for each other.

Kira: Iris told me you and Nick "porked"? Does that mean what I think it means? Why am I having to hear about this from Iris and not from you? Call me soon! I don't care what time it is!!!

I squinted at the phone. I had no idea what porking was, either, but based on Iris's text, she was assuming I had already slept with Nick.

My finger hovered over the texts from Robbie. Part of me wanted to just hit "Delete Conversation." Curiosity got the better of me, though, so I opened the text.

Robbie: I'm texting you from my corner office in LA. I got that promotion we were always hoping I'd land. Now the West Coast branch of Lockhart and Taylor is completely in the hands of yours truly. I've got a vice president position open and waiting for you. This is way more your speed than whatever you're doing with that silly dog company. Come to LA. There are other branches. You do a good job and one can be yours, next.

I sighed. I felt a sense of overwhelming relief after reading the first text. If I were still the same person I'd been just a couple of weeks ago, I don't think I would've cared that accepting his offer would mean working under my ex. I would've jumped at the chance for a vice president position with opportunities to work toward owning my own branch. That sounded as close to my dream as anything I would've imagined. But I felt nothing. No temptation. No draw.

I was happy where I was. I scrolled down to read the second text, which had come about four hours after the first.

Robbie: Ignoring me? That's cute. I forgot to ask what you thought of Max? Did you wonder why he chose to talk to you, of all people? Or how he knew which flight you'd be getting off of? Just some food for thought as you consider my offer.

What the hell was that supposed to mean? I tossed my phone onto the bed with an annoyed groan.

Then the door to the bathroom opened. I almost expected Nick to come out shirtless and clad only in a towel, but I was relieved to see he was already wearing black pajama bottoms and a tight-fitting gray shirt. Admittedly, it wasn't a whole lot less sexy than if he'd just come out topless.

"All yours," he said.

"Thanks," I stood up and did a goofy side-stepping walk to circle wide around him. I knew I probably smelled horrible after our trek through the woods, and I didn't want him to notice.

I walked into the bathroom and then popped my head back out of the door. "Uh, hey. I kind of forgot I need a change of clothes."

"I'll get them for you. Where's your key?"

I thought about declining, but the idea of him picking an outfit for me—and picking my underwear—sent a dirty tingle of heat through me. "In my purse. The small inside pocket."

Nick picked it up and headed out toward my room.

I closed the door and took a look at myself in the mirror. I was a mess. My hair was wild, my makeup had almost all been sweated away, and I had several ugly, irritated spots on my skin from where plants had scratched me. Despite my looking like I'd been given a makeover by a team of half-blind senile squirrels, Nick had still been looking at me like he could barely keep his hands to himself. Then again, after everything he'd seen me go through, from my candy binges to getting sloppy drunk, I was starting to see the truth about Nick.

He didn't care about my reputation or any of the show I put on for everyone else. Nick cared about me. The *real* me. Little by little, Nick was helping me see how good it felt to let go of the pressure to be perfect all the time.

With a little smile, I stripped out of my clothes and turned the shower on.

The hot water felt amazing, but my mind wouldn't leave Nick. I kept picturing how he'd looked at me, how he'd tasted, and I couldn't keep from imagining what he must be thinking. I worried most that I seemed like a tease. I'd been the one to kiss him on the bed, and now it probably felt like I was dangling that temptation in front of his face.

Once I finished up in the shower, I wrapped a towel around myself and stuck my head out the door just enough to look for him. "Did you find them?" I asked.

"Yeah," Nick said. He walked right up to the door and handed me a little pile of my clothes. "I wasn't sure what you prefer to sleep in, but I did my best. I also let Thug out for a quick walk and brought him to my room for the night too."

"Oh, wow. I'm glad you remembered him. Thanks," I said. Once I closed the door, I saw Nick had decided to pick out what probably seemed like my most casual top—a faded-blue tank top that I had to tie in the back to keep from sliding off my shoulders. He'd grabbed a pair of loose-fitting sweatpants, and . . .

I laughed softly. A lacy red thong with a matching bra. *Nick, you pervert.*

I thought about calling him on his choice, but the idea of him looking through my underwear and choosing *this* was oddly hot. I slipped into my clothes and stepped back into the hotel room. Nick was already sitting under the comforter on one side of the bed, with his phone in his lap.

"Hey," I said. "Do you mind if I borrow one of your shirts to sleep in? The knot on the back of this one isn't really comfortable to sleep on."

Nick dug out a white T-shirt from his suitcase. "How's that?" he asked.

I switched to his shirt in the bathroom and sneaked a few deep sniffs of the material. It smelled faintly like him, and I found the scent to be incredibly comforting.

The room seemed too quiet. Nick was lying on his back again, but I heard him put his phone down on the nightstand when I got in bed.

"Am I being a tease?" I asked suddenly.

"No. Why would you think that?"

"Because I wouldn't blame you for thinking so. I wanted to be upfront and honest with you. It's not that I don't want to . . . *you know*. It's that I am worried I'd be doing it for the wrong reasons. And I'm worried there'd be no turning back once we . . . *did*."

He chuckled. I twitched when his warm hand pressed into my shoulder, squeezing gently. "It's sexy how you're a formidable business-woman on one hand, but you're also too shy to say *sex*. You're worried there'd be no turning back once we had sex? I'm not going to lie. I have no idea what would happen, but I know what I'm hoping would happen."

"What?" I asked.

"I'm hoping it won't be the last time."

I smiled, even though he couldn't see it. "I guess that's a step in the right direction. At least you're not planning on the old 'hit it and forget it' strategy that seemed to be your MO lately."

"That wasn't what it probably looked like. I watched my brothers pair off and saw how happy it made them. Then when I looked in the mirror, I saw how much I wanted it. I wanted somebody who could make me feel like Kira and Iris make my brothers feel. Whole, I guess. And I didn't actually sleep with any of those women I dated the past few months. In case you were wondering."

I smiled to myself even more at that. "I might've wondered a little bit. Why not?"

"Whether I realized it or not, I think I only ever wanted you."

I swallowed hard at that. As much as my brain wanted to accept all the things he was saying, it was too much to process all at once. "You said you wanted to feel whole," I said slowly. "But how do you know you're not just shoving something in the empty spot? What if it's shaped like a square, and I'm a triangle? How would you know?"

He laughed. "I think I'd know if I tried to shove a triangle inside a square-shaped hole."

I groaned. "Okay. Bad example. What if I'm a small circle, and you have a big circular hole in you?"

"A big circular hole, huh?"

I turned around so I could swat at his arm. I wasn't ready for the sight of him lying so close beside me, though. "Can you stop acting like Cade for a second and take me seriously?"

"I am—sorry," Nick said. "I'll admit I'm a little distracted right now. You just smell so damn good."

I licked my lips. "Yeah, well, stop smelling me and listen."

He grinned. "Okay. I'm listening. No more sniffing, I promise."

"I'm just saying, How do you know we're a good fit? What if it's just a good-enough fit?"

Nick had a funny look on his face.

"What?" I asked.

"I shouldn't. You told me to be serious."

I sighed. "Just get it out of your system."

"I was going to say there's only one way to find out if I'll fit, and I think we'd both enjoy the experience."

I rolled my eyes. "Having good sex wouldn't mean we're compatible."

"Then why do you seem so afraid of trying it?"

"Because I don't want to get confused. I want to know this isn't a mistake."

"If people got to know whether a relationship was a mistake or not before they tried, it wouldn't be much fun. Would it?"

I closed my eyes and curled up until my head was against his chest. "Most guys can't hurt me like you could. The moment I stop holding back, I'd be giving you the power to do that again."

He stroked my hair slowly, sending shivers down my neck. "I'd never hurt you. Never again."

"I believe you," I said.

I let the slow, gentle pattern of his fingertips against my scalp pull me closer to sleep. It felt good lying with him. It felt *right*. And if I bought into his stupid analogy, it felt a whole lot like a medium-size circle fitting into a medium-size circular hole. But it still felt like I was waiting for something—some sign that it was time to take the final step. I knew one thing: I needed to find a way to tell him about Robbie's job offer. I didn't want Nick to think I was considering it or trying to use it to gain leverage, though. I'd need to make sure I chose my words carefully and found the right timing. Easier said than done.

Chapter 18

NICK

Miranda and I spent the morning completely ignoring work, which was starting to feel like business as usual on this trip. After we had breakfast in my room, we took an unofficial tour of Julian Ridge. We played a round of bowling so bad that one of the employees at the alley had to ask if we wanted bumpers in the gutters. After bowling, we watched a screening of *Die Hard* in the theater.

It wasn't until we'd sat down in a little pizza café around lunchtime that our conversation finally took a turn toward the business.

Miranda was still wearing my shirt from last night, and she had stopped by her room only to grab a pair of shorts in place of the sweatpants I'd picked for her. More than once, I'd wondered if she was wearing the red, lacy thong I'd picked out for her too. In uncharacteristic fashion, she hadn't even stopped to do her makeup or spend more than a few seconds throwing her hair in a ponytail. It was the most natural I'd seen her. Considering she normally used perfection like a wall to keep everyone at arm's length, seeing her like this felt like a sort of private invitation into her world.

I leaned back in my chair and took a sip of beer. "I've never had this much trouble focusing on work."

She smiled, then popped a bite of pizza in her mouth. "I'll take that as a compliment. But I'm in the same boat. Before you, I don't think I ever went a full hour without thinking about my career, let alone a few days. It has actually been nice. But I did think of something the other day. I was just too pissed at you to want to talk about it at the time."

I laughed. "Was it around the time of Max Frost?"

"Yes, and your jealous explosion."

"Are you implying I didn't have a right to be jealous?"

"No. I think I'm actually glad you were. It was like a wake-up call. Before that, I really believed you didn't have any feelings for me. Once I saw the way you acted when I showed up with Max, I wasn't so sure anymore. But I guess I was too much of a chicken to talk to you about it."

"So," Nick said. "What was it you were too pissed to tell me?"

"That Bark Bites might not just have failed because of some shady accounting tactics. Sure, it still seems like somebody was screwing with the finances, but we could just hire a new staff if we can't find out who. But maybe the problem is bigger than that. I've been watching everyone here with their dogs. What if the problem is that Bark Bites aimed too small? What if it was an all-inclusive, dog-friendly resort, like a Julian Ridge of our own, but amped up in every way to make it dog friendly? A dog movie theater, bowling alleys with lanes for dogs, and everything else you could think about."

I narrowed my eyes and leaned forward. At first, I couldn't decide if it was the dumbest idea I'd ever heard or one of the best. Then I thought about what I'd seen since we'd come to Julian Ridge with all the Bark Bites employees. Everyone had been having a blast terrorizing the typically no-dogs resort with their pets. I wasn't sure if it was the most representative sample of people to base a business decision like this on, but she might be on to something.

"We'd have to do some testing," I said slowly. "Surveys, test groups . . . we'd also need to talk to legal about potential pitfalls as far as liability goes. But yeah." I nodded as I felt the idea solidifying in my head. "I think that's an amazing idea."

"Really?" she asked. She flashed the most genuine, excited smile I thought I'd ever seen from her.

I wanted to reach across the table and pull her in for a kiss, but I was doing my best to respect the fact that she still wanted space. It was killing me inside, but I'd already made such a mess of things with her that it was the least I could do. "Really," I said. "I think that's exactly the kind of idea we needed. And I'm exactly the right kind of guy to make it happen."

"You mean because you're loaded?" she asked.

I laughed. "That's partly it, but I still try to fund our acquisitions with investors' money instead of our own, when possible. The ultimate goal is to hand the company off once we've made it profitable to sell, and we've found that investors are much more motivated to keep a business on the right track. Besides, paying for it all out of pocket takes some of the challenge out of it."

"I've always wondered what motivates someone in your position. Is that it, the challenge?"

"My position?"

Miranda shrugged, maybe a little self-consciously. She probably wasn't comfortable talking directly about money with me. Most women weren't, and I didn't blame her. It was a sensitive subject, where even a few careless comments could make somebody seem like a gold digger. "I mean somebody who appears to have it all. Most people are motivated to work hard because there's always something bigger and better they want to buy. I can't imagine there's anything you couldn't have with a snap of your fingers, so it made me wonder what gets you out of bed in the morning."

"Do you remember when I said my brothers and I had reasons for wanting to buy Bark Bites? Personal reasons?"

"Yeah," she said.

"I might've fibbed a little. The truth is that *I* had personal reasons. The companies Sion acquires are usually massive, almost faceless organizations. There's hardly any personal stake in the success of the business. It's just numbers and investor expectations—that sort of thing. For once, I wanted to feel like I was helping turn around a company people cared about. Instead of heartlessly streamlining it and turning it into a money printer, I wanted to make it better." I laughed softly. "I'm not sure that makes as much sense when I say it out loud."

"No. It makes a lot of sense, actually." She looked down at her fingers, clearly deep in thought. I wondered if she was disappointed in my answer.

"What are you thinking? That I'm an idiot to imagine what I'm doing with Bark Bites is any different?"

"Actually, I was thinking how the Nick King I knew back in high school must really be in there, after all." She narrowed her eyes at me and then laughed. "Did I just make you blush?"

I took a sip of my drink, partly to cover my face a little. "Life didn't go exactly as I planned, so I guess I had to change and adapt."

"What part weren't you planning for?"

Letting you slip through my fingers. "You know . . . You said there's nothing I can't have at the snap of my fingers, but that's not entirely true. There is something I never managed to get, even though I wanted it more than anything. Are you implying I should try snapping my fingers and seeing if she comes?"

She drew her eyebrows together in confusion, then her cheeks went red. "Unless she's a dog, I don't know if that would work. It might take more work to get her to come than that."

"Somehow, I don't think making her come would feel like work at all."

Miranda nearly choked on the sip of her drink she was taking.

I watched her, barely containing the urge to reach across the table for her hand.

"You never answered my question," she said a little awkwardly. She was clearly trying to change the subject. "What gets you out of the bed in the morning? Is it really just trying to make more money?"

"No. At this point, my brothers and I donate almost everything we earn. I couldn't spend a billion dollars in a lifetime, let alone several billion. I also have no interest in hoarding a giant pile of money to create a legacy of entitled children. I enjoy the work, and if I can take the money and do something good with it, then I see no reason to slow down."

"So you do want children?" she asked.

I nodded. "Eventually, but only if I find the right person to have them with. Then again, I wonder if anyone ever really knows."

"I've always thought it's like those kid toys. A circle fits in a circle-shaped hole and so on. And when you find the right hole, it just fits."

"Hmm," I said. "Why does that sound vaguely sexual?"

She flashed a wicked smirk. "Maybe because you're wondering if I could fit in your hole?" Miranda clapped a hand to her forehead. "Oh God. I'm terrible at flirting. I meant—"

I almost spit out the beer I'd just sipped. I coughed, then shook my head, smiling. "I feel like there's no way to answer that question without compromising my . . . *manhood*. But I'll say this: I have no way of knowing if we're right for each other. Maybe it's just feeling like I've wanted a chance with you for over seven years. I know what it feels like to regret missing an opportunity to be with you, and I don't want to have to live with that again. I don't know much more than that, except that I feel good when I'm around you. I feel like work isn't everything. I don't feel as lonely."

She was biting her lip. "You mean all that?"

"Yes. Every word."

"Oh God," Miranda said. Her eyes were focused on something behind me.

I rolled my eyes in preparation for seeing Cade strolling toward us, but it wasn't him. It was Max Frost, and he was wearing a smug expression I didn't like one bit.

"Hey, kids," he said. He grabbed a nearby chair and plopped it beside our table, then sat. "Yes, I survived the rabid bears, and I came back because my friend didn't hear back from Miranda about his offer. He asked me to come clarify some things for you two."

"I was holding Miranda last time I wanted to punch you," I said. Then I showed him my very empty hands. "You sure you want to keep talking?" I was starting to develop a working theory on this situation with Max Frost and the person named Robbie he'd been on the phone with, and it wasn't a theory I liked at all.

"You'll want to hear this," Max said. "So, that story I was working on was a little different than I led Miranda to believe. It was actually a piece about a spoiled playboy billionaire who forcefully took over a local company just so he could make a move on his old high school crush."

I stared at him in disbelief. My heart was pounding, and my blood felt cold.

Shit.

I rapidly played through what he'd just said again and again, searching it for any holes. There didn't seem to be any. He could very easily spin what had happened that way, and it would look horrible not just for me, but for Sion. Considering we were a company that relied heavily on public trust of our good intentions to do the right thing with the businesses we took over, the results of a story like that could be catastrophic.

Miranda looked at me with a questioning expression. I thought she was trying to silently figure out if what Max was saying counted as a valid threat. I gave her a small, grave nod.

"When are you going to run the story?" I asked.

"Never, as long as Miranda does what my friend wants."

I resisted the urge to grip his collar and squeeze until his face went red. Anger wasn't going to help anything here. "Does your 'friend' know you were trying to drunkenly sleep with his ex-girlfriend?"

Max looked a little startled at that. "According to you," he said.

I decided not to press the issue anymore. I at least knew Robbie hadn't sent Max to sleep with Miranda, which meant it might be an angle I could use later. There was no use in making that any more clear to Max at the moment. "And what does your friend want?" I asked.

"Robbie has a new company and a perfect position available for her in LA. All she needs to do is accept his job offer. That's it. No strings, no expectation of her taking him back. He just wants her for the job."

"Like hell he does," I said tightly. "She breaks up with him, and now he's, what, paying you to blackmail us to get his ex-girlfriend to move across the country and work for him? And you expect us to believe he doesn't have any plans beyond that?"

"Frankly, it doesn't really matter what you believe. The deal is on the table." He rapped his knuckles on the wood cheerily and then stood. "Your move."

Chapter 19
MIRANDA

Nick wanted to go back to his place and talk about what Max had said, but I told him I wasn't feeling well and needed a little time in my room.

I lay in bed for hours while I ran through the possibilities. My favorite was hopping on a plane, finding Robbie, and strangling the life out of him with some of the dental floss he never left the house without. As amusing as that idea was, I unfortunately didn't have the same murderous instinct that Iris did. I also couldn't floss my teeth without breaking a string, so I doubted I could choke a grown man to death with it, but a girl could dream.

Admittedly, the job offer *was* tempting. For starters, there would be nothing except a few hundred miles stopping me from dating Nick freely. I'd also be back at the kind of job everyone expected me to take. As much as I'd wanted the Bark Bites job to feel like I was actually contributing somewhere, part of me hated the thought that everyone would see me as a joke for working at a company based around making a dog-friendly restaurant.

Taking Robbie's job would also mean leaving behind everything I'd already started to build here. Bone Thug was contractually bound to the company as its mascot, as ridiculous as that sounded, so I couldn't take him with me. I'd also be leaving behind my plans for the future of Bark Bites Resort.

There was no easy answer. Staying would be selfish on so many levels, but leaving would feel like I was stepping back into being that person I was before everything with Nick happened. I'd be letting my obsession with my image take back over, and now that I'd had a taste of shedding that part of myself, I hated the thought of going back to it.

The question that kept tormenting me was whether I could really do it. Could I really keep going after what I wanted when I knew how much damage it could do to Nick's company? It wasn't even just Nick that would suffer from a story like that. Rich, Kira, Cade, and Iris were all tied to Sion now. With one selfish move, I'd be potentially harming everybody I cared about.

Potentially.

It was the little word that kept bringing me back full circle. Could a single news story really do any noticeable damage to a billion-dollar-business empire? Even if it did, would the King brothers miss a few million dollars or even a few *billion*?

I turned over and groaned into my pillow. There wasn't an easy answer. A few hours ago, I'd been on the fence about what to do with my feelings for Nick. Did I sit on them and wait to see what happened? Did I pounce on them while they were still so strong? Or did I shelve them entirely and focus on my career? Now that my options felt like they'd been stripped from me, the answer seemed so obvious it hurt.

I cared about Nick. I always had. Even when I'd been telling myself I hated him and was happy I'd sworn the oath to stay away from him, I'd still wanted him. The oath was just a defense mechanism. It had let me think the reason we weren't together was because I'd decided we wouldn't be. I hadn't had to face the fact that I was too scared to put my feelings out there for him and the idea that he might not feel the same way about me.

But now I knew he did. It was all right in front of me, and the only thing that had been left to do was reach out and take it. Except I'd waited too long. *Again.*

There was one option in the entire mess that might work for both of us, though. It was far from ideal, and I knew Nick wouldn't approve. I had a feeling he was going to tell me to let Max run the story and promise he'd take care of the damage.

I wasn't going to let that happen. I could fix this. I just needed a little time.

Chapter 20
NICK

I got tired of waiting for Miranda to stop pretending she wasn't feeling well around dinnertime. I reasoned that five hours was plenty of time for her to decompress. If she really wasn't feeling well, she would need to be checked on, anyway.

I knocked on her door and waited. *And waited.*

It took me five minutes before I peeked through the windows. I felt my stomach drop when I saw the room had been cleaned out. All her stuff was gone. I staggered backward and slumped down, racking my brain for an idea.

She was almost certainly trying to go to LA. The part I didn't know was *why*. I fired off a text asking what was going on, even though I suspected she was planning on doing something she knew I wouldn't like, or else she wouldn't have sneaked off like this.

I looked up Robbie's business and found the address. She'd probably be headed there. All I needed was to somehow intercept her before she got there and did anything stupid. I couldn't imagine she'd offer to get back together with him, even to stop Max from running his story. But I was worried he'd try something. *God*, I was worried.

I called Cade.

"I'm naked, unless nipple clamps count as clothing. Wait, didn't we have a debate on this once? I can't remember what we decided on."

"We decided you didn't need to brief me on the amount of clothes you were wearing every time you picked up the phone."

There was a short pause. "Oh. Right. Well, what did you need?"

"Can I use your helicopter?"

"I was planning on getting burritos when Iris and I finished up here. How am I supposed to get burritos without a helicopter?"

"I don't know, a car? Call delivery? Pretend you're a normal person for once in your life?"

He let out a long, dramatic sigh. "Yes. You can use the helicopter. The pilot said he'd be at the bowling alley. Apparently, he was going to go pro, but then he had some kind of butt cheek injury that screwed up his ability to put spin on—"

"Cade," I said. "Thanks." I hung up the phone.

Unfortunately, I got the tail end of the butt cheek story from the pilot himself while I walked him up from the bowling alley to the field where he'd parked the helicopter.

Flying cross country in a helicopter was hardly practical, so I used the flight to arrange for an airplane to take me the rest of the way. I wasn't sure how I'd find Miranda if she didn't want to be found, but if I got to LA before her, I'd at least know where she'd turn up eventually. All I'd have to do was wait.

Chapter 21
MIRANDA

The woman beside me on my flight gave me the third death glare in five minutes. I smiled tightly and squeezed my knees, hoping to keep my legs from shaking, but it was no use. They were shaking so badly that the little tray table in front of me kept getting jostled. I was a nervous wreck. It had finally seemed like my life was starting to fall into place, and now I was sneaking away on a last-minute flight to LA so I could grovel for a job from my ex-boyfriend. It sounded so far fetched it could've made me laugh, except all it made me want to do was cry.

I'd gone back and forth on telling Nick what I was doing. Ultimately, I decided I just needed a day's head start. I wanted him to know what was happening once it was too late for him to talk me out of it. He'd make some argument about how he and his brothers could easily survive this or how it really wasn't going to be a big deal.

I was surprised by how much the idea of leaving Bark Bites stung. Part of me had resented the job. I knew what everyone must've been thinking when they found out I'd been let go from Crawford and ended up there. *The great Miranda Collins must not have been so great, after all. Now she's so desperate for work that she'll sign on to that joke of a business.* But despite all that, I enjoyed working there. Sure, Nick was probably a big reason, but I thought it was more than that. My contributions at

Bark Bites mattered, and I still had big ideas I was never going to get to see through.

I hated admitting it, even to myself, but I knew there was one other reason I'd decided to run. Nick had proved before that he'd let obstacles come between us. I never knew if it was that he enjoyed the flirtation with me but not the idea of a real relationship, or maybe something else. All I knew was that it had almost broken me the first time. Feeling that much for him and then watching him disappear from my life had been one of the hardest things I'd ever done. Except this time, I had the chance to walk away before he could do that to me. If it wasn't for the blackmail and all the other circumstances, I knew I wouldn't have ever gone through with it. But it felt like fate was pushing me toward it already, and maybe this was the only way to protect my heart from the inevitable—to leave before he could leave me.

I let my forehead thump against the little oval window to my side. I didn't know why I had done this. When I found myself in a situation that might wind up taking control from my hands, I always ran from it. Except I ran in a way that let me keep the illusion of being in control. I couldn't kid myself. I wasn't *leaving* Nick. My feelings weren't going to evaporate just because I put half a country between us. Deep down, I think I knew the same was true for him. No, I *hoped* it was.

When Nick had asked out Kira, I was the one who had pushed for us all to swear an oath to stay away from the King brothers. A bitter realization settled in on me like noxious fumes: I cared so much about being in control of how I appeared to everyone else that I would have sacrificed anything to maintain my image.

The only thing I had really stood up for myself on was Robbie. He was exactly the guy people thought I deserved. But for once in my life, I'd put my foot down and said no. All those confusing emotions I'd felt were the sense that I might finally be carving my own path. And now I was riding a plane back to Robbie. It was exactly the path that everybody would've expected me to take. Worse, it was the path that protected me from Max's story, because I knew how eagerly people would jump headfirst into believing it.

I glanced at the text Nick had sent for the hundredth time.

Nick: Please tell me where you are. Whatever you're thinking, we can talk about it. Let's figure this thing out together. Please call me. I just need to hear your voice.

I pressed the phone to my chest and closed my eyes. I just had to believe I was doing the smart thing. After all, it was only a job. I was a big girl. Whatever Robbie thought he'd be able to pull by having me come work for him wasn't going to matter.

By the time I arrived in LA, it was in the early hours of the morning. I had wanted to get straight to Robbie's office and settle this whole thing right away, but I had to get a hotel and wait until he'd actually be there. Even the thought of looking at him after knowing what he'd resorted to made me feel sick to my stomach. I was still trying to wrap my head around how it was possible to have missed his darker side after all the time we'd spent together. Except maybe it wasn't so shocking. I'd thought of him more like a business partner or a convenience than a romantic partner. All I'd cared to see were the parts of him that lined up with the image I was trying to protect. And look where that had gotten me.

The receptionist at the hotel gave me a strange look when I told her my name, but I made it the rest of the way to my room without any incidents. I tossed down my small bag of luggage and collapsed onto the bed.

What the hell was I doing?

Chapter 22

NICK

I got a call just after three in the morning. I'd paid off every receptionist at every hotel within twenty miles of Robbie's building, and one of
them called to let me know Miranda had checked in.

I drove my rental to the hotel as fast as I could and stopped at the
front desk. "Hey," I said, handing over $500. "This is for you. Can you
tell me what room she's in?"

The girl—a dark-haired college-age kid with glasses—frowned.
"Don't you think that's a little creeperish?"

I gave an exasperated sigh. "Haven't we already crossed into creeperish territory by now? I just paid you five hundred dollars to tell me
when someone checked in. What if I was a hit man? You didn't have a
problem with any of that."

"Yeah," she said. "But I didn't tell you her room number, so . . ."

"For Christ's sake," I said. I dug in my wallet and pulled out another
couple of hundred-dollar bills. "Does this help?"

She took the money. "Room 212."

I took the stairs and found her room. It was only when I was
finally standing just outside that I had the first moment of hesitation.
Everything until now had been driven by pure adrenaline. She'd gone

off without me to make this decision on her own. The only thing that made sense was finding her as fast as possible.

But what if she was right to come here? If Max ran that story, it could ruin her career as well as mine. Some old part of me was afraid of that, but I was surprised to find it didn't matter to me anymore.

I knocked on the door and waited. When I didn't hear any movement inside, I put my mouth close to the door. "Miranda. It's me."

A few seconds later, she opened the door. Her face crumpled as soon as she saw me, and she practically fell into me. I wrapped her in my arms and squeezed. I had half a mind to lift her off her feet and carry her back to the car and then back to West Valley, never letting go until I got her back where she belonged. But I knew Miranda was too strong willed for that. If I pushed too hard, I'd only end up pushing her away. So I made myself let her go and took a step back to smile.

"Since I had to do some detective work and a lot of last-minute travel arrangements, can you reward me with an explanation?" I asked.

She laughed softly. "I have to admit, it's pretty impressive that you found me this quickly."

"Yeah, well, I was just starting to get used to the idea that you might be mine soon. Then you set off across the country to go take a job for your ex-boyfriend. I might've shot down your plane if I knew you would've survived."

She folded her arms and raised her eyebrows. "I don't remember talking about this whole ownership arrangement."

"There are some things you just take ownership of. It doesn't mean they are yours. It means you decide that taking care of them matters more than anything else—that you'll sacrifice whatever it takes to keep them happy and safe. I was kind of thinking more about that kind of ownership."

She chewed the corner of her lip. "How am I supposed to go through with this when you say something like that?"

I slid my hand around the small of her back and pulled her closer. "This is the part where I wish I used all that time on the flight thinking up a speech to convince you to stay with me. To stay in West Valley, where you belong. But I was really nervous, and I ended up playing a game on my phone to distract myself."

She laughed. "You really are Cade's brother. But I don't know anything you say can change the facts. Max's story would ruin both of us. You'll look like you care more about your cock than the company, and I'll look like someone who is willing to sleep her way to the top. Both our reputations will be completely trashed."

"If only I could think of something in the world I wanted badly enough to sacrifice my reputation for . . ."

She smiled, lowering her eyes. "I want it too. I mean, I think I do. I don't know how anyone claims to know this stuff. All I know is there's a crazy, jittery feeling in my stomach when you look at me. And—"

"You can't stop picturing me naked when you're in the shower? And the amount of times you've touched yourself while thinking about me is verging on unhealthy?"

She glared, but not without a hint of a smile. "This isn't the time to make jokes."

"Sorry, I wasn't trying to be funny. I was just trying to figure out if I was the only one."

"Nick . . ."

I was tired of playing nice and patient. Miranda was too practical. If she had her way, she'd wait and wait until some kind of divine sign shot straight down from space and landed in her lap. The only thing I could think to do was to show her exactly what we could be together.

I took a step toward her as I felt my thoughts growing hungrier by the inch.

She ran out of room to back up and bumped into the wall beside her bathroom. I stopped when I was so close I could feel her rapid breaths on my neck. I met her eyes and waited. Without breaking eye contact, she nodded and gave the faintest, sexiest half smile I'd ever seen.

I pressed my palms against the wall above her, and I bent my neck to kiss her. "I want to taste every inch of you," I whispered into her ear.

Her body shivered against mine. "Would it kill the mood if I asked to shower first?"

I laughed. "Seriously?"

She shrugged, smirking a little playfully. "I did just get off a long flight. If we're doing . . . *this*, I want to be clean for it."

"Maybe I like you dirty," I said.

"You can get all the figurative dirtiness you want. But I literally stink."

"Fine. You can shower, but only if I get to clean you."

"What?"

I lifted her hands by the wrist. "I'm a jealous bastard. And tonight, I don't even want these touching that body. It's all for me."

Her cheeks went a deep, gorgeous shade of red.

Chapter 23

MIRANDA

My heart was beating so fast that I thought I might pass out at any given moment. My head felt light and fuzzy, and no matter how many times I tried to blink myself awake or pinch myself, he was still there. The bathroom door clicked closed behind him, but he made no move to give me a moment of privacy to undress. I guessed I didn't know why he would think to look away if I'd agreed to let him bathe me.

God. I wanted to kick myself and give myself a high five at the same time. Yes, this was pretty much the culmination of every teenage fantasy I'd ever had about Nick King, and, *yes*, he wasn't the only one who might have had some dirty thoughts in the shower, but it all felt like it was happening at the speed of light.

After seven years, I guessed I would've thought it would take an equally long time to develop feelings for him. Instead, the bundle of confusing emotions I had when I thought of Nick all these years had just grown and grown. The moment I'd decided how I felt about him, all that emotional energy seemed to explode toward this overwhelming kind of magnetism I felt toward him now.

I reached and flicked off the lights, which left us in near-complete darkness.

Nick turned them back on. "No hiding."

I took a deep breath. Apparently, when Nick got turned on, he also got *very* bossy. Normally, that would've irritated me, but right now it just seemed intensely sexy. It felt like a relief, oddly enough. I'd spent so much time trying to hold on to control with a white-knuckle grip that letting go was never an option. But with him, I thought maybe I could let go. I could put my heart in his hands again, but this time, I knew I could trust him not to break it.

I pulled at the little bow that kept the collar of my dress tight, then undid the buttons. I had no reason to be self-conscious of my body. I took good care of myself, but I still couldn't stop my hands from shaking like this was my first time with a man.

Nick's sharp intake of breath at just the sight of my chest in a bra helped ease my nerves. He clearly liked what he was seeing so far.

"More," he practically growled.

I grinned, and with that grin, I felt most of my remaining nerves melt away. This could be fun. This *would* be fun. It didn't have to mean I was going to let Max run the story either. We were both adults, and we both wanted this. It could be that simple.

"You first," I said.

Nick's eyes were electric as he pulled his tie loose and dropped it to the floor with a silky whoosh. He undid his buttons next, giving me my first glimpse of his smooth, muscular torso. I wanted to reach out and touch him, but I wanted to at least maintain some semblance of dignity, even as I was stripping off my clothes.

"Now you."

I chewed my lip, then slid off my dress. I was wearing a white thong, and I kept myself from self-consciously glancing down to make sure it hadn't scrunched up awkwardly.

Nick's eyes roamed me so hungrily I didn't think he was going to be able to wait for this whole striptease to finish.

He stepped toward me and my breath caught, but he reached into the shower only to start the water. Now we were only inches apart. With him standing so close, I could feel the heat rushing away from his skin. *God.* He was like a furnace.

"Bra," he said.

I held up my hands playfully. "I thought you were too jealous of these to let them have all the fun. Or did you forget?"

He made a deep groaning sound as he pushed me against the wall and pressed his mouth against my neck. With skillful, quick fingers, he undid my bra and tugged it away from me. He didn't even take time to admire the view before plunging his mouth down around my nipple.

I sucked in a surprised breath and felt my neck arch back all on its own. Nick was always so deliberate and measured that seeing him this animalistic was unbelievably hot. I threaded my fingers through his hair, gripping hard and pressing his mouth against me. When he groaned, I could feel the vibrations run through my chest, spreading a wave of intoxicating heat all the way to my core.

"I think you got hot faster than the water," he said, grinning up at me, almost boyishly.

I knew I was blushing, but I didn't care. "You too." I half breathed the words because it was all I could manage. I felt like I was in the middle of a marathon—like my brain was starved for oxygen and running at only a tenth of normal speed. In reality, I suspected every available ounce of processing power was getting sent to recording and enjoying as much of Nick's touch as I could. I was savoring it like it might be the last time his hands were on me, because for all I knew, it would be.

He backed me into the shower, helping me balance as I stepped over the ridge of the small tub.

"I'm still—" I started.

"Fuck the clothes," he said.

"I think that's actually the opposite of how this works," I said.

"Smart-ass."

The water made a pattering sound against Nick's pants and soaked straight through my thong. He didn't even bother with our remaining clothes before hiking my legs up around his waist and pressing my back into the wall.

I put my hands on his cheeks and stared at his face, mesmerized by the rivulets of water tracing his carved features and running off his parted lips. "Tell me one thing," I said.

"Anything."

"What would you have done if my name was on that poem seven years ago?"

"I always wanted you, but I wanted you so badly I was too afraid of screwing it up. Seeing your name on that poem would've been too much to ignore."

I ran my thumb across his lips, marveling at how soft they were. "It's a little ironic, isn't it? We both wanted to be together so badly that we had to convince ourselves it was hatred instead of—" I cleared my throat. The awkwardness I felt broke the spell of his presence. I realized what I was about to say. *Hatred instead of love.* I hadn't been back in Nick's life long enough to throw around a word like that.

I couldn't read his expression, but Nick saved me the embarrassment by pretending he hadn't noticed. "Yeah," he said. "I guess we're both just cowards hiding behind false confidence, aren't we?"

"Something like that," I agreed.

His eyes started to get heavier again, almost like I could see the thoughtful, rational part of him retreating deeper inside. "Now," he said deeply. "If you're all out of questions, I need to fuck you before I explode."

"Is there an option where you don't explode? I've kind of started to like you."

"We'll have to work on the 'kind of' part," he said.

I let out a small surprised moan when he emphasized his words with his hips, driving the hardness of his erection into me in just the right place.

"These need to go," he said. With what seemed like no effort at all, he pulled my thong free, snapping the material in the process.

"Are you planning to replace those, Mr. King?" I asked.

"I'll buy you an entire lingerie company, if that's what it takes."

I smirked. "No. I don't want your money. I just want you."

Nick's eyes met mine for a moment, almost searchingly. He kissed me then, grinding himself into me until I could barely contain my need.

I couldn't reach to help him with his pants because he still had me pinned with my legs wrapped around him, but with one hand he managed to strip them and his underwear in seconds. They flopped to the floor of the tub, and he kicked them out of our way.

"I've been dying to taste you," he said. *All of you.*

I put my hands on the wall to steady myself as he raised me up and positioned my thighs over his shoulders. *Wow.* I had only a moment to marvel at how high I'd been lifted before the sensation of his hot tongue between my legs snapped me into focus.

Nick King was eating me out. The thought felt so bizarre that I had to replay it a few times before it stuck. I gasped and tightened my legs around his head. Before Nick, my experience of having a man's head between my legs had been largely unpleasant. One guy acted like he was trying to dial a long distance number on an old-school rotary phone with his tongue. Another used his tongue like an exploratory probe, and he wasn't sure which button turned the thing on, so he just slung it around without any form of plan or strategy. In both cases, I'd been left staring at the ceiling with a confused, slightly disturbed look.

Nick knew exactly what he was doing.

It was almost as if he could feel what I was feeling—like every time he found a rhythm or spot that drove me over the edge, he knew exactly how long to keep it up. Hottest of all was just the ferocity of his movements. I could *feel* the pent-up sexual frustration he must've had for years and years, and it was all getting channeled into me like an intravenous shot of bliss.

As much as I wanted to stay there all night while he explored me with his tongue, I couldn't wait any longer. "I want you inside me," I gasped.

Nick didn't wait for me to ask twice. He slid me down to his hips and let me guide his length into myself. It was *big*, and I had a moment of panic at the idea of trying to make that fit inside me. But he took it slowly, easing himself in inch by inch.

I threaded my fingers behind his neck and reveled in the sensations of our slick bodies sliding together—of him filling me more deeply than anything I'd ever experienced.

I caught glimpses of him as the steam rose from behind his head, and it was like something out of a dream. He was too perfect to be real. *This* was too perfect to be real. Maybe that was why a finger of dread snaked its way into my head, even as I was gasping and moaning his name.

People thought my life was perfect, but things like this didn't actually happen to me. There was going to be some kind of catch, and I needed to prepare myself for it.

But I couldn't think of that now. He was burying his face in my neck and breathing hard with each thrust. His hands were like iron around my waist, pulling me onto him so that he was completely buried inside me.

"I'm on the pill," I breathed into his ear.

He stopped just long enough to catch my eye and wait for me to nod.

He increased his pace until my world became a white blur. My skin felt like it was on fire, and it had nothing to do with the water pouring over us. Nick pumped himself into me deeper and harder until he finally tensed up. I could feel him pulsing inside me, and it made me feel like I'd just slept with a man for the first time. I'd never let anyone finish inside me before, and I'd never felt anything close to that much passion and emotion get tangled up in the act.

I put my hand on his face again, maybe just to reassure myself that he was really there. "It's going to be hard to beat that," I said.

"I look forward to trying. Night after night," he said. "And in the morning."

I grinned, but that little nagging fear came back to me. He must only be saying that. Now that he had what he came for, he was probably going to start distancing himself. "I'm not sure how you shower, but for me, I usually use more soap and less penis. I also clean more than my mouth, nipples, and pussy."

He smirked. "So you're still feeling dirty?"

"You could say that."

Chapter 24

NICK

I was already up and sipping my coffee when Miranda woke. She wasn't the woman everybody thought she was. Maybe that would've made some people feel deceived, but I liked it. Knowing more about the real Miranda Collins than everybody else just made her feel more like she was mine. I'd also come to see how she and I battled some of the same demons, even if we faced them in different ways.

She rubbed her eyes and sat up. We'd gone to sleep together when our hair was still wet, and hers had dried in a wild nest on top of her head.

"Morning," I said, not bothering to hide my amusement.

Miranda didn't appear to notice. She was staring at me with a strange look.

I frowned, then ventured a guess at what was going through her head. "Did you think I would run off once I slept with you?"

"The thought crossed my mind."

I got up and went to sit beside her on the bed. I tried and failed to get her hair to lie back down on her head, but I enjoyed running my fingers through it either way. "Like it or not, I think you're going to have a hard time getting rid of me now. Almost as hard a time as you'll have getting your hair to lay back down."

"If you can look at me like this and not run, then maybe you really aren't planning to."

I chuckled. "The only way I'm running is if I have to chase after you. Kind of like last night."

"Fair point." Miranda smiled, then closed her eyes and rested her head on my thigh. "Where do you think snails are going?"

"What?" I asked, laughing in surprise. "Have you been talking to Cade?"

"Not recently, no. It was just something he asked, and I was thinking about it. I think they're looking for love."

I tried not to grin. She sounded so damn serious that it made me want to laugh out loud, but something told me what she was saying was important. "If snails are looking for love, what does that mean?"

"I don't know, exactly. But what gets me curious is that it probably takes almost their whole lives to get where they're going. So what happens if they finally make it to this lady snail and it turns out she's not everything they imagined? Would they really just say, 'Oh jeez, I know I spent seven years slowly inching my way toward you, but now that I see you up close, I don't think this is actually going to work out.'"

I finally let some of my smile show. "Seven years is an oddly coincidental number."

She opened her eyes and looked up at me. "I'm just worried that I could be convincing myself this all feels right because it took so long to happen. I mean, admit it. It's got kind of a romantic feel to it, doesn't it? Seven years apart because of a stupid poem with the wrong name on the bottom. Then we reunite, and it turns out we both secretly wanted this the whole time? It just seems too perfect."

"And perfect things don't really happen to you," I said slowly. "People just think they do."

She nodded. "Yeah. Something like that."

"Maybe the trick is that you can either look happy, or be happy. I'd say breaking up with Robbie and going after this Bark Bites job were your first steps toward being happy. Neither of those lined up with everyone's idea of you being Miss Perfect."

"But I still tried to keep it all secret for as long as I could. I'm not sure it counts."

"Because it's new. You're not used to following your own heart, but look at everything you've done recently. Whether you realize it or not, you've been giving a big-ass middle finger to living by anybody else's rules. And I'm proud as hell of you for it."

She smiled, biting her lip. "Assuming you're right, which I'm not ready to admit you are, by the way . . . what would this new-and-improved Miranda do right now? About Max and Robbie and this whole mess?"

I thought for a long time before I spoke again. "I came here to talk you out of taking this job from Robbie. I didn't care what it took. All I knew was that I couldn't stand the idea of you going back to him, even if it was just figuratively. But that's not my choice to make. I just want you to know I'm here to back you up, however you decide to handle this. And I think the new-and-improved Miranda should do what's right for her."

Miranda sat up. "You mean that?"

"Yes. I'll even help you tame your hair before you go meet with Robbie, if that's what you want. Or we can go back to West Valley together and turn Bark Bites into what you imagined, shitty news story or not."

"Would you still help me tame my hair if we went back to West Valley?"

"Unless a bird mistakes it for a nest before then. I think it'd be a nature conservation issue at that point."

She swatted at me, then her expression grew serious. "I want to talk to Kira, Iris, Rich, and Cade before I make my final decision. But if they're okay with it, I think I want to give Robbie one of those big fat middle fingers."

"As long as that's not as dirty as it sounded, then I'm in."

Chapter 25
MIRANDA

We sat at Bradley's biggest table, which was a ten-seater in a corner booth. Between Julian Ridge and my brief-but-interesting trip out to LA, it felt like I'd been gone from West Valley for ages. It was fitting that today was Watermelon Day in West Valley, because there were few town events that embodied our collective weirdness better than Watermelon Day.

Even though almost everyone was already outside at the hill by the river for the main event, we all sat around the big table, waiting for Cade to finish his story so I could explain why I'd asked everyone to come. Bear was half-asleep in Cade's lap but occasionally cracked his eyes open long enough to take a bite of Cade's ice cream.

Cade was leaning forward with both elbows on the table. He was in the middle of a story about some "dick nozzle" he'd met at Bear's day care the other day. "Seriously," he said, "it was perfect. Like you know when you read something and just hope you'll have a chance to use it someday? Well, this guy tried to sound smart quoting some Bukowski line. I think he said people are dumb because we run from the rain, yet we sit in bathtubs. It just so happened that I saw that exact quote on the internet a couple years ago, and my favorite comment was somebody who asked if it's also strange that we'll eat when we're hungry but duck if you throw an apple at their face. But guess what I happened to be holding?"

Rich sighed. "Did you throw your apple at his face?"

"No," Cade said. "But I *was* holding a zucchini that Bear and I cut up to look like George Washington for a school project. And, yeah, a zucchini should hardly be classified as food, since it's basically just a phallic-shaped bag of water, but I did throw it at him."

"It also looked nothing like George Washington," Iris added.

"Yeah, well," Cade said, "the joke went over his head anyway." He drummed his fingers on the table and grinned like an idiot. "Actually he had really bad reflexes, and it kind of hit him right in the forehead, but, figuratively, he just didn't get it."

Iris was shaking her head slowly.

Kira was frowning. "Is that a true story?" she asked.

"Unfortunately," Iris said. "The worst part is that I'm friends with the guy's wife. The man was just trying to make an interesting comment about the rain."

"Interesting," Cade said. "Or pretentious. You be the judge."

"So," I said. "Speaking of interesting, I didn't actually ask you all to meet us here so we could hear about Cade throwing things at people. Robbie actually sent a friend of his to gather dirt on me and Nick while we were at Julian Ridge."

"Okay, wait," Cade said. "Can we pause here and just get a solid confirmation for the curious listening audience? Did you two bone yet, because she's kinda got this glow thing going on, and Nick looks a couple inches shorter when he's sitting down, which I can only assume to mean he's no longer sitting on his catastrophically swollen blue balls."

Iris elbowed him. "Don't talk like that in front of Bear."

"What?" Cade asked. "I used code words. Did you understand what I was talking about, bud?"

"Something about dog toys?" Bear asked.

"See?" Cade said, and then he turned his eyes expectantly back on me. "Dogs love blue balls. Just ask the innocent mind of our child."

"That's beside the point," I said. "Anyway—"

"No," Cade said. "The point we're concerned with right now is between Nick's legs. Inquiring minds want to know if *you got the point*, if you catch my meaning."

Iris elbowed him but didn't take her eyes from me.

"Let her finish," Nick said.

"No, it's fine." I looked at Bear and tried to think of an appropriate way to say what I wanted to say. "I got Nick's point. Loud and clear." I felt an unexpected grin spread across my face as soon as I said it. The old me would've held that in as long as I could. I would've been too worried they'd think I was easy or desperate. Today, I was happy to realize I didn't really care much what they thought—at least not more than I cared about the fact that I was happy, and I wasn't going to apologize for that or try to hide it. "And it was great," I added.

Nick stifled a laugh from beside me.

Cade and Rich shared a look with their lips pursed, then gave Nick a brotherly nod of approval.

"As much as it's slightly disturbing to casually talk about this," Rich said, "I am happy you two are working things out. It's kind of like we completed a circle here."

"Not entirely," Cade said. He held up his hand and tapped the ring on his finger.

"Can you just let her finish, please?" Nick asked.

I cleared my throat. "This friend of Robbie's, Max Frost, is—"

Cade burst out laughing. "Wait a second. Seriously? The guy's name is Max Frost? Does he work as a character in a video game on the side? Maybe a bad guy in a cheesy straight-to-DVD movie?"

Iris pulled out her Taser and aimed it at Cade. "I know you've been up to no good, *Max Frost*. Drop the freeze ray and come quietly, or I'll aim for your nipples."

"Do that and you'll regret it," Cade said in a deep, goofy voice. "Because Max Frost loves a little Taser action on the—"

Iris jabbed him in the shoulder with her knuckles and cleared her throat.

Cade sighed. "All I'm saying is that Max Frost is the kind of name a seven-year-old boy would give himself if he got a chance for a redo. This was a grown man, right? Not a child?"

I closed my eyes and wished for the patience to survive this. "Yes, his name is Max Frost. I'm pretty sure he changed his last name at some point after he became a TV reporter."

Rich's expression darkened. "A reporter? What did he want?"

"He figured out that Nick and I had a past back in high school. Now he's got this story put together that'll make it look like Nick only bought Bark Bites so he could hook up with me."

"Dirty bastard," Cade said, winking at Nick. "But nice. I gotta admit it. *Nice.* I was wondering why you were interested in a dog company. But now I see it's because *you* were the dog all along."

Nick groaned. "He's making it up, dumbass. Did you forget the part where we didn't even know Miranda was coming to interview before we bought the company?"

"I mean, she did walk in the door *right* before you handed Dan the check. An argument could be made—"

"An argument could be made that you're dumber than the snails you spend all day thinking about," Nick snapped. "It's bullshit. He knows it, and we know it. It's that simple, but it won't matter to anyone else. Good gossip spreads, and people will eat the story up."

"Okay, first of all," Cade said. "Way out of line. You really have no way of knowing how dumb a snail is. They could have an entirely different method of communication from us. Shit, for all you know, you just gave me a compliment. Would we even know it if snails had colonized other planets? Mastered interstellar travel? No. They're so small we wouldn't even see their factories or spaceships. So, yeah, now who's the dumbass?"

Rich put his palm to his forehead. "I'm pretty sure it's still you, Cade."

Cade held up his palms. "Whatever you say. Just don't come crying to me when it turns out I was right all along."

From the look on Rich's face, he knew arguing the obvious was futile.

"The point is," I said, "he's going to run the story if I don't go work for Robbie in LA. And since my decision could possibly impact everybody here, I wanted to talk to you all before I made a choice."

Cade put his hands over Bear's ears. "Fuck Robbie," Cade suggested. "Figuratively, I mean," he said quickly once he saw the look on Nick's face. "Though, I do think fucking Robbie—or this Max Frost character, for that matter—would be a potential solution as well. *Not that I'm recommending it*, Nick, so stop glaring at me." He pulled his hands off Bear's ears once he'd finished talking.

"You know we're with you," Kira said. "I could never ask you to go work for your douchebag ex, even if somebody had a gun to our heads."

"Well," Iris said. "If somebody had a gun to my head, I might ask Miranda to suck it up. But yeah, ditto. Minus the gun part."

"This wouldn't be the first publicity hit Sion has suffered," Rich said. "We've survived before, and we can do it again. Besides, I don't want that asshole to think he can get what he wants by blackmailing you. Teach him a lesson and let the story run."

Cade looked surprised when we all were looking at him. "Oh, my turn. The moment that assclown changed his name to Max Frost, he basically invited every human being on the planet to hate him. And guess what, Mr. Frost? Invitation accepted. Let him run the story. So, can we go look at watermelons now? I've been waiting all day for this."

"Yeah!" Bear shouted.

Nick and I lagged behind while everyone filed out to head for the river, where the main event was taking place. He put a hand on my shoulder and gave a little squeeze. "Did that help you make a decision?"

"Mostly," I said. "Now that I know you and your brothers are okay with your end of the fallout, I just need to decide if I can handle my own end."

"You mean what everyone around here will think?"

"Yeah," I said. "I clung to my image for so long that letting Max's story destroy it feels . . . I don't know. I guess that's the problem. I don't know how it'll feel to lose that part of me, and I don't think I will until it happens."

"I think life is full of doors. Some are labeled so you know exactly where they'll take you. You can have a pretty normal, just-fine life if you only ever go through those doors. But I think the best stuff is behind the blank doors. You just feel a pull toward them, but you have no way of knowing what'll be on the other side until you go for it."

"Couldn't I just stick my head in and peek around?"

"Don't try to deconstruct my little metaphor. You know what I mean."

I smiled. "I do. And maybe you're right. I just need to decide if I'm ready to open that door."

"That sounds like a decision that can wait until after the watermelon festivities," Nick said. "Come on. Let's get your mind off it, even if it's just for a couple hours."

There were two pleasant surprises at this year's Watermelon Day. Surprise number one was a brand-new event—which was rumored to have been sponsored by and invented by none other than Cade King himself. The other surprise was that Robbie had apparently made the trip back to West Valley to attend. A small part of me was still afraid of taking the final leap and letting Max run the story, but something about seeing Robbie skulking around the crowd while glaring daggers at Nick and me was helping push me to it.

Nick wanted to go talk to him, but I had a feeling there'd be a more satisfying opportunity to let Robbie know what our decision was going to be if we bided our time.

We made our way past rows of vendors, who were selling everything from watermelon-flavored adult beverages to watermelon ice cream. There was even a place where you could get yourself fitted for a custom watermelon helmet to take part in Cade's event. Basically, they punched a head-size hole out of a hollowed-out watermelon and then made eye holes and a mouth hole.

Roughly a quarter of the people walking around the event were wearing watermelon helmets.

We found Kira and Iris up by a roped-off gladiatorial-style ring in the center of a grassy field. There were remnants of shattered watermelons and zucchinis everywhere.

"I'm guessing Cade is planning to participate," I said, nudging Iris. "Did we miss it already?"

"No," she said. "Cade and Rich are actually up after these two."

Nick squinted. "Rich agreed to this?"

"Cade got under his skin until Rich just wanted an excuse to whack him in the head with a zucchini a few dozen times," Kira explained. "He was trying to convince Rich that dinosaurs were actually made up by museums to sell more tickets. I don't think he actually believed it, but he argued with Rich until it came to this." She gestured helplessly to the circle, where two people who appeared to be in their seventies were limply whacking each other in the head with zucchinis.

"What happens if the . . . *fighters* are too weak to crack each other's helmet?" I asked.

"Sudden death," Iris explained. "First one to poke the zucchini in the other person's mouth hole wins."

Nick snorted.

I turned to make sure the sound had actually come from him, and, sure enough, he was smiling like an amused child.

"Really?" I asked, grinning.

"Sorry. Something about the phrase *mouth hole*—well, that and the idea of people forcefully jamming zucchinis into each other's mouths. Where else would this be condoned by an entire crowd?"

"You're right," I said. "Probably nowhere." And, sure enough, the referee called for sudden death, and the two elderly combatants switched from overhead swings to short thrusts until one landed a direct mouth hole hit.

Cade and Rich walked out next, looking somehow intimidating even with giant watermelons thrust over their heads. I leaned on the ropes, eager to watch the match.

Cade was walking in a semicircle around Rich with an impressively sized zucchini in one hand and a makeshift watermelon shield in the other. "Dinosaurs are a lie," he shouted.

Rich took a few deep breaths and squeezed his weapon tighter. "Come a little closer and say that."

"Dinosaurs," Cade said, advancing toward Rich. "Are." He took one lunging swing at Rich when he got in range. "A lie!"

Rich easily ducked Cade's swing and swung the zucchini at Cade's head like it was a miniature baseball bat. With a single blow, the watermelon cracked open, and Cade was left standing there openmouthed and covered in watermelon juice.

Before Cade could even close his mouth, Rich jabbed the zucchini in his mouth, which drew a roar of approval from the crowd.

I turned to Nick and saw he was practically dying with laughter. When he noticed me looking, he casually reached out and took my hand. After what had *happened* last night, it shouldn't have made butterflies explode in my stomach like it did. Either way, I was happy to lean into his shoulder.

I don't know who, if anyone, even noticed that we were practically announcing we were together to the public, but it felt like putting my hand on that metaphorical door Nick had been talking about. All I needed to do now was give it a push and take the step.

Once the sun set and the majority of families with kids went back home, it was time for the drinking contest. Hollowed-out watermelon halves were loaded with several shots' worth of liquor. The game was simple. Whoever drank the contents first won.

Nick and I were waiting nearby to watch when we spotted Max Frost standing with Robbie near the tables that were being set up for the event.

"I have a really childish idea," I said, nudging Nick as we watched the two of them.

"If it involves pissing those two off, I don't care how childish it is. I'm in."

"Then we need to convince them to participate in the contest, because I need them to be sloppy drunk for this to have a chance."

A few minutes later, Nick watched from a distance while I approached Robbie, who had split off from Max. I wasn't sure how long I'd have him alone, so I knew I needed to be fast. I put on a little show of stumbling and slurring slightly once he saw me coming.

"Hey," I said.

Robbie was clearly confused—and sober, from the looks of it. "Did you reconsider my offer?"

"Maybe. But I'll make you a deal. Win the drinking contest, and I'll do that thing you always wanted me to do."

His eyebrows shot up. "Wait. You're serious?"

I nodded. "Super serious." It took everything in me not to burst out laughing on the spot. I'd just told Nick about Robbie's deepest, darkest secret fetish, which I'd never even come close to agreeing to. He had this weird fixation with food being eaten off his dick. When I'd told Nick, it had taken him a long minute to stop laughing, and just thinking of how amused he'd been was making it almost impossible to keep up my act right now. "And there's plenty of watermelon here. All you've got to do is win. We could meet in the town hall building. They never lock the back door."

As I hoped, Robbie's horniness seemed to override his good sense. He left to go enter the competition. I looked to Nick, who was still red in the face and covering a wide smile with his hand. He pointed at something behind me and nodded. I turned to see Max Frost coming back with a big soft pretzel in his hands.

I kept up my drunken act and stumbled toward him. "Hey," I said.

Max sized me up, and once he seemed convinced I was drunk, there was a predatory glint in his eyes. "Hey, Miranda. It's been a while."

"I need a favor."

"I don't do favors for free," he said.

I wiggled my eyebrows in what I hoped was a convincing sloppy-drunk-seductress look. "I need you to enter the drinking contest and come in second place. Robbie needs to win. Do that for me, and I'll let you have what you wanted at Julian Ridge."

Max drew his eyebrows together. "Why do you care about who wins the drinking contest?"

"Does it matter? Oh, and if you do what I ask, then meet me in the town hall building. They leave the front door unlocked. And I want you to show up wearing nothing but a watermelon," I added. I nearly lost my composure at that, but through a heroic effort, I held my cool.

"Wearing nothing but—you're serious?"

I walked off and waved. "Second place. Don't forget," I said over my shoulder.

I met Nick once I was done planting the seeds of chaos, and I finally burst out in laughter. Nick was smiling wide. "You really think they'll do it?"

"The good thing is we don't need to wait long to find out. The drinking contest starts in ten minutes."

As much as I wanted to watch the drinking contest, Nick and I spent the next few minutes spreading word that a secret, hilarious show was going to be taking place in the town hall building immediately after the drinking contest. With Cade's help, we convinced a relatively large group of people to follow us there.

After that, all we could do was wait.

We had to wait for only about twenty minutes in a darkened town hall meeting room before we heard somebody struggling at the back door. We had convinced everyone that no matter what, they had to stay absolutely silent and that nobody could move. I wasn't sure it would work, but the meeting room was big enough and dark enough that I thought we at least had a chance.

Nick and I motioned for everyone to be quiet.

A moment later, the back door opened. It was so dark that we couldn't see anything except the silhouette of a dark figure walking slowly and uncertainly into the building. The door closed behind him.

"You here?" Robbie whispered. "Are you here?" He whispered again, only louder this time. There was a thump when he bumped into something and a few curses. "Damn it. Come on out and eat some of this watermelon off my dick!"

I had to bite my fist to stop from laughing. As much as I wanted to flip the light switch right away, I was waiting in hopes that Max would arrive soon enough.

Luckily, the front door opened just a few seconds later. I saw another dark silhouette of a man creep into the room. "Hey," he called in a deep voice I recognized as Max's. "I brought the watermelon you asked for. I hope you're hungry."

Before Robbie could reply, I flicked on the light switch. Suddenly, the twenty or so people gathered with us in the small room had an unfiltered view of Robbie—who had skewered about five pieces of watermelon with his erect penis and was otherwise naked. Max, on the other hand, was clutching a full-size watermelon with what I assumed must've been a small—*very small*—penis-size hole in it. Both men were butt naked and staring wide eyed at all of us.

"This isn't what it looks like," Robbie said.

Cade burst out laughing, along with everyone else who had come to watch the surprise show.

"Hey," Cade said. "I think Max looks hungry. Give him some of that watermelon like you were planning."

Max decided the wisest course of action was to turn and run for the front door. Robbie paused just long enough to glare at me before he ran toward the back door and shuffled out with one hand covering his ass crack.

Nick looked down at me. "Do you think he knows you're not going to take his job now?"

I grinned. I hadn't thought of it when I was quickly coming up with this plan, but in a way, I'd made a final decision without realizing it. Robbie was almost certainly going to tell Max to run the story now. Maybe that should've scared me or made me feel sick to my stomach, but I was surprised to find it didn't.

"Maybe he could give Max the job instead. They could have Watermelon Wednesdays every week if they wanted."

Nick laughed. "They're going to have a hard time living that down, aren't they?"

"I hope so."

Chapter 26

NICK

West Valley was a town of rolling green, pristine hills. Wildflowers and gently blowing grass were often no more than a few steps from any given building, and in some places, you could travel only a few feet down a hill and find yourself with a view of nothing but the valley and the hills in every direction.

Once we'd finished getting payback on Max and Robbie, we were able to easily slip away from the festival without being noticed. Everybody who had been at the town hall with us had been busy recounting increasingly embellished versions of what had happened.

To be honest, I wasn't sure it would've mattered if we'd had an audience. It had been less than a day since I'd had her in the shower in LA, and I was already ravenous for more.

I had dragged her by the hand to a place on the hill. Once I'd looked around and decided it was good as any, I'd gestured to the ground.

The setting sun caught her face as she smiled, highlighting just how breathtaking she was. I could even see the faint silhouette of her body through her summer dress. It was far more girly and casual than what she normally wore, but I was absolutely enjoying the look on her.

"I know you mentioned wanting a chance to get to taste me," she said. When she slowly got down on her knees in front of me, I think my heart rate doubled. "But . . ." Her hands went to my belt and started working on getting my pants loose. "As your business partner, I don't think it would be an equitable exchange if you got to taste me last time and I didn't get the same opportunity."

"I never expected dirty business talk to turn me on," I said. "But I accept your offer."

She grinned, then pulled my already hard cock free. Watching her study it for a moment before taking it in her mouth gave me goose bumps. She felt so unbelievably good. Her lips were so warm, and her hot tongue slid across my crown, making my knees nearly give out.

I gripped her hair and watched, transfixed, as she bobbed her head back and forth. She'd occasionally open her eyes to gaze up at me, and those moments of eye contact were enough to nearly push me over the edge.

"I want to come inside you again," I said, pulling her back.

She put her hands on the grass behind her and spread her legs so that her dress rode up, giving me a spectacular view of her pink panties, which were visibly wet. An involuntary growling noise rumbled in my chest as I crawled on top of her.

"I can't believe I wasted seven years without you," I said.

Miranda's hands went to my face. She seemed to have a habit of roaming my features with her fingertips, which I was quickly beginning to find sexy as hell. "I was thinking the same thing. I was also thinking if we wrap this up quickly, we could still see some of the heavier watermelons at the end."

I glared. "Just for that, I'm going to take my time."

"*Damn*," she said sarcastically. "Nick King taking his time while he sleeps with me. That sounds like torture."

I smirked. "No, but telling you that you're not allowed to come until I give you permission might qualify."

"What?" she asked. "How am I supposed to control that?"

I answered her question by pulling her panties to the side and guiding my still-wet cock into her. The way her tight walls had to gradually stretch and relax to fit me felt sublime.

Her eyes closed, and her lips parted.

"*Oh,*" she gasped. "I don't think I'm going to be able to stop it for long."

I hiked her legs up so I could get even deeper and didn't hold back. The idea of making her hold her orgasm was driving me wild, especially when I saw how much she already appeared to be struggling. Her fingertips dug into the grass, ripping small paths of dirt in their wake.

I increased my pace relentlessly, watching her face all the while. The wet sounds of our sex seemed particularly out of place among the distant chirping of birds and the soft breeze rustling the flowers. I grinned at the thought. I couldn't have said how many times I thought of desecrating these same hills with Miranda Collins back when I was a teenager. The fact that I was finally doing it seemed too good to be true.

But it was more than that. The sex felt like an extension of something deeper. Something pure. Even back then, I think we both knew there was a connection between us that we couldn't find anywhere else. We were wired the same way, but we'd taken different paths and still wound up circling back together.

Doing this. Being here. It all felt so fucking right that it hurt. It was almost frightening. My feelings for her were growing so quickly that I wasn't even sure I was in control of them anymore. Stupid, hopelessly romantic thoughts kept bubbling up in my mind, threatening to turn into spoken words. *Love. Marriage. Kids.* I couldn't tell if those ideas were coming to me because I was practical and they were the logical result of a relationship if it didn't fail. But I'd never thought about them seriously with any other girlfriend.

Miranda's eyes closed tight, and her hands clenched into fists, squeezing clumps of dirt out from between her fingers. "Nick—I can't—" she gasped. "I'm going to—"

I slowed down and bent to kiss her neck. I pulled free of her but let the length of my cock rest on her clit so that each small movement of my hips would stimulate her. I took my time kissing her—tasting her—and just when I could feel her start to come down from the edge of climax, I'd use my hips to bring her back.

She was gasping for breath and moaning with each exhalation by the time I pulled her dress down and took her nipple between my teeth.

"Nick," she breathed.

I wouldn't admit it, but it was me who couldn't hold back any longer. I brought my mouth to hers and buried myself in her as deeply as I could.

She felt so damn good. It was only minutes before she clenched tight around me. Her body curled up, and she dug her fingers into my back as she cried out. Watching her come pushed me over the edge. My balls went tight, and I filled her for the second time in twenty-four hours, which was a particularly enjoyable thought.

"Sorry for the mess," I said, rolling off her.

She was lying on her back, staring up at the sky. "With you, it's kind of hot . . . 'the mess,' I mean," she added.

I smirked. "You like when I mark you, is that it?"

Miranda rolled to her side and returned my smile. "Something like that." She bit her lip, then kissed me. "You know Robbie probably isn't going to let us just walk off into the sunset together, right?"

"I was thinking the same thing. His deal with Max was an attempt to scare you into his control again. But if he was willing to go that far, I'm worried he'll have something else planned."

"I'd feel a lot better if I knew what it was that he was planning."

I took her chin between my thumb and forefinger. "We'll handle it. Whatever it is. *Together.*"

She nodded, then closed her eyes and nuzzled into me.

I let out a long, contented sigh. I might not know what Robbie was planning, but I finally knew what I wanted. I was done hiding behind half truths. It didn't matter what label I wanted to put on my feelings for Miranda. Maybe it was already love, or maybe I was an idiot for thinking I even knew what that was. It was stronger than anything I'd ever felt, and it turned my life on its head. All the things that had taken priority were now in the back seat to this—*to her.*

I needed her, and I wasn't going to let anything come between us. Not this time.

Chapter 27

MIRANDA

Max Frost's story went live on the air three days after I left LA. As promised, it was salacious, sensational, and utterly ridiculous. Everybody in West Valley was buzzing with gossip the following day when I met Iris and Kira at Bradley's. They had suggested we move our morning ritual to one of their houses to avoid stares, but I wasn't going to hide.

"You sure you don't want to go to my place?" Kira asked. She had even ordered her bagel in a to-go bag, I noticed.

"No," I said. "I want them to have to look me in the eye while they spread their gossip. The story was a lie. Anybody who wants to believe it instead of asking me to my face is welcome to think what they want."

Iris whipped out her nightstick, which she didn't seem to have quite the same fondness for ever since finding Cade. "Or I could use the power of the law to compel them."

"Isn't that what they say during exorcisms?" Kira asked.

"I'm pretty sure it doesn't matter what I say if I whack them hard enough in the boobs with this," Iris said.

"Thanks, but really," I said, "it's okay."

Iris studied me for a few seconds, then pointed at me. "What happened to you in Julian Ridge—other than getting T-boned by Nick, that is?"

"T-boned?" Kira asked. "You got in a car accident?"

"No. It's when the woman does a split lying down on the edge of the bed, and the guy kind of . . ." She tried to demonstrate with her hands, but failed. "I mean, it's more like a lowercase *t*, I guess. The top of the *t* would be the—"

"We get it," I said. "And I just finally realized I don't need to worry so much about all that. Let them gossip. I'm not going to lie: it still bothers me. But I'm not going to let it dictate my life anymore."

"Hell yeah," Kira said with a grin. "You should've got laid a long time ago."

I laughed. "It's not like I was a virgin. This isn't about sex."

"But," Iris said, wiggling her eyebrows, "this conversation just became about sex. How was it? Genetically speaking, Kira and I are riding the same dick, so it's no fun asking her."

"Ew!" Kira said. She threw a crumpled-up napkin at Iris. "That's disgusting."

"What? Don't tell me it never occurred to you," Iris said. "They are genetically the same. *Identical.*"

"Well, I didn't marry Rich's DNA. I married the man."

"You did kind of marry his DNA too," I said. "Just playing devil's advocate here."

"Changing the subject!" Kira announced quickly. "How was everything with Nick? Not just the sex, obviously. But . . . that too."

"Hot?" I said. "I don't know what you want me to say."

Iris made a disgusted noise. "Come on. I gave you the dirty details. Don't make me beg. *Or torture you,*" she added under her breath.

"I feel stupid saying it out loud. But it felt special," I said. "I mean the passion was there, and it was everything you'd want it to be. But it felt like there was something else. It was different. Like if you'd only ever seen a movie with the sound muted for your whole life, and then suddenly somebody cranks the volume up."

Iris and Kira turned to each other with raised eyebrows and knowing smiles.

"What?" I asked.

Kira shrugged. "You're falling for him harder than I thought."

"Maybe I am," I said proudly. "I'm not going to apologize for that."

"Coincidentally," Iris said, "I think Harper and Edna King are about to ask you to do more than apologize. Prepare your butthole; they like it rough and raw."

I followed her gaze and saw that she wasn't kidding. Harper and Edna King looked completely out of place in Bradley's, which was very much a working-class kind of restaurant. Harper had on his usual fresh-off-the-yacht-style clothes with oversize buttons, a sport coat despite the heat, and his rich-guy hair. Edna looked like she wasn't above kidnapping a few dozen dalmatians and using their coats to update her wardrobe.

I had to admit to being a little satisfied to know the King brothers had all finally cut them off financially. I knew Harper and Edna would never let it show to anybody, but they were being forced to downsize their home and let go their "service" staff. Rich thought it would be better for them in the long run. Cade was just happy he didn't have to write checks anymore, because he said his hands were cramping from all the writing. I hadn't picked Nick's brain on the topic, but I thought he probably agreed with Rich.

Harper and Edna sat down at our table and smiled.

I grimaced. I'd heard the horror stories from Kira and Iris about them, and I'd even witnessed some of it firsthand. They had fought tooth and nail to keep Rich from marrying Kira and Cade from marrying Iris. Now Nick was their only remaining son who could possibly give them the kind of prestigious, wealthy match they would've wanted. I braced myself for what was about to come.

"Hi," I said innocently.

"Don't worry," Harper said. He flashed an easy smile. "I know what you're probably thinking, but we wanted to come personally to tell you what Robbie asked us to do."

I felt my stomach sink. "What did he ask?"

Edna didn't look quite as gracious as Harper, but she sat silently, nose pointed upward and lips pursed. I decided it was a good sign that she was letting her husband do the talking, at least.

"He asked us to help him with his little scheme to get you back to LA. He wanted us to make it look like Nick was seeing some other woman so you'd want to break things off and go back to Robbie," Harper said.

Edna rolled her eyes, which told me all I needed to know. She'd been all for the plan, but Harper had apparently overruled her.

"Why are you telling me this?" I asked.

"Because we made the mistake of thinking we knew what was best for our sons twice now. We tried to keep them away from these two," he said, nodding to Iris and Kira. "But look at them now. I've never seen them happier. Well, I've never seen Cade *weirder*, either, but I guess he's happy too. Nick has had a dark cloud around him for years now. If you make him happy, then we are going to support that."

"Oh," I said. I felt honestly touched. After everything Iris and Kira had gone through with these two, I had already been planning which chair I'd bash them over the head with before I made a mad dash to the exit. But they were just coming to give me their blessing? *And* they tipped me off to what Robbie was planning next. "Thank you. Really, I mean that. Thank you so much."

Edna leaned forward. "It's a good thing you look like you have a solid future ahead of you. If you were just another country bimbo, I wouldn't have let Harper do this. Maybe you'll be able to talk our son out of this nonsense about 'bringing us down to earth,' even."

Harper made a bored sound, then hugged her with one arm as if she'd said something cute.

"I may be a country bimbo," Iris said, "but at least my boobs are still winning the battle with gravity."

Edna didn't give the slightest indication that she had heard Iris as she got up and left with Harper.

I laughed once they were gone. "Do you seriously talk to her like that?"

Iris shrugged. "Only when she's being vile. I treat her like a kid. She gets a fresh start every day. If she's being a raging bitch, she gets it just as hard as she gives it. If she's nice, then I'm nice."

"I just avoid her," Kira said.

As she suddenly straightened in her seat, I realized that Kira had appeared to shrink a few inches while Edna had been here.

"Were you going to hide under the table?" I asked.

"Maybe," Kira said.

A couple I recognized from high school passed by our table and then stopped to turn around when they saw me. The woman was Beth Stevenson, who had always been a bit of an academic rival of mine. She wound up working for Crawford around the same time as me but never saw the frequent promotions I did.

"Beth, hey," I said, smiling.

She gave me a tight, unfriendly smile. "Just wanted to say I always knew you were sleeping your way to the top at Crawford. I guess you're fine with everybody knowing you're still doing it now that you're at Bark Bites, huh?"

Iris stood up and reached for her nightstick.

"It's called freedom of speech, Iris," Beth said snootily. "And if you hadn't slept through history class every day, you might know a thing or two about it."

"Oh," Iris said, "I know all about freedom of speech. Just like I know all about my freedom to kick your ass and deal with the consequences later. But if you ask me, you were looking at us with some crazy eyes, and I thought the only reasonable thing to do was nightstick you in the throat."

Beth made an appalled face and touched her throat with her fingertips.

"Iris," I said. "Thank you, but it's fine. And, Beth, I really don't give a shit what you think or how you think I got promoted over you. But if you're really curious, you could start with the fact that you were always too busy flirting with the delivery guy."

The guy I assumed was her boyfriend looked over at her as she started dragging him away from our table. "What delivery guy?" he asked.

"Kira," Iris said. "Have some self-respect and get out from under the table."

Kira popped up with a napkin a second later. "Found it," she said meekly.

Iris and I shared a grin.

"You okay?" Kira asked.

"Surprisingly, yes," I said. "I might actually survive if Beth Stevenson doesn't think I'm perfect."

"And what about Robbie? Do you really think that was his big plan? Set up Nick and make it look like he was two-timing you?" She blew an unimpressed raspberry. "Like you would've fallen for that."

I smiled a little nervously. "Yeah, totally wouldn't have worked." I wasn't as confident as I made myself sound, though. The truth was I didn't like the idea of Robbie scheming to split Nick and me up one bit. And after the stunt we pulled last night, I had a sinking feeling that Robbie wasn't going to give up anytime soon.

I opened the door to Nick's office after knocking twice. "Mr. King?" I asked with a mischievous grin.

He stood and approached me without saying anything. "You know how I feel about being interrupted," he growled.

I finally cracked a smile, which he returned. Nick gave me a quick kiss, which turned into several kisses and then a light mauling, which probably would've turned into sex in the middle of his office if I hadn't told him to wait.

"What is it?" he asked.

"I was hoping to pick your brain on something."

"Is it about the permitting? Because I was actually going to tell you we got that all sorted out last night. There's a spot about ten minutes out from West Valley with over a hundred acres we can use. It'll be the perfect site for Bark Bites Resort."

"Oh, that's amazing." I took a seat behind Nick's desk, just because I liked seeing the hint of danger in his eyes when I stole his spot. He leaned against the bookshelf, crossing his arms in a way that made his rolled-up sleeves and forearms the perfect eye candy. "But that wasn't what was on my mind."

He frowned. "What is it?"

"It's about everything, I guess?"

He pulled a chair out and sat down, eyes growing even heavier. "You're not going to break up with me, are you?"

I laughed. "No. *No.* It's more that I'm still worried. I feel like I should be able to relax and just enjoy where we are, but instead I keep thinking how everything could still go wrong—how Robbie might not be done trying to split us up or how my idea about the dog resort could be the dumbest thing ever. Or how maybe I'll regret letting Max trash my reputation."

"Hey," Nick said. He came to stand behind me and wrapped his arms around my shoulders, putting his head by my ear. "The only thing that could split us up is *us.* And I don't know if you know this yet, but I would give every last thing I have to stay with you. I haven't felt good like this ever. I feel complete when I'm with you. Happy. It's—" He stood up straight and walked in a small path around the desk, arms folded and eyes searching the floor for the right words. "It's like I was spending my whole life trying to solve more-and-more-complicated problems because I was hung up on what happened between us. It was the original puzzle." He spread his hands like he was reading off a billboard. "Why didn't we end up together?"

"Because I was too chicken to sign my name on a silly little poem?"

He chuckled. "No. More like I was too afraid of the real answer. So afraid I looked for answers in every place but the one I should've been focused on. *Us.*"

"And what was the real answer?"

"That you were the one challenge I was too scared to take on. Maybe I just wanted to get enough practice before I decided to tackle it—or you," he added with that boyish smirk of his.

I stood up and turned to look him in the eyes. I chewed my lip as I idly ran my hands over his tie. "You know you never had anything to be afraid of with me, unless the idea of somebody falling hopelessly for you is a spooky concept."

"Very spooky," he said, studying my lips from beneath those long lashes of his. "Because you do things to me I didn't think were possible. I don't wake up restless and angry, just waiting for something complex to bash my head against. Now I just want you."

"How do you want me?" I teased.

"Vertical. Horizontal. In a boat or in a moat."

"Hmm. I think the moat gets my vote for least desirable."

Nick's eyebrows were pulled together as his eyes roamed my face. He put his thumb to my eyebrow and moved it softly as he spoke. "You want spooky? I think I'm falling in love with you."

Love. Suddenly I thought my knees might actually be made of melted butter, because it felt like I was going to collapse. It was the word that had floated around in my own head and made me feel silly. I'd said it with boyfriends before. *Love you too.* It was casual, almost.

Like a little obligatory catchphrase to signify a relationship had gone from infancy to adulthood. But Nick made me realize how empty those words had been.

"I feel it too," I said so quietly I wasn't sure he could hear me. "Maybe that's what has me so scared. I thought my heart was broken seven years ago, but what happens when I feel like *this*?"

"What happens is we fight for it. Nobody comes between it, because we can't live without it. So this shit with Robbie is meaningless. He can try whatever he wants, but it's not going to matter."

I nodded. "You know, if this is how snails feel, I think I can finally understand why they spend their whole lives just gooping along at two inches an hour in search of it."

He chuckled. "Did you really just turn this into a snail conversation again?"

"Maybe," I said. "You have to admit there are some parallels to be drawn."

Nick walked over to me and kissed me so tenderly that I thought I might just turn into warm, runny liquid and slide out of the chair. "I love you," he said.

"I love you too."

Chapter 28
NICK

My brothers and I were in the middle of our annual fishing trip. It had been a tradition since we were kids, and even the rinky-dink boat with a single engine and rust spots was part of the ritual.

We'd spend most of the day trying to catch whatever we could with cut-up hot dogs as bait, because that was what we'd used as kids. It was a perfect day for being on the water. There were enough clouds for the shade to let us cool off from time to time and not so much wind that our crummy little boat was getting blown all over the lake.

Cade, as usual, was wearing some monstrosity of an outfit, complete with suspenders, pins commemorating his make-believe achievements in fishing, and a floppy hat. He tugged impatiently, shaking his rod around.

"Are you sure there are even fish in here anymore?" Cade asked.

Rich was dressed like a normal human being would dress to go fishing. He tugged his hat a little lower and sighed. "Maybe if you didn't make it look like your bait was having a seizure, the fish would bite."

"I don't see them biting yours," Cade said.

Rich mumbled something under his breath and stared back out at his line.

In fact, none of us had caught anything all day, but that didn't bother me.

"Hey," I said after a while. "How did you guys know with Kira and Iris?"

"Know what?" Cade said. "That we wanted to smash?"

I shook my head in disbelief. "That you loved them."

"It felt way more intense than anything before it," Rich said. "The kind of thing that doesn't even give you a choice, you know? Like it has a gravity all of its own that sucks you both in."

"For me," Cade said, "it was the first time I saw her ass in that uniform." He licked his finger and mimicked touching something sizzling hot.

"Seriously?" I asked.

For once, Cade's smirk faded, and he looked a little more serious. "I mean, there was the other part too." He looked down at the splintery wooden bench he sat on and picked at a loose chip of paint. "Normally, I was already looking for the next woman as soon as I'd get with somebody. It was this restless, never-ending kind of thing. Honestly, it was exhausting. Then once things got serious with Iris, that part of me just shut down. The idea of looking for someone else seemed pointless, because I was good with where I was."

Rich nodded. "I can't believe I'm saying this, but Cade said it pretty well. It goes from feeling like you're looking for something to feeling like you want to protect what you've found at all costs."

"Yeah," I said. "That's pretty much how it feels."

Rich raised his eyebrow. "You think you love her?"

"I do. I said as much the other day, at least."

Cade punched me on the arm and grinned like an idiot. "Look at our little brother, growing up so fast."

"Shut up," I said, but I was smiling. "You know, ever since you talked to her about snails, Miranda won't stop bringing them up. You poisoned her mind."

Cade perked up. "Really?"

"Yeah, she even brought it up after we talked about the whole love thing. She said something like she can understand why snails spend their whole lives searching for love if this was how it felt."

Cade mimicked wiping a tear from his eye. "I'm so proud of how far she has come. I've always thought snails were such a perfect metaphor for life. And now I know I'm not the only one who believes it."

"What if they are just like simple little machines?" Rich asked. "If condition X is met, then behavior Y will be applied. That sort of thing. Who says it has to be about snail love?"

Cade looked at Rich like he had just said something unbelievably stupid. "If you think snails are robots, you're even dumber than I thought."

Rich sighed and went back to focusing on his fishing line. "That Max Frost story really did cause a few problems," he said in an almost bored voice. "The Southpoint deal fell through, and I think it's due to reputation concerns."

"Fuck 'em," Cade said. "That place was going to lose us money anyway."

"Did you even read the report on it?" I asked him.

"No, but my intuition is almost always right. Most of the time," he said.

"I really am sorry I brought all this shit down on us," I said.

Rich waved me off. "We'll survive it. People are going to pay the most attention to it now, while the story is still fresh in their minds. Give it a few months, and I doubt anyone will really care. Besides, I've heard a lot of people actually like the story. They think the idea that all of us moved out here to chase after our high school sweethearts is romantic."

"Yeah," Cade said. "Especially if you and Miranda manage to turn Bark Bites around. It looks a whole lot better if the company you bought to score some pussy ends up profiting and creating new jobs, after all."

"Oh," I said. "While we're on the subject. I needed to ask you two about something before I pull the trigger."

Chapter 29

MIRANDA

I stared at the stack of papers Nick had shown me and gave him a questioning look. We were in a hotel in LA again, but this time for an entirely different reason.

"You don't think this crosses a line? Or maybe it's just a little too petty?" I asked.

Nick frowned. "Of course it crosses a line. It's also extremely petty. But he deserves it. And once you told me how worried you were about him still coming after us, I knew I needed to think of something to put your mind at ease. This will protect us. It's perfect, as long as you can swallow the slightly questionable morality, that is."

I pushed the stack of papers back and closed the pen Nick had given me. He'd spent the past few minutes explaining the complicated business workings that allowed him to perform a hostile takeover of Robbie's new employer. He figured we could let Robbie know by firing him, and he wanted me to technically own the company so I could deliver the bad news.

"As much as I want to," I said. "I don't think this is the right move. What if we just show him that we're capable of this? Couldn't we make a threat and let that hang over his head so he'd be too scared to ever screw with us again?"

Nick grinned. "I thought you might mention that. And, yes, that would make more logical sense. I mean, if we nuke his career, all we're really doing is giving him a ton of free time to think of something really stupid to piss us off. But if we blackmail him, he might just leave us alone forever. I'll be honest, though. I really wanted to watch you fire his ass."

"It *is* tempting."

"You're right, though. Let's do it your way. Do you want me to come with you, or do you want to go by yourself?"

"As much as I'd appreciate the backup, I think I want this to be something I do on my own."

Robbie's secretary let me into his office a few hours later. He was waiting behind his desk with a smug look. He was still handsome, but the way he'd acted since our breakup made me see his good looks in a new light. He reminded me of the corrupt politicians you'd see in movies—sneering and gnashing their teeth in one scene only to smile for the cameras in the next.

"Miranda." He stood, smiling and spreading his arms to hug me.

I put my hand up and motioned for him to back off.

Still smiling, he straightened his tie and gestured for me to sit. "I knew you'd come around eventually. Max really did run quite the story."

"Actually," I said, "I was here to let you know a few things. One is that I broke up with you for a reason. It wasn't a mistake. It wasn't an accident. It wasn't the kind of thing that you can change my mind on. I thought I could be with somebody who made financial sense and who would be good for my career, and the feelings would come all on their own. But that never happened."

Robbie leaned forward with an irritated look. "Wait a minute. If you think all of this was about trying to win you back, you're just flattering yourself."

"Another thing," I said, interrupting him, "is that Nick's parents told me what you were planning when the Max Frost story didn't work. Which is why I'm here today."

"I have no idea what they are talking about. I haven't spoken to his parents in ages."

"I am here to lay this out to you, not to listen. So if you don't mind, stop trying to make excuses and just listen to what I have to say."

Robbie glared, but he sat back in his chair and watched me.

"So I decided you were probably going to keep trying petty, childish things to spite me. That's why Nick and I worked up a plan to buy out Lockhart and Taylor. All we'd need is twenty-four hours, and we would have the power to fire you and anyone else we choose. We could shut the whole thing down, for all we care."

"Bullshit."

I shrugged, standing up. Nick thought Robbie would try to get the details of our plan, but we decided we'd have to keep them secret in case he tried to warn his bosses. "It's up to you. Believe it's bullshit if you want and test us. Maybe you'll lose your new, cushy job. Maybe you won't. But I feel confident that you'll be smart enough not to find out. Won't you?"

"I don't think you'd risk your reputation to get involved in something like this."

"The reputation you ruined? Thanks for that, by the way. You didn't really give me a choice, but I realized it wasn't everything I made it out to be."

"Miranda," he said, changing his tone entirely. "You're not really considering that, are you?"

I shrugged. "All I'd need is a little motivation. So maybe think really carefully next time you want to interfere in my life."

Robbie gripped his pen so hard I thought the top was about to pop off, but I managed to keep from smiling smugly to myself until I turned to leave.

Epilogue
MIRANDA

Six Months Later

I could hardly believe I was looking at the nearly completed version of Bark Bites Resort. I knew Nick had more money than he could spend in a lifetime, but it still made my heart swell to think he'd risk his reputation and his money on my idea like this. Nick met me at the dog-bone-shaped swimming pool.

He hugged me tightly and slid his hand behind my back in that possessive way he had, then kissed my neck.

I secretly liked the way Nick always made sure to mark me as his own when we were out together. He never seemed jealous or insecure about it. It was more like a simple statement of fact. *This one is with me, so forget it.*

I grinned at the thought. "You smell nice," I said into his shoulder.

"You taste better."

"Stop," I whispered. "There's a lot I have to show you, and if you start talking dirty, we're going to end up in a janitor's closet somewhere."

"You say that like it's a problem."

I jabbed my finger in his chest. "You're supposed to be looking over the pool with me to make sure we don't have any complaints to take to the contractors."

"You know, usually this sort of thing gets delegated to your underlings. I think having the vice president and CEO personally inspect a pool is a little overkill. Although they apparently didn't think using a level would be a good idea when they did these pavers." He knelt and pulled a coin from his pocket, then set it on edge and watched it roll down the slope of pavers that should've been flat.

"See?" I said. "This is why I brought you."

"I just came for the ass," he said.

"You better be talking about mine."

Nick nodded to a worker who was bending down to work on some pipes a little way away. "Actually, I was talking about him."

I slapped his arm. "Could you try acting like my boss for a minute so we can get this over with?"

"I actually meant to talk to you about that. I've been doing a lot of thinking, and I don't think I can let you work for me anymore."

I laughed at first because I thought he was kidding, but he didn't even smile. He just looked down at me with a grave expression.

"What do you mean?"

Nick sighed. "It's just . . . well, I've never stayed on at a company this long after Sion acquired it before. Part of what I do is find a suitable replacement CEO to take over when I walk away from the company. And I've found someone who is perfect for the job. *You.*"

"Nick," I said slowly. "As much as I want that—and I *really* do. But it's too much. I can't accept that."

"Miranda, this isn't a gift. It's not some trinket I went and bought at the store to try to impress you. It's a job that you earned. You earned the hell out of it. Just look around you. This whole thing was your idea. Your dream. So I want to give you the keys and the ability to know you made this. When it works, you'll be able to know it was because you put it together and ran it as amazingly as I know you will."

I blinked a few times, trying not to let the tears I felt stinging my eyes come. "For the record, there's a lot of pollen out today."

Nick pulled me into a hug. "Cry if you want to," he whispered. "You can stay right there for as long as you want. Oh, but there was one more thing." He whistled sharply, catching me off guard.

I heard the sound of a dog approaching. When I pulled away from Nick's chest, I saw Bone Thug trotting up to us with a goofy little pink ribbon tied around his head. There was a pillow on top and a . . .

"Is that?" I asked.

Nick got down on one knee and reached for the ring. Bone Thug tried to bite him, so Nick yanked his hand back and swore. "We practiced this, you big asshole." He tried again, but then Thug thought he was trying to play and started running sprints. Thankfully, the ring fell off, and Nick was able to awkwardly crawl a little to retrieve it.

He cleared his throat. "Not exactly as smooth as I planned, but now that we're not colleagues, I figure there's nothing stopping this from being a great idea. So what do you say, Miranda Collins? Will you marry me?"

Epilogue
NICK

The sound of clattering bowling pins filled the air. There was also a distinct dog smell floating around. Miranda and I joined my brothers and their wives for a game of bowling to celebrate opening day of Bark Bites Resort. The bowling alleys were shaped like big dog bones—supposedly, at least. I personally thought they looked a little phallic. Each lane was flanked by a padded doggy lane where the dogs could carry plush bowling balls down and smash into the pins at the end.

We invited all West Valley to stay for the weekend for free to celebrate the grand opening. There was some slight drama concerning the fact that this weekend was supposed to be when the yodeling games were held. Eventually, we worked it out so the yodeling games could still take place, and it'd just be a Bark Bites–sponsored event.

Miranda looked casual in a silky Bark Bites polo and khaki pants that made her ass look too good not to grab. She sat down beside me with a tray of chili cheese fries and wiggled her eyebrows. "Hungry?"

"Not for those," I said, nudging her leg.

She bit her lip, then lowered her voice. "I'm not on the menu until tonight. As a big, important CEO, I have a lot of work to do."

"Oh, absolutely. I can see how hard you're working right now."

She shrugged. "Work-life balance is one of my keys to success. If I don't have a little time to bowl with my fiancé, what am I even working for?"

I smirked. I still wasn't used to hearing her call me her fiancé. A little jolt of excitement spiked through me every time I heard that, and every time I glanced down at the engagement band on her finger.

"Hey, nerds," Cade said. He was standing at the computer dressed like he was in a biker gang from the eighties. There had apparently been a miscommunication about the dress code, he claimed. When he turned to look at us, I couldn't help laughing. He had on a fake, thick black mustache, sunglasses, and a red headband. He had also ripped the sleeves off a leather jacket and wore pants so tight I didn't really want to look below his waist. "You two gonna pick a name, or am I gonna have to pick it for you?"

"What's with the accent?" I asked.

He made a dismissive sound and typed our team name into the computer. *Balls of Fury.*

"I figured I'd go easy on you guys. I did win fifty dollars from Iris when you got together, so I probably owe you."

"He's not kidding," Iris said. "I tried telling him there was no way in hell our Miranda would ever go back on the oath she tried so hard to bang over our heads when Kira and I were thinking of breaking it. It was just *sooo* important until it was her turn."

"Okay," Miranda said. "For the record, it stopped being an oath when you two broke it. And my King brother didn't actually do anything bad to deserve it. If he hadn't thought Kira signed that poem, I never would've wanted to swear the stupid thing in the first place."

Kira ducked her head. "Awkward," she whispered.

"Sorry," Miranda muttered. "I'm just saying that me falling for Nick was probably the most forgivable sin here. I waited the longest too."

"It's not a competition, Miranda," Iris said. "But if it was, I'd win because I at least arrested my King brother first."

Cade nodded wisely. "She wouldn't even frisk me properly. The woman was made out of restraint. I think if I hadn't had a kid up my sleeve, I would've been doomed."

"Speaking of your kid, where is he, exactly?" I asked.

"Taking advantage of the free day care, thank you very much."

Rich cleared his throat. "Kira tried pretty hard to throw me off too."

"Gee, thanks, Rich," she said with a sideways smile. "You make me sound really tough."

He shrugged. "I knew you wanted me from the get-go. I just had to be patient enough for you to admit it to yourself."

"Liar," Kira said, laughing.

After a few minutes, Cade, Rich, Kira, and Iris were all laughing about something that happened at a King family barbecue a few weeks back.

Miranda leaned her head into my shoulder and smiled. "I really am happy."

"Because you're winning?" I asked.

"There's that. Yes. But I'm happy I got you. And you're the first guy I've ever been with who encourages my ambition. You don't get intimidated or weird about it. I really appreciate that."

I kissed the top of her head. "As long as your ambitions also include a side of wanting to get into my pants, I'll always be there to help push you along."

She laughed. "I was thinking it would be easier to take them off instead of trying to fit inside them."

"You're the boss."

She didn't answer right away, but when she did, her tone was slow and thoughtful. "I am, and I finally found something that matters to me more than that."

"Chili cheese fries?" Cade asked. He picked one out of her tray and popped it into his mouth. "You should really free both your hands before you give sappy speeches. I mean, wouldn't setting that tray down kind of kill the mood before you go in for a romantic kiss?"

I thrust the tray into his chest, and he happily took it.

"Hey, weird question," I said suddenly.

"Is it about snails?"

I grinned. "No. It's just that you said you never understood people who had kids before they got what they wanted out of their careers. So now that you seem to have done the whole career thing . . ."

She pulled her bottom lip into her mouth, eyes darting across my face like she was waiting for a punch line. "If you don't mean what I think you mean, I will literally murder you. I won't even wait until you're asleep. I'll make sure it's painful and messy."

"I mean it all. But you can bet I'd haunt your ass. And you can also bet I'd be a perverted ghost."

She grinned. "A baby?"

"Sure, we could start with just one if that's what you wanted."

She laughed, hopping up on my lap and hugging me tightly. I ran my hands through her hair, holding her like I was afraid she'd slip away if I didn't squeeze her tight. I knew one thing. I'd never let her go. Not again. Not ever.

Five Years Later

Even if the view of West Valley had changed quite a bit since our high school days, Overlook Point was still the same. There were more stores and more houses in West Valley than there had been. If you squinted, you could even see the massive, glinting building Sion called headquarters past the trees outside town. But for all the ways it had grown and changed as we had, West Valley still felt like home.

More and more, the time my brothers and I had spent out in California was starting to feel like a footnote. Everything that mattered had happened here.

I'd met Miranda, let her slip away, found her again, and started a family. Every last one of those things had happened in this same scenic little valley.

We'd come out here with my brothers, their wives, and their kids and brought enough fireworks, picnic blankets, food, and camping gear to keep us until morning. Cade and Iris had pumped out kids so fast over the past few years that I was almost certain they weren't respecting the whole "no sex for six weeks" after pregnancy rule. The two of them had a small, terrifying little army of Cade and Iris clones now. God help the world if any of their kids were even half as wild as their parents.

Rich found me looking out over the town and nudged me with his shoulder. We were all finally starting to age out of that near-stasis period in our twenties when it felt like time couldn't touch us. The only signs that Rich had aged were the faint lines appearing at the corners of his eyes.

"Deep in thought, like usual?" he asked.

I grinned. "Just thinking how crazy it is that we all wound up back here. How we all got the girl in the end, you know?"

"Yeah," Rich said, nodding seriously. "It's just too bad only one of us could get the best girl. But the early bird gets the worm, you know?"

I punched his shoulder and grinned. "I'm going to give you a pass because you've got an infant, and you're probably sleep deprived as hell."

"Hey," he said, gripping my neck and giving a little squeeze. "It took Kira and I a long-ass time to get pregnant. A long-ass, enjoyable time, okay? So don't sweat it. Just keep doing your husbandly duty, and it'll come."

I chuckled. I hadn't meant it to come out that way, but I could see how Rich would think I was bitter or resentful that he and Kira had managed to get pregnant. Miranda and I had been trying for four years now. I had to admit that trying to get her pregnant and failing easily qualified as one of the most enjoyable activities to fail I'd ever found, but it still stung. We were both so damn ready to have our own kid, but month after month, we were let down. It didn't stop us from doing all the things we wanted and loving it, but every year that went by made me wonder more if it would ever happen for us.

"Not all of us can be Cade, the sperm bank, I guess," I said.

Rich laughed. "No. I have to give him credit, though; he's really taken well to fatherhood."

"In his own way, yeah. I walked in on him sitting with all the kids in a semicircle a couple weeks ago. He was basically giving a lecture on snails to them, and all the kids were enthralled. Even the infant."

"You're right. Maybe he's only taking so well to it because he likes the idea of building a small army of Cadelings."

"Exactly what I was thinking."

"Look on the bright side. If you guys never manage to get pregnant, Cade will have so many extra kids that I'm sure he'll be happy to lend you one whenever you want."

I groaned. "That's exactly what we don't need."

Rich patted me on the back and smiled before he headed back to where Kira was lying beside their newborn, Erik, who was currently asleep in his carrier.

Something hot shot me in the ass, making me jump and grab my butt cheek. I turned to see Cade and Bear aiming two lit roman candles at me. I ducked for the nearest bush and hoped they would have enough brain cells between the two of them not to set it on fire.

Once they were out of ammunition, I cautiously stepped out of the bush and raised my arms. "Are you two done?" I asked.

Bear lobbed one of those little white exploding packets my way and made me flinch. He and his dad cracked up laughing at how scared I'd been, but I knew enough to fear Cade and his son, who was growing up to be unfortunately similar to his dad.

Bear even looked like a small version of Cade. At ten years old, he'd apparently worked his way through most of what he called the "cream of the dating pool" at his school. He was also big for his age, which meant he enjoyed dominating all the team sports he had time for.

"We saw you trying to brood over here and decided you could use a little fire in your ass," Cade said.

"I just don't ask questions when Dad says I can aim fireworks at people, so . . . sorry, Uncle Nick."

"Don't apologize," Cade said. He put his arm around Bear's neck and started leading him back to the tents. "Apologies are only for girls you really, *really* like. And even then, they are a last resort. You apologize when all the other tools in your tool belt won't work, and if . . ."

I couldn't hear the rest of Cade's undoubtedly bad advice as the two of them walked off.

A few hours later, when all the kids had fallen asleep for the night, Miranda and I met our brothers and their wives at the edge of the hill overlooking town.

Miranda gave my hand a little squeeze.

Cade yawned. "What are we doing here, exactly? Snail hunting?"

"No," Rich said. "Why would any of us want to go hunting for snails?"

Cade shrugged. "Because maybe you got your heads out of your asses and realized we could learn a lot from them? Miranda is pardoned from that, by the way. She's the only one who really appreciates what our shell-backed friends have to offer."

Iris rolled her eyes.

"Actually," Kira said, "I wanted us to come out here so we could make one last oath."

"Oh, cool. This is like *The Lord of the Rings* now," Cade said. He stuck his fist into the center of our little circle. "I'll ride with the dwarves. I enjoy their humor and drinking songs."

"I'm being serious," Kira said. "I want us all to make an oath."

"I *oathe* to never believe dinosaurs are real, no matter what Rich says," Cade said.

"*Oath* isn't a verb, dumbass," I said.

"What is the verb form, then, Mr. Genius?" Cade asked.

"Vow, maybe?" I said.

"Okay, I changed my oath," Cade said. "I vow to buy a big-ass dog, teach it to poop on command, and then take it to Bark Bites Resort and command it to poop in that big, stupid bone-shaped swimming pool for dogs."

I sighed. "I vow to make sure you and your dog never step foot in one of our resorts."

Iris raised her hand.

"You don't have to—" Kira said, pinching the bridge of her nose. "I was kind of planning to tell you guys what the oath was, not ask everyone to just throw one out there."

"Well," Iris said, ignoring Kira. "I vow to never lose the keys to the handcuffs again. Especially when Cade is tied to the bed."

Cade nodded his head sadly. "Good vow, Iris. Good vow."

"Rich?" Cade asked. "Do you have a vow for the class, or do we need to call home?"

"I'm planning on letting Kira finish what she was going to say, unless Miranda had one."

"Actually," Miranda said, "I did have one little oath. I vow to do everything in my power to make this little thing growing in my belly the happiest baby on the planet."

It took me a few seconds to realize what she'd said. Cade was already squatting down with his fist over his mouth when it dawned on me. I turned to face her. "You're serious?"

She nodded, biting her lip. "Serious," she said.

I picked her up and then promptly set her back down as carefully as I could. "Oh shit. I shouldn't be picking you up like that if you're pregnant."

She laughed. "I think it's safe when it's this early. I just found out two days ago. Since we were planning to meet here, I thought this would be the best place to tell you."

Iris and Kira leaned in to hug and congratulate us, and when they were done, Kira cleared her throat.

"So," Kira said. "Tonight, I wanted us all to swear just one oath. No matter what happens, I'll never love anyone but Rich. *And Erik*," she added with a little grin, then squeezed Rich's hand.

He smiled and bent down to kiss her.

Cade took Iris's hand and knelt in front of her. "Sorry, baby, but I've got to swear the oath. Kira's orders." He scooted over to kneel in front of Rich and tried to take Rich's hands in his. "No matter what, I'll never love anyone but Rich."

Kira groaned. "You're supposed to modify it to fit the person you love, Cade."

Iris gave Cade a little whack on the back of his head. "No matter what, I'll never love anyone but Cade and our little army. *So help me God*," she added with a little sarcastic grin.

Miranda reached out for my hands. "And no matter what, I'll never love anyone but Nick. And our baby on the way."

"Not to be a downer," Cade said, "but we all know how the last oath sworn up here went. Are we sure this is really the best symbolic gesture?"

ABOUT THE AUTHOR

Penelope Bloom is a *USA Today*, Amazon, and *Washington Post* best-selling author whose books have been translated into seven languages. Her popular romances include *His Banana, Her Cherry, Savage*, and *Punished*.

Her writing career started when she left her job as a high school teacher to pursue her dream. She loves taking her imagination for a spin and writing romances she'd want to live. She likes a man with a mind as dirty as sin and a heart of gold he keeps hidden away. Her favorite things include getting to wear socks all day—pants optional—and being a positive example for her girls. Showing her daughters that no dream is too big, no matter what anyone tells them, is worth all the late nights, doubts, and fears that come with being a writer.

Stay connected! For giveaways, goodies, updates, and extras, join the mailing list: http://eepurl.com/chOOEX. Follow her on Facebook at PenelopeBloomRomance, and check out her website at www.penelope-bloom.com.